Standard of Care

D1009196

Standard of Care

a novel by David Kerns

SENTIENT PUBLICATIONS

First Sentient Publications edition 2007
Copyright © 2007 by David Kerns

All rights reserved. This book, or parts thereof, may not be reproduced in any form without permission, except in the case of brief quotations embodied in critical articles and reviews.

A paperback original

Book cover designer: Kim Johansen, Black Dog Design
Book design: Nicholas Cummings

Library of Congress Cataloging-in-Publication Data

Kerns, David, 1944-
  Standard of care : a novel / David Kerns.
    p. cm.
  ISBN-13: 978-1-59181-054-4
1. Physicians--Fiction. 2. Patient advocacy--Fiction. 3. Medical care--Quality control--Fiction. 4. Medical ethics--Fiction. 5. Hospital management companies--Fiction. I. Title.

PS3611.E763S73 2007
813'.6--dc22

2006028150

Printed in the United States of America

10 9 8 7 6 5 4 3 2 1

SENTIENT PUBLICATIONS
A Limited Liability Company
1113 Spruce Street
Boulder, CO 80302
www.sentientpublications.com

In loving memory of
Morgan and Andrew

Contents

The very first requirement in a hospital is that it should do the sick no harm."

—*Florence Nightingale*

"...and now a retail business you've begun."

—*Johann Wolfgang Goethe*

Prologue

———

A DISMAL CONSOLATION, A SLENDER MERCY, SHE HAD remained conscious for only fourteen seconds. The call button to the nurses' station, inches from her left hand, lay untouched. As her blood pressure and oxygen levels plummeted, Kerry's body answered in reflex desperation. Nerve centers in the chambers of her heart, and in her aorta and carotid arteries, sent their special instructions. The adrenal glands disgorged emergency hormones. A blood pressure-promoting chemical from the kidneys, and another from the pituitary gland, poured forth. In one coordinated voice, Kerry Jameson's five-year-old body was screaming. Save my heart, save my brain.

Her blood vessels responded. Circulation to her skin was diverted, leaving her cold and ashen. Arteries constricted and blood was re-routed. Past the kidneys, past the intestines, past the liver. Precious oxygen-rich red blood cells, fewer by the millisecond, were shunted toward the coronary and cerebral vessels. To save her heart and save her brain.

She was alone and she was losing. Her airway was obstructed with gelatinous chunks of clotted blood. The bleeding from her throat, from the site of her surgery, had abated, but only because she was in shock. Instead of water and carbon dioxide and precious energy, her tissues were producing worse than useless substances. Acids. Toxic waste that, in a downward spiral, poisoned not just the sacrificial organs. The blood sluggishly coursing through her coronary arteries was foul—acidic, oxygen-depleted, and under failing pressure. The contractions of her heart weakened by the second, and became erratic. First, with long irregular spaces between the beats, and then slow by half. Abruptly, one minute and seventeen seconds after she lost consciousness, there was no cardiac activity at all. Her circulatory system had collapsed.

Now every cell in her body was suffocating. In her brain, the live-or-die energy molecule ATP was in free fall, unleashing neurochemical chaos. Calcium ions—the cheery stuff of mother's milk and strong bones and teeth—poured unmodulated into her cells, activating poisons with names like lipase and calpain and arachidonate, each wreaking havoc on this astonishing organ, the paragon of evolution.

The cells began to fall apart. Membranes burst into fragments and proteins disintegrated. Millions of brain cells—coordinated, precise electric miracles four minutes earlier—were dead or dying. And in their catastrophe, they couldn't sustain a paleozoic reflex, much less a sentient being.

Then she was penetrated. First by latex-covered fingers excavating the back of her throat. And twice more, scooping out the clots. A metal blade displaced her tongue while the blood, oozing blue-black now, was vacuumed away. Needles searched for uncollapsed vessels in her left groin and at the flesh in front of her right elbow. A curved rigid tube slid down her gullet, and cold oxygen-rich air pushed its way through ever-smaller tunnels to the tiny lung sacs where breathing actually happens. A wooden board for leverage, hurriedly shoved beneath her, abraded the pallid clammy skin over her shoulder blades and tailbone. A powerful hand compressed the center of her chest, while salt water and drugs rushed into her punctured veins. Her flaccid sac of a heart began to ineffectually wriggle. Crushed once a second between breast bone and spinal column, it passively extruded a pitiful current. A spit in her circulatory ocean.

A burst, a trillionth of a lightning bolt, electrified her chest. Nothing. The jellied defibrillator paddles fired again, and again. Nothing. A silver needle, a half a foot long, pierced her skin and, riding the upper surface of a rib, traversed muscle and sinew and membrane and muscle again, this time cardiac muscle, and entered the chamber of her right ventricle. A clear stream of adrenaline exited the beveled opening and dissipated into the brackish blood. It did its job. Shocked one more time, the special circuitry of bundles and fibers in the walls of her heart—the neural network responsible for a lifetime of perfect rhythm—took over.

Kerry Jameson, what was left of her, was alive.

Part 1

Berkeley, California, two years later

Daniel

—

DOCTOR DANIEL JEROME FAZEN WAS NOT A MAN GIVEN TO primping at bathroom mirrors or obsessing about meetings with hospital administrators, yet here he was doing both.

Memorial's CEO had surprised him. "There are some things going on around here that you might not be aware of. Any chance you'd be open to a career change?" Aside from his interest in the opportunity itself, there was something flattering and pleasantly conspiratorial about being entrusted with closely held information.

He tied his tie for the third time, moved in close to snip a few more nose hairs, adjusted the tuck of his shirt. He checked his look and, without altering a thing, re-combed his thick salt-and-pepper hair.

He had not said aloud, even to Susan, how burned out he felt and how much he wanted a change. Sure, he had talked about the boredom and repetition of his practice. But feeling that it arose from some kind of personal weakness, he had not expressed what in truth was an emerging sense of disappointment and desperation about his professional life.

—

The reverse commute from Berkeley to the east seemed to worsen by the week. Dan slowed to a crawl as four lanes squeezed into two through the Caldecott Tunnel. Then he broke out into the sun and weaved and surged, inattentive, ignoring the gold of the Golden State, the bleached hillsides of Indian summer. His once silky 535i had loosened up over the years but the sound system masked most of that. Distracted, he barely noticed NPR droning on about Argentinean wheat futures. After a quarter of a century, this drive was embedded in his nervous system.

He could see the Walnut Creek Memorial Hospital miles before he got there. The glass and steel tower dominated a hillside just to the southeast of the burgeoning little city. Hospital Administration was on the top floor, with coveted views of the Contra Costa Hills and Mount Diablo. He got a perky welcome from the CEO's secretary. Waiting, he leafed through an old issue of *Hospital Medicine*. He was looking at the pictures.

"Dan, it's good to see you. Thanks for coming in."

Marty Sullivan was setting the tone for the meeting, personally coming out to welcome him. He rose to greet his favorite administrator and they shook hands.

"Hi, Marty. I've been looking forward to this. You've got me intrigued."

Martha Sullivan led the way into her big corner office and gestured him to a chair at the conference table by the windows. He'd known her since the early nineties when she came out from Boston to run Memorial. Heralded as a brilliant businesswoman and a passionate patient advocate, she didn't disappoint. Small in stature, this working-class, Harvard-educated Irish woman was as tough as she had to be with executive counterparts or the most arrogant of docs. You did not intimidate Marty Sullivan. On this morning she radiated warmth and accessibility. She was recruiting.

"I understand that you're doing a great job on QI," she said. "I know I'm not supposed to know what goes on there, and actually I don't know the clinical details, but I hear that you're willing to call 'em as you see 'em, regardless of who you piss off."

She was talking about the confidential Quality Improvement process where, among other things, physicians reviewed the quality of care provided by other physicians.

"Well, actually it's not all that dramatic," Dan said. "Most of the process is really pretty dull. Churning for the regulators."

"Well, that's not what I hear," she said.

"You're not supposed to hear."

"Right. I just wanted you to know that your effort is appreciated."

"Thanks. I mean, you're welcome." He executed a nervous exhalation, a chuckle.

Marty dropped the preliminaries. "Mark Rader is leaving." She let it sink in.

He could not have been more surprised. Rader, the Vice-President for Medical Affairs, was ten years his junior, an MD/MBA doing a first-rate job as the full-time senior medical executive at Memorial. He had left his private practice, taken a year off to get his Master's from the Sloane School at Stanford, and returned as VPMA. Everyone figured that Mark was the heir-apparent to Marty.

"He's going to Olympia Pacific," she said.

Another cortical jolt. Dan took a moment to focus.

"As what?"

"Chief Medical Officer."

"But that's a lateral move."

"Not financially it ain't."

"Christ, he's joining the evil empire," he said.

"Fuckin' A." Marty liked being one of the boys.

OHC, the Olympia Healthcare Corporation, was the biggest player in the hospital industry in America. Following a consolidation of three small multi-hospital companies in the mid-1980's, it had, through acquisition and predation, become the 550 hospital, for-profit darling of the New York Stock Exchange, a juggernaut. Olympia Pacific, formerly the venerable Vista Pacific Medical Center in San Francisco, was acquired by OHC several years earlier. Once a quality-driven and prestigious University-affiliated hospital, Vista Pacific had been annually losing millions in the competitive frenzy of the 1990's. Olympia bought it for a song and, through desiccating cost-containment and aggressive pricing, was bringing it back to at least financial health. Mark Rader had certainly assimilated the business acumen to hold his own there. What his conscience might tolerate was another matter.

Marty made her pitch. "Dan, I'd like you to think about Vice-President for Medical Affairs. Over the years you've demonstrated a staunch commitment to quality of care and an ability to work well with both the docs and the administrators. As a past president of the medical staff, you're intimately familiar with credentialing, with quality management and all the regulatory imperatives. You're highly respected in the community and you know this marketplace as well as or better than anyone out there."

He was surprised and pleased by her formality. This was rehearsed, this was serious.

"This is a critical time for us," she said. "With the intensity of competition externally and the challenges of re-engineering and cost-containment internally, I need a strong physician on my administrative team."

She softened and spoke through a smile.

"You know, you and I have always had an easy and productive working relationship and that's invaluable. I appreciate the magnitude of the change, just how different this would be for you. But if you're at all ready for a new experience, I think it's a terrific job."

She stopped. He wasn't sure if she was going to continue. She didn't. He smiled.

"Well, I'm really flattered. And you're right, this would be a very big change for me." He could feel the little surge in power, the temporary upper hand. "I hope it's obvious how much I care about Memorial and its mission. And I appreciate the acknowledgment that this offer represents."

He already knew what he was going to do. Awash in boredom and restlessness, and harboring more ambition than he would care to own up to, this was an easy call. But he kept his stillness and crafted his demeanor. Thoughtfulness seemed just right.

"Look, how about I take a few days, let it incubate, talk to Susan, and get back to you about whether I want to seriously explore it. I'm very flattered and very interested."

"Great. I can't ask for more than that." Marty stood up as she changed the subject. "Hey, did you hear about that death in the Presbyterian waiting room?"

The conversation about the job was over. He assumed that, like him, she did not want to appear too hopeful or remotely obsequious.

"Yeah, I saw it in the paper," he said. "There but for the grace of God. I didn't read the details. Apparently this poor guy keeled over dead after waiting like ten hours in their Emergency Department." They might as well have been talking about the weather. "You know, I really tend to avoid medical stuff in the media, particularly clinical stuff. And I never watch *ER* or any of those. Even when they get it right, who needs an extra dose."

Marty extended her arm in his direction. "Well, thanks for coming by. I'll look forward to hearing from you."

As he suspected, she didn't really care about the troubles in someone else's Emergency Department.

He squeezed her hand. "Thanks, I won't drag this out."

⟶

He got in the car, started the ignition, and sat. He could feel the lightness of being extricated from his office, the adventure of a new career experience, the anticipated financial freedom. He relished the escape from his practice. The relentless parade of physical and emotional complaints, the rote spiels of instructions, side effects, and precautions. His life had become a blur of conversation, palpation, auscultation, penetration, dictation, and a deluge of paperwork. And managed care? Don't get him started.

For the time being, he did not worry about his or anyone else's patients. Nor did he think about unintended consequences, slippery slopes, corporate misadventures or the fate of good deeds. For the time being, he felt great. After three decades of private practice and ascension through the hierarchies of medical staffs and teaching faculties, Dan Fazen was going to hang 'em up.

Ben

H E SPEED-DIALED HOME.
"I'll give you the gory details later, but I just had the meeting with Marty and she told me that Mark Rader is leaving and she wants me to think about quitting practice and becoming Vice-President for Medical Affairs."

"Jesus," Susan said.

"My head's kind of spinning. Look, I'm going up to Ben's for lunch. Can't wait to hear what he'll have to say."

"Say more about how you're feeling." Ever the shrink.

"Pretty jazzed, actually. I know I have to be mature, analyze it, blah, blah, blah. But it feels pretty damn good right now."

"We'll talk," she said.

He tossed the cell phone onto the passenger seat and drove down the hill to pick up 680 South to Alamo.

As usual, Dan found him with his orchids. For Ben Berman, breeding orchids had been more a parallel career than a hobby. He had served for several years as a board member of the American Orchid Society, including a term as president. He had more publications describing research on orchids than on his medical specialty neurology. The AOS had even named a hybrid he'd created in his honor: *Albus bermanensis*. Dan saw him in the greenhouse as he walked up the gravel path from the road. Carrying a bag of take-out, he crossed the lawn and rapped on the glass. His old friend waved him in.

"Boychek!" Ben put down his trowel, wiped his hands, and welcomed him with a bear hug and a wet kiss on the cheek. He was several inches shorter than Dan with wiry arms and legs, a pinch of gut hanging over his rumpled chinos, and an angular face with twinkling blue eyes. With his prematurely acquired shock of white hair, he had often, as a younger man, been mistaken for Leonard Bernstein. As usual he smelled like cigars. He would smoke anything, but he particularly liked cigars, a passion he had only been able to fully indulge since his wife Libby's death. "Whaddaya got?"

"Chinese," Dan said.

"Great. How 'bout a beer?"

"Soda's fine."

"Let's sit out there." Ben led him inside to the refrigerator, then outside again to a redwood picnic table under a live oak behind the greenhouse. They ate and drank without speaking, their friendship easily incorporating a minute or so of silence.

"Hey, how about your pal, the junior senator?" Dan said.

He never passed up an opportunity to tweak his old friend's political nerve endings. Dan's mother would have called Ben "a real Bolshevik," and it would have been a compliment. Not actually a communist, but lavishly left-wing, Ben still referred to his favorite misanthrope often and only as "that prick Nixon." His loathing was engendered during Nixon's congressional red-baiting Alger Hiss period, well before his presidency and Watergate.

"The little putz is getting what he deserves," Ben said. Edward Norton (not the movie star, or for that matter the Ralph Kramden sidekick, but Edward Norton, the ultra-conservative senator from San Diego) had just been indicted for insider trading with information from his Texas oil friends. "This is a guy, talk about hypocrisy, who spun an entire political career out of outrage over non-existent Arkansas land deals. Norton got more mileage out of the Clinton-haters than anyone I can think of."

"Well, how about Karl Rove?"

Ben thought about it. "You've got a point."

"So, how are you?"

"I'm okay," Ben said. "My damn hands have been bothering me, especially if I don't take a break at the work table."

He would work for hours in the greenhouse and his knuckles would become stiff and painful. Dan would advise him to pre-medicate before these sessions with something like ibuprofen, and Ben would agree but rarely comply, saying that the pills upset his stomach. Dan would suggest that perhaps the frequent schnapps, cigars, and chopped liver and onions had something to do with his gastric distress, and Ben would shrug him off. They'd go on like that.

"I hate to ask," Dan said, "but are you taking anything for the arthritis?"

"Please."

They had met when Dan was a junior medical student doing a neurology elective and Ben was serving on the voluntary teaching faculty at UCSF. But the friendship between these two doctors, a generation apart, was forged in their political and ethical resonance, not in their medical dialogue.

"So how's my boy?" He meant his namesake, Dan's second child.

"We're pretty sure he's still at Yale," Dan said. "We send stamped self-addressed envelopes."

"Hey, he's a great kid."

"I know."

"Danny, how are you?"

"I'm good." He started to gather his thoughts. "I've got something to tell you about."

Ben leaned forward to listen.

"I had a meeting with Marty Sullivan this morning, like an hour ago. She told me that Mark Rader was leaving, by the way to go to Olympia Pacific, and she asked me to think about being the new Vice-President for Medical Affairs. I have to confess that I'm pretty interested. I've told you about being bored with the office. To tell you the truth, I understated it."

He tried to read Ben's face. He was looking back at him benignly, nodding.

"If she really offered it, and if I really took it, which I'm not saying I would, I'd have to learn a lot. But I already have plenty of experience in quality improvement and utilization management, and that's a big part of the job. I would need to get up to speed about things like risk management, treatment authorizations, managed care contracts."

It seemed to him that Ben was now staring at the bridge of his nose, the way that he himself would feign listening when his patients told him, in remarkable detail, about their bowel movements.

Dan had his own judgments about leaving practice for an administrative job, something that is "less than," not really being a doctor. The culture of medical practice was traditionally contemptuous of administrative chores for physicians, and of administrators themselves. *Who would spend ten years in pre-med, medical school and residency, only to waste their time on this shit?*

He knew that Ben had never been interested in the business side of practice. But it was a sad surprise when he saw him withdraw from his once beloved clinical work. Libby, his wife of forty-five years, had died of ovarian cancer. Were it not for her illness, Ben might still be conducting his neurology practice in Berkeley. He took nearly three years off to take care of her, and after her death recaptured neither his passion for patient care nor the desire for the office routine. He spent most of his time these days listening to Mozart, watching political talk shows, reading, writing letters to the editor, and working in the greenhouse. Dan knew that his regular Thursday visit for lunch was the high point of Ben's week.

"Tell me more about how the office feels," Ben said.

"Jesus, you sound like my wife."

Ben waited.

"It's not that it's terrible or anything. But it's boring. I'm mostly writing prescriptions, giving a little more or a little less of this or that for the same common stuff. Reassuring the worried well. At this point it's no great accomplishment to make a routine diagnosis, and almost all the diagnoses are of course routine. I enjoy seeing some of the patients, really because I like them personally. Has nothing to do with the doctoring."

Dan shooed a bee as he spoke, one of Ben's little helpers.

"I do spend a hell of a lot of time filling out forms, though. The HMOs are ratcheting down the rates. Christ, Medi-Cal is looking better all the time. For four years now I've made less money each year than the year before."

"So what do you like?"

"I don't know," Dan said. "There's something comforting, I guess, about the routine. I like the residents and the med students, the conferences at the hospital. But the typical day in the office is a countdown of remaining patients. I'm relieved at the cancellations, annoyed at the walk-ins. You know, when I say this stuff out loud, it sounds pretty bad." He paused and shook his head. "It feels like turning off to clinical practice is some kind of failure, something to be ashamed of. How was it for you?"

"It was different. I pretty much enjoyed it right up until Libby got sick." Ben wasn't going to shift the conversation to himself.

"I guess I'm burning out or having a mid-life crisis or something," Dan said.

"So is there anything positive about this job, or are you just looking to be rescued from practice?"

"Jesus, you're an annoying bastard."

"I love you, boychek."

Dan had always been his own toughest critic. As a resident he would obsess about each small error in fact or judgment, no matter how inconsequential. He was ruthless in the analysis of his own performance. He thought that he was just all right and that the faculty had an overinflated opinion of him. The interns and junior residents had idolized him and unanimously chose him as the recipient of the Outstanding Senior Resident Award, bestowed before the entire faculty at the resident graduation dinner. In typical form, Dan was completely surprised.

While he had softened on himself over the years, he still had a reservoir of suspicion. In response to accolades, he felt both pride and a sense that he had fooled them again, that he was part Daniel Fazen, M.D., mature, capable senior physician, and part impostor. With the solicitation from Marty only an hour old, Dan had found his harsh inner voice. Now he began his defense.

"Look, maybe I can do more good in a leadership role than I can as an individual practitioner. With all the push to control costs and limit care, someone in authority needs to try to ensure that quality doesn't go out the window."

He got up from the redwood bench and began pacing, hands in his pockets.

"The pressure to do less for the patients comes from every direction. That's what managed care is about. The payers, by one mechanism or another, pay less for everything, and the HMOs and hospitals press for less care at every opportunity. It's less, less, less. I'm not in favor of unnecessary anything, but there needs to be some kind of balance between all this cost-containment and the well-being of the patients. Striking that balance in an influential role with the physicians and hospital administration is worthwhile work. I have good relationships with the administrators and with most of the docs who matter. I'm not saying I will do it, but I think I could do it."

"Your abilities, Danny, are the least of my concerns. I am, however, plenty worried about the assholes."

With the same consistency that he bestowed upon the thirty-sixth president, Ben uniformly referred to hospital administrators as "the assholes," even the ones he liked.

"I have nothing against Marty Sullivan," Ben said, "but she answers to the Board. And yes, the current Board of Directors is okay. But in this *industry*," he hissed the word, "how do you know who's going to be where? Does Marty stay at Memorial? And who comes onto the Board? The Vice-President for Medical Affairs will work not just for these assholes, but for the next set of assholes. And who knows when?"

Dan had not thought about that. He sat down again. "Look, I know that anything can happen. But Marty is very popular and powerful. The hospital has been there for decades and is fundamentally stable. I don't see anything disruptive on the horizon."

Ben challenged his dear friend with his eyes.

"Look, I'm not going to do anything impulsive."

It would not be through naiveté that he would err on the side of taking this job. He would do it for the exhilaration of the change itself. Weary of private practice, this was the new thing in front of him—a career adventure, a fresh start. The risks were off in the future, and theoretical. The rewards were immediate, and not simply about his professional emancipation. There would be executive compensation—salary and benefits—and a legitimate senior leadership role. Money and power were in play, more than he was inclined to acknowledge to himself, or certainly to Ben. He looked at his watch and changed the subject.

"Well, I need to get to the office. So when are you coming to the house for dinner?"

Ben went along. "I don't know. When is Susan making the risotto?"

The Elmwood

HE THREE OF THEM—DAN, SUSAN AND CARLY—WERE clustered at the end of the dining room table lingering over Susan's notable chocolate layer cake. This room, with its bay window to the garden, parquet floors and dark oak moldings, had been the clincher in their decision to buy the house in 1985. The classic brown shingle, built in the mid-twenties, was tucked into a cul-de-sac three blocks from the heart of Berkeley's funky-chic Elmwood neighborhood. With Sarah across the Bay as a freshman medical student and Ben in his sophomore year at Yale, their once bustling and congested home had become quiet and roomy.

Susan was smiling. "I think it's great that Marty wants you to do it. It impresses the hell out of me."

"To be honest," Dan said, "it does feel good to be asked."

He had described with considerable precision the conversation with Memorial's CEO, and with less detail the visit with Ben. He knew he was shading the information, particularly anything that sounded like he was fleeing the practice, running away. He would come clean with Susan, about his ennui at the office and about Ben's concerns, but not in front of Carly.

Carly—Carlotta Maria—was named for her mom's paternal grandmother. She had inherited Susan's beauty and musical talent, was precocious at math, could hold her own at soccer, and, arising from somewhere in her Jewish-Italian gene pool, had difficulty seeing and writing language. Elementary school had been a struggle, with special education classes, a particular strength of the Berkeley school system, and private tutors. Now, as a freshman at Berkeley High, she continued to receive special instruction in reading. All of this in remarkable contrast to her mastery of the cello. By age twelve she had already aced her audition for BAYO, the Bay Area Youth Orchestra, and was under the weekly tutelage of Serge Rosenberg, the first chair of the San Francisco Symphony. Carly was brilliant, often frustrated, and not just a little bit volatile. She didn't respond well to change, and was becoming agitated as she listened to her father's news.

"I don't see why this is so good. Don't you like your patients anymore?"

"I like my patients fine, honey. But I've been doing exactly the same thing for a very long time. This new job would give me the chance to have new experiences, to have more variety. I'd be able to make a difference for lots of patients, but I'd be doing it differently."

Carly was staring at the table. "Does this mean that we have to move?"

"No, not at all. If I took the job, I'd be working full time at the hospital instead of dividing my time between the hospital and the office. There'd be fewer emergencies than there are now, and no need for me to live closer to the hospital. I'll probably have more control of my time than I do now."

It wasn't lost on Susan that he had just shifted from *I'd* to *I'll*.

Carly looked directly at her father. "Will I still be able to work with Serge?"

Susan weighed in. "Of course, honey. If daddy does this, it won't change any of the things that you're doing."

Like it was her own nervous system, Dan watched his wife navigate the microterrain of their daughter's voice and expression, the smallest departure. He knew too well the momentum of Carly's fragility. Susan was trying anyway. "This wouldn't affect your work with Serge at all."

He took her hand. "Carly, I wouldn't do anything to interfere with your music. You know that. That's a promise."

Carly's eyes welled with tears. Susan slid off her chair, pivoting, and Carly sank into her arms. He knew that there was nothing he could say, at least in the moment, that would matter. A variation of this scene had played out hundreds of times over her childhood. Carly's sensitivity to whatever—change or fear or disappointment or criticism—was exquisite. The exception was for Serge. His criticism and demands seemed only to steel her intensity to play better.

Dan watched them on their knees on the dining room rug, Carly's face pressed into Susan's neck, her shoulders aquiver. He joined them, sitting cross-legged next to Susan, his hands folded in his lap, eyes closed, listening. Being next to them, quiet, was the best he could do.

Throughout their relationship, they had their most serious conversations in bed in the dark. Their decision to get married, to start a family, to buy the Elmwood house. In 1990, with their "2.0 children doing just fine, thank you," as Susan liked to say, and their lives on track, she became pregnant despite meticulous use of a diaphragm. They'd had no intention of having a third child and Susan was just starting to get her life back as Ben entered pre-kindergarten. After a wrenching all-nighter, she was clear that she could not choose an abortion, and he was clear that he would support her decision.

Tonight they pecked and hugged, but neither initiated any familiar preludes to sex or sleep. He knew that she would wait for him to talk.

"Toni, this is a big one."

Her name was Susan Antonia Giuliani Fazen. He rarely called her Susan.

"I know," she said.

"Did Carly say anything else after dinner?"

"Uh uh."

"You know, realistically there's nothing in this job that threatens her in any way."

"What does realistically have to do with it?"

Now he waited for her.

"Look, help me understand this, about how you're feeling at the office. You don't need to win me over, just tell me what's going on." This, just above a whisper, her mouth at his ear.

One of the many things that Susan gave him was the freedom to be defenseless when it mattered. And this was true well before she was a seasoned psychotherapist. He knew that he could trust her with his feelings, that she admired him without idealizing him. When she asked him to really talk, and he did, there were no ambushes. It was one of the ways that she loved him exceptionally, and he got it.

"Do you remember when I started moonlighting in the emergency room in the early years of the practice? I'd be on call one or two nights a week and it didn't bother me. The money helped and I was used to sleeping in the hospital anyway. I did it for almost three years. And then, without any particular event or premonition, on one busy Sunday shift, exhausted, hustling from patient to patient, I just couldn't do it anymore. Do you remember? Not one shift more."

The insight crystallized as he spoke.

"Like I think I try to make something okay even as it's getting worse. So I can avoid the conflict, just not deal with it. At some point it just surfaces, unacceptable. I mean right then and there. I never did another ER shift again."

She was kneading the back of his neck.

"Starting about a month ago, I began consciously dreading the office. I know I've said a few things about it, but I haven't told you just how bad it feels. The first thing I do when I get there is count the appointments. I tell Karen to shunt the add-ons to the ER, even when there's space in the schedule. As I see each patient, I'm doing the math, watching the clock. I'm not present with them the way I used to be. I mean I'm not grossly rushing them or making mistakes. But it's just get 'em in and get 'em out. An experienced nurse practitioner could take care of ninety-five percent of what I'm seeing, or more. I just want to get to the end of the day. It's depressing. And the thought of another five or ten years of it?" He let the thought incubate. "The way it feels right now, I don't want to do it for another week."

He exhaled, quiet for several more seconds.

"I've been seeing patients for over thirty-five years. It just doesn't feel like anything anymore. You know, like I already gave." He was crossing a line, testifying aloud to the depth of his discontent, giving it the hardened reality of speech, of a witness. And his voice was rising.

She followed his lead and stopped whispering. "So what about this position? What's Marty talking about?"

"I haven't seen the job description yet, but I pretty much know what it is."

He went on to describe that there would be no direct patient care, but that there would be a major responsibility for review of the quality of care. He said that one of the reasons that Marty approached him was his performance as Chairman of the Quality Improvement Committee. He talked about being ultimately responsible for the whole quality review process and for the management of the medical staff office, which oversees the credentials and privileges of all the physicians. He described roles in the negligence suits against the hospital, and in the preparation for visits by the various regulatory agencies.

"It's an administrative job," he said, "but it has a lot to do with what kind of care all of the hospitalized patients get."

"So what's the problem?"

"Well, for one thing, it isn't doctoring."

"You just said that you're bored with doctoring."

"Well, yeah."

"So what's the problem?"

"Well, part of the problem is that it just seems weird to become an administrator, even though it's a medical administrator. And we didn't get into it a lot, but Ben thinks it's risky."

"Like how?"

"I don't know, he said he was worried about changes in Marty's position, the board members. Eventually. I told him that I thought the leadership at the hospital was pretty stable. He didn't say anything, but he looked at me like I was, uh..." Dan tilted his head back as though he could find the word on the ceiling, "...like I was naive or something."

"Is he right?"

"I don't know. Maybe. I don't know. Look, if I'm going to extricate myself from practice and try something new, it's not going to be completely without risk. I think there's plenty of upside here. It would be a big change for me, which I need. And no bullshit, I think I could do some genuine good for the patients." He hesitated. "It wasn't discussed but I'm sure there'll be a significant increase in income, a big fringe benefit package. Pension and deferred compensation, maybe even a signing bonus." He was up on his elbows.

She brought down the volume. "Look, you don't have to sell me. I just want to know what's going on."

"I need to make a change."

"I get it."

"I'll have a job description to look at in the next day or two, and presumably a written offer if I tell Marty I'm interested. There's no need to decide anything now." He needed another increment of clarity. "Are you okay with this?"

"Danny, you need to play this out."

That he was going to take the job seemed a certainty. On balance it made sense. Above all, he could not spend another decade doing something he didn't like. They kissed softly, once, and whispered their goodnights. The Fazens, the three of them, had a fitful night.

VPMA

—

H E GOT THE CORNER OPPOSITE MARTY. IT WAS NEWLY carpeted and painted, and furnished in dark walnut and grey nubby upholstery. The office was divided it into three areas—a workstation, an oval conference table and chairs, and a soft sitting arrangement. His accumulated stuff was scattered about. Family photographs, degrees, awards, a buddha, a menorah, nameplates, artwork large and small, and a half dozen plants. One wall, corner to corner and floor to ceiling, was crammed with his books and journals. Susan raved about it, especially the view of Mount Diablo. Even Carly liked it. It was no oversight, though, that he had not invited Ben in. His cranky mentor would be merciless about the domain of the assholes.

He had not worked like this since residency. Twelve hour days were routine, and with evening events at the hospital, fifteen and sixteen hour days were common enough to matter. While he had an alleged rule about leaving work at work, he violated it regularly, bringing unfinished business home on the weekends.

The central activity of the medical administrator was the meeting. There was email and phone, journals and paperwork, but mostly there was the meeting. There were standing meetings, project meetings, personnel meetings, ad hoc meetings, emergency meetings; there were casual encounters that turned into meetings; there were meetings to plan meetings and meetings to evaluate meetings; there were even meetings to decide if there were too many meetings. The meeting was the place where information was as likely to be thrust as shared. Regardless of content, these ubiquitous events were in one way or another expressions of hospital politics, the overt and covert play of authority in the organization. The atmospherics were infinitely variable and depended as much on the cast of characters as on the subject matter itself. The presence of legitimate authority packaged in a powerful persona, Marty for instance, rearranged the molecules in the room. While Dan was treated respectfully and given a quantum of deference, he did not have Marty's kind of gravitas.

There were days when there was nothing but meetings. On this particular Tuesday Dan went from a seven a.m. monthly standing with a medical department chairman, to a secretarial job interview, to a utilization management committee meeting, to a standing weekly with the QI Coordinator, to a prep session for a regulatory visit by the State Department of Health Services, to a lunch meeting to discuss an HMO contract renewal, to an unexpected hour with a distraught OR nurse who was alleging verbal abuse by a neurosurgeon—this instead of an hour of desk time to catch up on the various forms of mail—to an Executive Management Group discussion of a budget challenge by the Board of Directors, to a reception honoring long-time employees, to a meeting that he himself chaired exploring a consolidated cancer center adjacent to the hospital. At three minutes to six he got to his desk. He had barely started to click through his email.

"Got a minute?" Marty was leaning against his door jamb.

"Sure." He would have preferred to stay seated and gesture her to the chair facing the desk. Etiquette lifted him up and they settled at the end of his conference table.

She had come at the end of this long day to schmooze about re-engineering, the in vogue cost-containment process that Memorial was embarking on well after most of its competition. Marty and her management team were preparing for an all-day retreat three days hence with their Board of Directors.

"Dan, you know re-engineering is going be the most difficult thing we've taken on since I've been CEO. It's going to shake this place right down to its shoes. It's all well and good to talk about re-designing processes, creating new efficiencies, emphasizing utilization management, yada, yada, yada. In the end, no matter how you package it, you're talking layoffs and less skilled people. And that'll mostly be about nurses. That's where the costs are."

She left a space but he remained quiet, more of an administrative novice than he liked to let on.

"The unions are gonna go nuts," she said, "and I guarantee you the media'll be all over us. The Board needs to understand the kind of shit that's gonna go down. I don't want them blind-sided. As much as anything, the purpose of this retreat is to manage the expectations of the Board members. Most of these people haven't a clue about what it means to try to take thirty million out of a three hundred million dollar operating budget."

In his brief tenure as VPMA, Dan had come to realize that the role of the Chief Executive Officer was quite different from what it seemed at a distance. Though most people in a large organization see the CEO as the big boss, the one who tells everyone else what to do, the good CEO manages mostly up and out rather than down. Marty's energy and creativity were focused on the Board, the media, the regulatory agencies, the unions, local government and businesses, the philanthropic community. For the most part, she let her senior staff, including Dan, run the place day-to-day. While she might occasionally meddle in the nuts and bolts of cost-containment, her attention would be on managing the responses of the Board and the external environment.

"Dan, I need you to be a ferocious quality champion. We're going to be trying to wring every last cent out of the budget, and I'll be the loudest cheerleader in the room. I want you to push back hard on medical quality issues. Don't give in. And don't worry about me."

He was thinking that she had gotten awfully perky for this late in the day. He kept his eye contact and nodded.

"If we let the cost-containment imperatives and the medical quality imperatives collide, as messy as that might be, we'll end up with a budget reduction that's acceptable, that peels away some of the cost but doesn't go too far. As our senior physician, you're the right person to be our outspoken quality conscience and patient advocate."

Now his thoughts wandered to professional wrestling. His CEO was choreographing a mock battle between them for the sake of a moderate outcome. She had no intention of making it to the full quality-crushing thirty million dollar reduction. She would allow herself to be body slammed and pinned at fifty or sixty or seventy percent of the goal. She would read the media, the unions, the employees, the medical staff, the Board, and she would tank when she thought the time was right.

"It'll be tough," he said, "but okay, I'll take the moral high ground."

"Dan, I'm serious."

"Don't worry about it. If you were asking me to eat the cuts regardless of the risk, then you and I would have a problem. What you're asking is who I am. Don't sweat it."

"I guess I'm sweating it in general," she said. "You know we've had losses for three consecutive quarters. Not big losses, but losses nonetheless. The managed care rates are killing us. And the number of hospitalized patients lately has certainly been less than breathtaking. The Board hasn't been openly critical, but they haven't been exactly overjoyed either. Given what we're about to undertake, the chemistry could be better."

"You're thinking that the Board may really bring the hammer down on cost-containment?"

"That's what I'm thinking." She got up.

"Well thanks for the tasty assignment," he said. "I'm going to be on point resisting reductions. Have I got that right?"

She was almost at the door when she turned back, smiling. "Don't worry about it. You're a doc, they won't hurt you. Besides, you've got me."

Memorial's re-engineering retreat was hosted by its most famous and formidable Board member. C.J. Corbett was a high-technology executive dynamo one level below the likes of Gates, Grove, and Ellison. His company, Redwood Solutions, had moved from obscurity to international prominence in the early nineties on the strength of its development of security systems for internet commerce. At Redwood's initial public offering in 1993, Corbett personally made over three hundred million dollars in a single day—in those days, a big score. His net worth was now estimated at nearly eight billion.

C.J. had a remarkable early resume. Valedictorian of his high school class in San Diego; NCAA national wrestling champion at 160 pounds in his senior year at Stanford; Rhodes Scholar; Master's from Cal Tech; and an MBA from the Sloane School, the latter acquired while working as a member of the Macintosh design team in the early eighties. He built Redwood Solutions from scratch with three friends from Apple and $500,000 in venture capital.

His public persona nowadays was shaped by his visibility as an outspoken conservative Republican. But he was not so easy to categorize. He was pro-choice, pro-nuclear power, pro-gun control, anti-national health insurance, pro-environment, and he thought the religious right were mostly bigots and idiots. His personal charities included AIDS research, the State of Israel, the Sierra Club, the Catholic Church, and Habitat for Humanity. Corbett's conservatism was related to the free market, about which he was ferocious. His hero was the late model Barry Goldwater.

Marty had confided her reluctance when C.J. offered Redwood for the retreat, but a refusal would have been a frontal insult. A gorgeous facility, it was still his turf. Corbett could be a load in any environment, but especially in his own setting. His Board Room was meant to impress with its centerpiece, a massive circular mahogany table, its vaulted skylit ceiling, gallery-quality southwestern artwork, and a herd's worth of swiveling, rocking calfskin on wheels.

"Good morning everyone," C.J. said. "It's my pleasure and honor to welcome you all to Redwood. I believe that the work we will begin today initiates a new era in the history of the Walnut Creek Memorial Hospital." Dressed down for the retreat, he wore a navy knit short-sleeved shirt, tan pleated cotton pants and suede tasseled loafers. He had a lean powerful upper body, a reminder of his college wrestling days, blue-gray eyes behind frameless glasses, and a blond buzz cut. Dan thought that he looked like a jet fighter pilot.

After a few more remarks by Corbett, a greeting from the Chairman of the Board, and the standard around-the-table introductions, the floor was Marty's. She began with what was described in re-engineering jargon as "the burning platform," the scenario that demanded action not just for the improvement of your hospital, but for its very survival. You are standing on a platform, the basic ground of your organization, and it's in flames. If you don't decisively extinguish the fire, you're dead.

"In the past decade, the business, the literal *business,* of hospital care has changed radically. At the end of the 1980's, despite the early inroads of managed care, and even in California, the acute care hospital with a decent physician catchment area and good name identification operated comfortably and expansively with a steady flow of fee-for-service dollars through commercial insurers and Medicare."

With her resonant voice and JFK inflections, Marty had the room in two sentences.

"We were building facilities and expanding services. And we were starting to learn to control utilization, that is, to control the length of admissions and the number of diagnostic studies ordered and medications prescribed. We did this because

Medicare paid for hospitalizations by diagnosis, regardless of length of stay or services provided. For the time being, anyway, this is still the case."

This was Hospital Business 101. She wanted to be sure that the less experienced board members got it.

"The external business and financial environment has changed profoundly, and at the heart of that change is the health care financing mechanism called *capitation*."

Marty, using projections from a laptop, detailed the dramatic transition that was taking place in health care financing. She described the shift away from fee-for-service reimbursement by insurers who paid for medical expenses in exchange for premiums. The actuaries figured it all out so that the insurers could make money, plenty of it, by raising the premiums. The problem was that fee-for-service powerfully encouraged the medical and hospital providers to do more of everything, and the costs for health care, borne mostly by government and the employers who buy coverage from the insurance companies, have gone through the roof. The response has been managed care—managed cost— which uses capitation, in Latin *per head*, as its principal financial mechanism.

"In capitation, the health care providers get a fixed amount of money per insured person per month from the insurer, which is usually a Health Maintenance Organization, an HMO. While there's a large variety of complex financial arrangements through which this can be done, they all add up to the hospital being financially at risk for excessive care. This, in and of itself, is not necessarily a bad thing. We all know that the dark side of fee-for-service was over-consumption—unnecessary surgery, medications, hospital days."

Marty moved to the heart of the matter.

"The HMOs own the so-called lives, the insured members. And the intense competition between the hospitals leads to our acceptance of contracts with the HMOs that require dramatically discounted rates for our services. So, we are not only at financial risk for excessive care, but we are providing services for deeply discounted reimbursement. After all, the whole point of managed care is to lower the cost."

She shut off the projector, turned up the lights and waited several seconds. With her arms folded across her chest she spoke quietly.

"So here it is. While the details are complex, the bottom line isn't. In order to get contracts to take care of patients, we need to accept deeply discounted rates from the HMOs. To do that and survive, we must reduce our expenses, dramatically and soon. And we must control the costs of care once the patient is in the hospital. If we do not do these things, we will not be financially viable." The burning platform.

Dan listened to Marty finish on a high ground, talking about the mission of Memorial and its history of service to the community. The Chief Financial Officer gave an overview of the hospital's performance over the prior five years, including the worrisome data of the past year. Then the senior re-engineering consultant spent an hour describing in detail how aggressive cost-containment would be implemented. This was dry stuff and Dan was having difficulty staying focused. Throughout these three long presentations, and the Q&A following each, C.J. Corbett remained attentive but said nothing.

After lunch it was Dan's turn. He had given serious thought to Marty's advice about his function in the process and to what he was going to say. He spoke without notes.

"Marty has eloquently described the dark side of fee-for-service, the over-utilization of services that drove health care costs through the roof in the 1980's and 90's. Well there's a dark side to managed care and its imperatives, and that is under-utilization: barriers to access and minimal care once you're there."

This was a pep rally for dramatically cutting costs, and here he was, the voice of moderation. That's what Marty said she wanted.

He went on to give examples of poor service and medical complications ascribed to severe labor reductions in other Bay Area hospitals. He talked about the complexity of controlling costs for hospitalized patients. And he spoke at length about maintaining the loyalty of the large cadre of physicians who referred their patients to Memorial.

"Believe me, I fully understand that we have to improve our business position. No market, no mission. This is understood. But it is essential that we strike a balance between cost-containment and our historic commitment to the patients and physicians of our community. For all the energy that we put into saving money, there needs to be a balance created by our efforts to protect patients. I believe that that is the real challenge and I believe that we can do it."

After Dan finished, he sat down. Neither Marty nor C.J. said anything. He had no idea how he had been received.

He was followed by two long technical presentations, one by hospital counsel and the other by a labor specialist from the consulting group, and at the end of the afternoon there was a wrap-up session. When it seemed that most of the energy had gone out of the room, C.J. Corbett got up to speak. Throughout the day everyone had spoken from their chairs, or at least standing at their place. C.J., hands in his pockets, slowly circled the perimeter of the big round table as he quietly began. Dan imagined that Corbett had worked this room hundreds of times in precisely this fashion.

After expressions of praise and pride for the hospital, its leadership, and its efforts in the re-engineering endeavor, C.J. went for the last word. "Let me tell you something about quality, folks. It does not distinguish you from your competition because your patients, your customers, cannot see it. Doctor Fazen, I hope you'll forgive me for calling your patients customers. I know that each time I do that, an angel dies."

With Dan as his involuntary straight man, C.J. got the biggest laugh of the day.

"Being a health care consumer is like being an airline passenger. You can't have the slightest idea about the level of performance in the maintenance hanger or the cockpit. Likewise, the patient is not equipped to assess what the doctor, the nurse, or the hospital is doing. What they can appreciate is service. How long are they on hold when they call? How easy and quick is registration? How good is the food in the rooms and the cafeteria? How easy is it to find a parking space? If you look at the complaints that the HMOs get from their members, 95% of them are about service, not quality."

C.J. talked about tales of service excellence. Nordstrom, Disney, and, proudly, Redwood. He mused on financial discipline, courage in decision-making, the intensity of competition among hospitals, and on the commonalities between health care and other service businesses.

"You'll sink or swim on three things, folks. The first is brand name. Do not underestimate the power of that. Coke hasn't won a blinded taste test with Pepsi for decades, but guess who dominates the market? Second is customer service, and third and by far the most important is, guess what, price. The purchasers of health care, primarily the HMOs or their contracted partners, for all their talk of quality, are interested in a hospital with low prices, a decent brand name, and not too much aggravation with service complaints by their members. As Marty clearly articulated this morning, the path to low pricing is cost reductions. Not just containment, folks, reductions. I think we're definitely on the right track."

After C.J. finished, Marty did the benediction and everyone headed home. Dan had a moment with her in the parking lot. She was effusive. "Hey, you were great. Those folks needed to hear what you had to say."

"Thank you." He was relieved. "Were you happy with how it went?"

"It was fine," she said. "C.J. was on good behavior. He did his little thing at the end, which he enjoys, but he's certainly behind what we're trying to do. Mission accomplished, I think."

Into the Fray

—

DEFYING PROBABILITY, DAN WENT NINE MONTHS AS VPMA without a major crisis with a member of the medical staff. He knew that his period of grace was over as he started to review the medical record of a twenty-eight year old diabetic man who had been found dead in his hospital bed a week earlier. Clare, Dan's secretary, had given him the chart with a note from the Chairman of the Department of Medicine. It read simply, "Let's talk." When he saw the name of this unfortunate patient's attending physician, he understood.

Doctor Walton Hill was a fifth-generation blue blood from nearby Orinda, the ritziest town in the county. He'd been in practice for over four decades, and as a much younger man, been considered a fine clinician. Always a cranky humorless sort, he'd become in his later years increasingly eccentric in his practice of medicine. Though Memorial was a teaching hospital with first-rate interns and residents, Walt Hill insisted that no trainee examine or even talk to his hospitalized patients. He practiced with stealth, avoiding consultations whenever possible. Because hospitalization in the intensive care unit required automatic involvement of critical care specialists, Hill was inclined to avoid the ICU by putting seriously ill patients in routine rooms, and therefore with less sophisticated nurses. His care had been criticized in a handful of cases over the past several years, for use of outmoded medications and failure to seek consultations. But until now, none of his decisions had led to a catastrophic outcome.

Dan began to sift through the chart, searching out the patient's medical history and physical examination, and particularly the preliminary autopsy report.

The review of a medical record could be a tedious business. In an older patient or any patient with complex problems, the chart itself could be huge, at times several volumes. In pediatrics, the chart might actually weigh more than the patient. While there was considerable talk about voice recognition technology, electronic medical records and paperless hospitals, most places still had conventional manila folders stuffed with an olio of forms, typed dictations, computer printouts, photocopies, and handwritten physician and nurse entries, which varied from meticulously legible to incomprehensible. These records, for better or worse, constituted the focal point of all case reviews. In professional performance evaluations, regulatory oversight, and malpractice considerations—where errors of omission were far more common than those of commission—the general principal was "if it isn't in the medical record, it didn't happen."

Doctor Hill's deceased patient, Dennis Barber, had been a juvenile diabetic since age twelve. Considering his sixteen-year history of the disease, he'd had a relatively benign course. He was hospitalized only twice after his initial admission, and he did not have advanced complications such as severe eye or kidney disease. As Dan scanned the record, he was surprised to see that Barber had weathered the tumultuous adolescent years far better than most diabetics. This was not a patient that an expert, an endocrinologist, would have identified as being at risk for an acute lethal event.

Even with a cursory review, Dan knew why the man was dead, and he knew why it was Walt Hill's fault.

His first phone call was not to the Chairman of the Department of Medicine or to Marty or even to Doctor Hill. His first call was to a lawyer. Richard Reynolds and his partners had for years been on retainer to provide legal services for Memorial. Reynolds, a specialist in medical staff issues, was a frequent advisor to Dan and the members of the Quality Improvement Committee.

"We've got an ugly one, Richard. A preventable death involving Walton Hill."

"Shit."

"Right."

"Can you give me a two minute summary?"

"Right off," Dan said, "there's the question of immediate suspension of privileges while we do a formal evaluation. We need to make a decision about at least that without much delay. In a nutshell, Hill admitted a twenty-eight year old diabetic man with DKA, diabetic keto-acidosis, hid him out on the general medicine floor, sought no consultation, and dramatically mismanaged his IV fluids and electrolytes. Specifically, he broke a cardinal rule and let the patient's serum potassium fall to dangerously low levels. His death was almost certainly due to a fatal cardiac arrhythmia secondary to hypokalemia. That's low potassium."

He decided on the fly to spare this lawyer the minutiae of cellular ion transport.

"I've seen the numbers and I'm comfortable with my interpretation. As we go through the formal review, we'll get an endocrinologist to give an opinion. But frankly, I'm confident that he'll agree."

"Jesus, Dan. Hill's son-in-law is on your Board of Directors, right?"

"Yes indeed. And that's not all. Hill still has plenty of influence with the county medical society, especially the older country club guys. And he's genetically mean."

"Look, why don't we sit down with Marty. You know, tease out all the considerations and come up with a plan."

"We better include Jack Jensen," Dan said. "He's Hill's Department Chairman. Jack thinks the guy's a menace."

"All right. You know we need to do this quickly. This will almost certainly get reported to the state, and if we delay in protecting Hill's other patients, they'll want to know why."

"That's why I called, Richard. I'll have Clare set something up within the next day or two."

Marty had been in a foul mood for weeks. The hospital had lost money for yet another quarter, making it four in a row for a collective loss of nearly nine million dollars. Re-engineering efforts, even if they were fruitful, wouldn't hit the bottom line for at least another six months. The Board's Finance Committee, which normally met quarterly, was at C.J. Corbett's insistence now meeting monthly. Dan knew that the last thing that Marty would want to hear was that an ultra-connected medical staff member was about to face a humiliating and possibly career-ending chain of events.

There was no informality to the meeting. Dan was the first to arrive but was not invited in until both Richard Reynolds and Jack Jensen were there. When the three men were ushered in, Marty remained seated behind her desk, apparently finishing a task on her computer. Without looking up, she told them to sit down. The congeniality that Dan had grown accustomed to in this office was not remotely in evidence.

Marty had been told only that there was a serious quality issue with Hill, that they needed to meet with her right away. The three of them, sitting side by side facing her desk, waited for her to start the conversation.

"All right, what's going on?"

Dan began. "Marty, a young man, a twenty-eight year old diabetic named Dennis Barber, was found dead in his bed on Two Center ten days ago. His attending physician was Walton Hill. Barber was first diagnosed as a juvenile diabetic at age twelve. He was able to self-manage his insulin almost from the start and had, as these things go, a pretty smooth time of it through high school. On two occasions he—"

"Dan, I know how you guys like to present cases," she said, "but could you give me a break. Give me some bottom line, some context, so that I know why the hell I'm listening. Please, don't torture me with the goddamn medical student presentation."

While Marty was making no effort to conceal her agitation, Dan did his best not to reveal his. This meeting was entirely for her benefit. She had no formal authority over Hill's medical staff status and, strictly speaking, did not have to be included in any disciplinary considerations. Dan and Jensen and Reynolds were there because the case was a political, legal, and public relations time bomb. They were there to give her the opportunity to do damage control, to protect her from being blind-sided. Dan appreciated that she was under financial pressure from the Board, and that her instincts had already told her that she was about to hear something horrific. Still, he thought she was being an asshole.

"All right, "he said, "we're here because it's a virtual certainty that we're going to have to suspend Walt Hill's privileges, at least for now, because of the way he managed a patient who died. And we're going to have to report it to the State Department of Health Services. Okay?"

"Thank you. Go on."

Well, thank you for allowing me to speak in your fucking condescending presence.

"Marty, I think that you do need to hear some background and detail to appreciate that this clearly was a patient who should not have died." Jensen and Reynolds remained quiet, content to have Dan in the lead.

"All right, go ahead. I'll just listen. For a while."

While Dan didn't throw a tantrum—it wasn't in his workplace repertoire—his anger was uncamouflaged.

"As I was saying, Dennis Barber was a twenty-eight year old juvenile diabetic who was initially diagnosed at age twelve. It matters, and I wouldn't mention it, Marty, if it didn't, that he had a relatively benign course over his sixteen years with the disease. Only two prior hospitalizations and remarkably minimal long-term effects. It matters, Marty, because he was not metabolically volatile, or non-compliant with treatment, or riddled with complications."

He was over-enunciating.

"He should not have been at risk for death with what appears to have been a routine episode of DKA during a viral illness, a flu syndrome of some kind. Now do you understand why his past history matters? No disrespect, Marty, but we're not conducting an amateur show here."

She exhaled with a flourish. "Look, I'm sorry guys. There's a lot going on. You're trying to inform me about a genuine problem, a crisis really, and I'm giving you shit. I am sorry. Dan, go ahead. Help me understand what happened. And chill a little bit yourself, okay?"

He waited a few beats. "To understand what happened to this patient, we've got to get into some biochemistry. No way to avoid it. I'm sure that you know that the fundamental problem in a diabetic is the lack of insulin. And that diabetics make up for this by giving themselves insulin injections and taking measurements of the sugar levels in their blood and urine. They also measure ketones in the urine. When a diabetic gets an acute illness, say the flu, they actually need more insulin. That's true even if they're eating less, even if they're throwing up. And it's counter-intuitive. The diabetic thinks, 'If I eat less, I need less insulin.' And that makes sense. Except when they're ill."

As Dan spoke, he was tracking Marty's temperament. She didn't appear to be reloading.

"When they're ill, the cells in their body, by mechanisms we don't understand very well, become relatively resistant to insulin. So they need more insulin rather than less. When Dennis Barber called Walt Hill and told him he had a fever and that he was throwing up, Hill told him not to take *any* insulin. That decision was the one that got him sick enough to be in the hospital. It was, however, not the one that killed him. Are you with me?"

"It's not so complicated."

"Well, it does get a little more complex. Jack, would you go through what happened in the hospital?"

Now that Marty had softened, Jensen seemed happy to join in.

"Hill meets the patient in the Emergency Room and finds that his blood sugar is elevated, in the six hundreds, and that he looks dehydrated and has significant acidosis. He makes a decision, a bad one, to admit him to the general medicine floor. Before he goes—"

"Wait a minute," Marty said. "You better give me a little primer on acidosis."

"Acidosis is sort of what it sounds like. Too much acid in the body. When diabetics don't have enough insulin, they can't use sugar, specifically glucose, in the biochemical reactions that manufacture energy in the liver. The liver, as a second choice, breaks down fat to make energy. The by-products of those reactions are acidic, and if enough of those substances accumulate in the tissues and the blood, the body becomes more acidic. Acidosis."

Marty was following intently now. "So the patient died because of severe acidosis?"

"No, that would be too easy," Jack said. "The patient died because of low potassium."

"Low potassium? You didn't say anything about potassium."

"One step at a time. Here's where it gets a little tricky. When the patient has acidosis, the measured potassium level in the blood overestimates the actual amount of potassium inside the cells of the body. There is less, and possibly much less, potassium in the body than is reflected in the potassium levels measured in the blood. Barber's potassium level came back from the lab in the low normal range, which meant that at the beginning of treatment on the ward, his body potassium levels were already dramatically low. Doctor Hill gave him enough insulin and a reasonable amount of IV fluid, but he barely gave him any potassium at all."

"That seems kind of esoteric to me." Marty's tone wasn't combative. She was just prospecting for some reasonable doubt.

Dan spoke up to validate Jensen's analysis. "Marty, the false high potassium in DKA is basic knowledge in the care of these patients. It's been a board question for thirty years." He was referring to the internal medicine board certification examination. "This is not top secret information."

"Well, then why didn't the nurses catch it?"

"They're not critical care nurses," Dan said. "They're general med/surg nurses. They shouldn't be taking care of DKA, and usually they don't. Barber should have been in the ICU. This wouldn't have happened there. And this wouldn't have happened even on the general ward if there'd been an endocrinology consultation. Anyway, Jack do you want to finish the story?"

"Sure. There's not much more. At about eighteen hours into treatment, he was found dead in bed. We're presuming that he had a fatal cardiac arrhythmia. We know that dramatic hypokalemia is associated with severe disturbances of cardiac—"

"What's hypokalemia?"

"I'm sorry. That's low potassium. We know that very low potassium levels can cause severe abnormalities of cardiac rhythm. Christ, even with the mismanagement of the potassium, if he'd been on a cardiac monitor, which he would have been in the ICU, some EKG abnormalities would have been detected before he had a fatal arrhythmia. Anyway, the serum potassium drawn post-mortem was 1.1, and that may have been still falsely elevated."

"What's normal?"

"About 3 to 5.5."

Another loud sigh from Marty. "Is there any plausible alternative explanation for why this man died?"

Dan was shaking his head. "Not really. The preliminary autopsy report describes nothing except some dehydration and modest chronic diabetic changes in some of the tissues. I can't see it."

"Jack?"

"Nope."

"Christ. All right, Richard. What are the options?"

The hospital lawyer broke it down. "We don't have many. From a medical staff standpoint, the case needs to be formally reviewed by the QI Committee. From what I've heard today, they'll surely recommend limitation of Hill's privileges. Unless he voluntarily resigns from the medical staff, which I doubt, there'll be a full due process hearing. In the meantime, Jack, as his Department Chairman, needs to suspend his privileges immediately. Which of course triggers a formal notification of the state, which also needs to occur immediately. I don't see how you can avoid it."

Reynolds paused, leaving room for argument. Marty moved him along, "What about risk management?"

"Well, we're the deep pocket here. He died in the hospital. Dan, you need to notify the hospital's liability carrier, and you need to try to come up with some kind of damage control with this poor guy's family. Marty, the media and the Board are your bailiwick. I haven't seen anything in the newspapers, but of course someone can always drop a dime. As far as the Board is concerned, this is a pretty unique situation. What are you going to do about Hill's son-in-law?"

Marty ignored the question. "What about the patient's family?"

Jack responded. "He was single. Lived with his mother. I haven't spoken to her, but I think I'd better. Richard, I'd like to talk with you and the liability folks before I have that conversation."

Marty was talking as she came around her desk toward the three men. They pushed themselves out of their chairs.

"All right. Dan, you deal with the QI review, the state notification and contact the malpractice carrier. Jack, you need to take care of the suspension of privileges and you've got to do it today, this afternoon. I don't want our Doctor Hill slipping a patient in here over the weekend. And you also need to create some kind of contact with the patient's mother." Marty hesitated, shaking her head. "I'll deal with the Board. I don't know how the fuck I'm going to do that, but it's mine. Maybe we'll get lucky and stay out of the newspapers. Oh, and Dan, you'd better work with Richard on a due process sequence for Hill. I really don't think the old fart's gonna resign. Anyone have any other ideas?"

—

Driving home in the Friday evening crush, Dan's thoughts about the Barber case gravitated not to the patient or the negligent doctor, but to Marty. While he was impressed by her grasp of all the elements of the situation that required action, and quickly, he was disturbed by her behavior at the beginning of the meeting. He had never seen that kind of raw hostility from her. On his list of reasons for taking the job at Memorial, working with Martha Sullivan had been right at the top. Feisty and tough were fine, but nasty was something else. She had only been obnoxious for a few minutes, and she had apologized, but in some way it shook his foundation. Later, in bed with Susan, she asked him how he was feeling about what happened. He thought for a while, struggling to capture it.

"Unsafe, I guess."

The Four Bridge View

A FEW YEARS EARLIER, CARLY WOULD NEVER HAVE MISSED ONE of her mom's performances. These days, when she wasn't practicing the cello or doing her homework, she was inseparable from her coed clique of high school confidantes, her "peeps." Attached as Carly was to her parents, the last thing this edgy ninth-grader wanted to do was socialize with them. So Dan, in jeans and tee-shirt, sandals off, sat alone on a blanket under a cloudless Sunday sky in Live Oak Park in North Berkeley.

Over the decades this lovely bit of greenery, not much more than one square block nestled in a middle-class residential neighborhood, had hosted hundreds of weekend events, expressions of East Bay politics and culture—from free speech to free Tibet, women's rights to gay rights, save the whales to save the rain forest; from impeach Nixon to re-elect Clinton to re-defeat Bush. And scattered among these national and global agendas were countless local causes like speed bumps, bike paths, and the neighborhood recycling center.

Susan's band, Heart To Heart, was one of several acts playing in support of a fundraiser for the struggling Berkeley Contemporary Cultural Center. The Center had recently, and with considerable fuss, lost its funding from the National Endowment for the Arts. The U.S. Congress somehow failed to appreciate the artistic value of exploding sculpture busts of Jesse Helms and Strom Thurmond, accompanied by the love theme from *Gone with the Wind*.

Heart To Heart, named for the opening line of a Stanley Brothers classic, was a traditional bluegrass cover band, and one of Susan's many musical incarnations. She played rhythm guitar, sang a few leads, and powered the harmonies. They took the stage, lining up five across with Susan in the center, flanked by mandolin and fiddle, with bass and banjo on the ends. She stood tall in her cowboy boots and hat, embroidered white blouse, string tie and brown leather vest. Dan had fallen in love watching her play and sing, and through the years he never failed to melt at least a little when she performed.

The band rolled smoothly through a short set, opening with their namesake song at breakneck tempo. They mixed in a Patsy Cline number, flaunted their instrumental chops on "Clinch Mountain Backstep," did a four-part gospel harmony with spare accompaniment by Susan's D-28, and finished big and fast with Bill Monroe's "Molly and Tenbrooks." For an encore, they got the crowd on their feet singing "Will the Circle Be Unbroken."

Guitar case in tow, Susan made her way through the crowd. Dan stood and greeted her with a long hug and a soft peck on the mouth. "You rocked 'em, Tone."

"Thanks. How was the sound out here?"

"I thought it was fine," he said. "Good balance, the leads were on top, plenty of volume, no distortion that I could hear."

"Good. Hey, I'm starving. Can we get outta here?"

They headed for Saul's, a kosher deli a half mile away on Shattuck Avenue. Ben liked to say that if it weren't for Saul's, you'd have to go to L.A. for chopped liver. They settled side by side in a maroon vinyl booth, ordered a bowl of matzo ball soup, a corned beef sandwich, and a plate of potato latkes, all to share, and Susan started to decompress.

"So, you were pleased?" Dan asked.

"Yeah, we were fine. The stage mix was really good. I heard everything. And the guys played great. Avram just exploded on "Clinch.""

In a genre laden with Earls, Clems, and Jethros, the banjo player, improbably, was Avram Goldbloom. A multi-instrument wizard, teacher, and session man, Avram had been Susan's friend and collaborator since their undergraduate days at UC-Berkeley.

She was just getting started. "The crowd was very cool, really quiet, acknowledged the good breaks. And it wasn't an automatic encore, they wanted it."

"You sang great," he said. "The harmonies were really pretty, especially on the quartet."

"Don't you love that gospel stuff. Noah puts that gorgeous bottom under it."

Noah Sampson played the bass and usually didn't sing. But on the gospel quartets he would lay the big instrument down and sing the classic bass harmonies. That deep resonant voice had plenty to do with his day job. He was the morning news anchor on KTVU, Oakland's independent TV station.

Susan was abuzz. "One thing about playing a gig on a big stage. You get the giant monitors and the full, gorgeous stage sound. I just love it. People don't have any idea how difficult it can be up there. We play gigs in clubs where we can't hear a thing. It can be an unbelievable struggle." She hesitated. "I've told you that a million times, haven't I."

"It's okay. I like hearing you talk about performing. I get the vicarious high. It's fine. Besides, I love you. You know?"

She put her hand on his cheek, leaned in and kissed him in front of his ear. "So what's going on?"

"Well, I have got a little bit of news." He overdid a coy expression.

"What?"

Teasing, he made her wait.

"What?"

"The Grizzly Peak house is on the market."

"You're kidding."

He strung it out.

"You're not kidding."

"Nope," he said, "I'm not kidding. I drove past this morning after jogging up at Inspiration Point. There's a sale sign up. In fact, there's an open house this afternoon. 'Til five, I think."

It was three-thirty.

—

Grizzly Peak Boulevard is Berkeley's Corniche, its Mulholland Drive. At the very crest of the hills, it is relentless ess curves on a ledge facing arguably the world's most beautiful urban eyeful, San Francisco and its Bay. As it winds north to south, it shifts from regional park trailheads to barren no-man's land to residential oases. The few parking turn-offs with spectacular views are packed with tourists by day, teenagers by night, and everybody at sunset.

It was Dan and Susan's regular Saturday morning bicycle route. They'd load their ten-speeds into the back of her Volvo station wagon, the ubiquitous family folkswagon of Berkeley, and haul them up one of the steep avenues to the top of the hill at Grizzly. Once on the bikes, riding the curves was a little dicey, but the East Bay motorists were more than accustomed to and even intimidated by the local cyclists. These were the people, after all, who from time to time paralyzed thousands of vehicles with rush hour bike-ins to protest unequal road access, particularly to the bridges. They felt entitled to a piece of the road, and they weren't kidding around. Benign bikers like Dan and Susan benefited from the general reign of terror.

It had been two years since they first saw the house. Marked only by a mailbox, a heavily wooded little road dropped steeply off the Bay side of Grizzly, veering to the left within ten yards so that you saw nothing but vegetation from the edge of the road. After noticing it on several excursions, on a whim they decided to go exploring. Chaining their bikes to the mailbox post, they headed down the driveway on foot. They followed it to the left where it widened and straightened for fifty feet or so, and then turned back to the right. As they rounded the corner, her "Wow!" and his "Jesus!" were separated by a split second. In front of them was a large vertical-barred electronic gate through which they saw a house on a remarkable piece of property.

The lot was shaped roughly like a piece of pie on a slightly downhill plateau, nearly coming to a point where they stood at the gate, and opening to and ending at an arc of sheer cliff some fifty yards across. The house occupied the outer third of the lot and beyond the house to the west they could see, well, everything.

Straight ahead was Alcatraz Island, almost perfectly aligned with the midpoint of the Golden Gate Bridge beyond and the Pacific Ocean beyond that. Panning to the north, Angel Island was in the foreground, with Marin County angling up to Mount Tamalpais and down to the Richmond-San Rafael Bridge. To the south of the Golden Gate was the full skyline of San Francisco itself, punctuated by the Transamerica needle. Connecting east and west, the Oakland Bay Bridge with its clunky industrial east section and graceful silver west span was in full view. Looking south past Candlestick Park—no one had stopped calling it Candlestick—and San Francisco International Airport, they could see the entirety of the eight mile causeway, the San Mateo Bridge. In the parlance of real estate brokers, the four bridge view. It was dazzling.

The house itself, by no means small, was not huge by hill house standards. From their view behind the gate it wasn't that distinctive. Typical tan stucco, red Monterey tile roof, probably less than ten years old. There was a double attached garage to the left and a circular driveway aligned with a short walkway to a wood and opaque glass front entry. They could discern by the arrangement of the few small windows that there were at least two stories in there, but it was clear that this east side of the house was private, not designed to reveal much to those in or out.

With treasure-hunt determination, they pedaled back to the Volvo, deposited the bikes, and set out to see if they could get a look at the cliff side of the house. They cruised several of the small residential streets below Grizzly for almost a half hour, and just as the fun was fading and they began negotiating giving up, they spotted it. The entire west side of the house was glass and redwood decking. While they weren't close enough to make out much detail, from below they could see that the back of the house was convex, curved to match the arc of the cliff. There was roof to floor glass on the upper level with an uninterrupted railed redwood upper deck running the full width of the structure. The ground level was likewise all glass panels and an even larger railed deck that appeared to overhang the cliff edge. They agreed that it was the coolest house in Berkeley.

The Grizzly Peak house had become part of their patter. "Honey, the toilet's running." "Yeah, it ain't Grizzly." "Did you read about this Oakland homeless guy who hit the lottery for thirty-two million?" "Yeah, if that was us, we'd be talkin' Grizzly." When Dan told Susan that his income would go up with the VPMA job, she asked if he would be making Grizzly money. He said that he seriously doubted it. Still, there wasn't the slightest question that they were going to this open house.

They parked behind four other cars in the circular driveway and walked through the open front door into a small foyer. A perky, well-dressed fortyish woman introduced herself as the agent and guided them to a table with a guest book, a glass bowl filled with business cards and a stack of one page ecru handouts with a sketch and a bulleted description of the house. At the bottom center, in the smallest font on the page, it read,

Offered at 3.2 million dollars

Susan asked quietly if he was surprised at the price.

"Actually, I thought it was going to be more."

They stepped out of the foyer into the main body of the house. Though the ceilings were nine or ten feet at the most, there was a remarkable sense of light and space. Except for the foyer, which had a connecting half-bath and an enclosed room apparently intended to be a small office or den, the entire main floor was a Wrightish open plan of contiguous spaces for cooking and eating and sitting, all grounded on white oak, which transitioned beyond the huge windows to redwood decking, which in turn visually ended in the wide-angle landscape of San Francisco Bay. With the late spring sun still high in the west, the Bay was a glare of silver-blue-green with hundreds of tiny white slashes, the throngs of sailboats always present on fair-weather weekends. There were two other couples exploring this level of the house, one on the deck and one in the kitchen. For now, Dan and Susan soaked it in without commentary, although there was a good deal of hoohah pantomime.

There were three bedrooms upstairs. Two were small but the views provided a sense of spaciousness. The master bedroom suite was between the two smaller rooms, and occupied at least half the upper floor of the house. The ceiling was vaulted to twelve feet. The sleeping area with its big fireplace opened to a salmon-marbled, double-sinked, limestone floored, brass-hardwared miracle of a master bathroom. From the toilet seat there was an unobstructed view of the Golden Gate Bridge. To their surprise, through a slider from the bathroom, there was an outdoor redwood hot tub which blended with the decking and had never been apparent to them on their numerous reconnaissance missions from below.

They sat alone facing the Bay on the tiled edge of the covered redwood tub. Not knowing if they could be overheard from the deck below, they spoke in animated whispers. "Danny, I can't believe this place. That office and bath off the foyer are absolutely perfect for my practice. And this master suite is unbelievable. We could put a refrigerator and microwave up here and never leave. I mean I thought I loved it from the outside."

"I agree. It's even more amazing than I expected."

They gushed for a while longer, took a second attentive walk around both floors, and headed down the hill. He was already doing the math in his head, estimating the potential profit from the Elmwood house, the price that the new house might actually go for, the savings from the additional tax shelter, his salary expectations, the long-term equity at Grizzly. His immediate thought when he saw the price on the flyer had been "no way." Now he was thinking it through.

⟶

They'd had dinner and watched an old Sopranos rerun, the one where Tony tells Bobby to "consider salads." In bed they read the Sunday paper, doubled-teamed a Merl Reagle crossword, and turned the lights out by nine. He was flat on his back with Susan on her side, snuggled in, face to neck. They had not talked about the Grizzly house since getting home. Without any need for cautionary cues, they'd each understood the importance of being quiet about it in front of Carly.

"Do you think that we could actually buy it?" Susan finally said.

"Not really. I mean we could probably do it. But between the tuitions and all the rest for Ben and Sarah, and everything that's ahead for Carly, we'd be creating a pressure cooker for ourselves. Even if we got top dollar for this house, and stole the Grizzly house, we're still probably talking about at least a million of new mortgage. Even at today's rates, that's another five or six thousand a month. And that doesn't count the taxes, which would probably be another twenty-five thou a year. As much as I loathe fucking Prop 13, we're paying incredibly low property taxes on this place."

"Yes, Doctor Dan. You can be one linear son of a bitch."

"You know I love that house as much as you do. Maybe more. I'd love to live there. But I hate financial pressure, and so do you. One of the great things about the new job has been the financial freedom. Everything's paid for, we're saving and investing. For the first time we're making decent donations to things we care about. I love not having to worry about money. I don't want to lose that."

"Hey bub, I'm on your side. I don't want to feel pressured either. It's just such a great house."

"I know." He rolled up on his side and they merged, arms and legs interlocking.

She shifted the focus. "Aside from the financial stuff, there's Carly. I really don't know how she'd handle a move, even if it didn't disrupt her school or her music. She's just so damn fragile."

"You know," he said, "the one time we showed her the house, from below on Keeler Avenue, she liked it a lot. Remember? I think she said it was 'hecka cool.' "

"Well, she thought she was sightseeing, not house hunting."

They were together on this. They thought the house was fabulous, but neither wanted to create financial hardship, and they shared a loving and serious concern for their daughter. The consideration of the Grizzly house was exhilarating but short-lived. They grieved for a couple of days, had a few rueful exchanges, and then stopped talking about it.

Special Session

———

To NO ONE'S SURPRISE, WALT HILL REFUSED TO RESIGN FROM THE Memorial Medical Staff. Through his attorney, he demanded an appeal of the suspension of his privileges before he was even formally notified of his due process rights. His lawyer also sent a grievance to DHS—the state Department of Health Services—as well as five chest-beating letters, one each to Marty, Dan and Jack, one to the President of the Medical Staff, and one to the Chairman of the Hospital Board of Directors. He was threatening to litigate for damage to his client's professional reputation and for restraint of trade. Hill's attorney wanted the appeal within thirty calendar days. The Medical Staff President, in consultation with Richard Reynolds, agreed.

Doctor Carol Tessler, a mid-career practicing obstetrician, was the chairperson of her department and the President of the Medical Staff. This position differed from Dan's VPMA role in that it was a two-year position elected by the docs from their own ranks. Dan had served in the role several years earlier. Tessler's principal responsibility was the leadership of the Medical Staff

Executive Committee, which was an aggregate of all the medical department chairpersons. In that capacity, she would preside over Hill's appeal.

A full day had been set aside for the hearing, which was about to begin in the large conference room on the main floor of the hospital. The rules of procedure, which in many ways mirrored a civil trial, were defined by the Medical Staff by-laws. The suspending party, Jack Jensen, was required to present a justification for his action through the submission of evidence, basically medical records and witnesses. Doctor Hill and his lawyer likewise had the right to present a defense by the same means. The jury would be the Medical Staff Executive Committee. Following each presentation, the parties could cross-examine, and the Executive Committee members, in the fashion of a grand jury, could also ask questions. The Executive Committee would in the end determine, by simple majority vote, whether the suspension of Hill's privileges was upheld or reversed. The fundamental question, as always, was whether Hill's management of Dennis Barber fell within the standard of care of the medical community.

The hearing had been called for eight o'clock. It was ten minutes past and Hill and his attorney had not arrived. The room was arranged with a large rectangular oak table in the center, and approximately two dozen stacking chairs distributed against the walls. Doctor Tessler waited alone at the center of the long edge of the table. Directly opposite were two unoccupied chairs for the witnesses. Jack Jensen and Richard Reynolds were seated to her left, and to her right were two more unoccupied chairs, these for Hill and his lawyer. A court reporter was at the ready behind and to the right of Tessler.

At 8:20, Hill strode in with a second man at his heels. He greeted Carol Tessler and quietly introduced his lawyer William Ferris, who gave her a business card. She gestured them to their places. The room quieted after her third "Good morning."

"This is a special session of the Medical Staff Executive Committee, convened in response to an appeal by Doctor Walton Hill regarding suspension of his privileges. I don't think I need to say this, but I will anyway. This proceeding is confidential and privileged and should not be shared outside of this room."

Dan was watching the accused from one of the stacking chairs at the periphery. While Hill's late arrival was uncamouflaged passive-aggression, there was nothing contemptuous in his manner. He paid attention to Carol Tessler's opening remarks, calmly looking directly at her. Even seated, you could see that Hill was a tall angular man. He had thinning gray hair, a sailor's wrinkled tan, and was adorned, preppy chic, in navy, grey, and cordovan.

"Jack, we'll begin with you," Tessler said. "Would you please present your justification for the suspension of Doctor Hill's privileges?"

Jensen took nearly three hours to orchestrate his presentation. Hill's attorney attempted to interrupt four times early on, and Tessler, with growing impatience, told him that he would have ample opportunity to ask questions later in the proceeding. Jensen distributed a synopsis of the Barber case, including details of the patient's history prior to the final hospitalization. He then led the pathologist through his findings and distributed copies of the autopsy report. The UC-Davis endocrinologist gave a lucid explanation of the intricacies of potassium management in diabetic keto-acidosis, and concluded that this was a "preventable death," that appropriate IV potassium supplementation would have kept the patient out of trouble. Jensen's last witness was Harry Rice, a well-known internist in private practice in Walnut Creek.

"Doctor Rice, could you please tell us a little about your practice?"

"Sure. I think I have a run-of-the-mill suburban general internal medicine practice. Particularly in the last ten years it's been disproportionately geriatric. But I still see some younger patients. I divide my time, approximately eighty percent in the office and maybe ten percent each in the nursing homes and in the hospital."

"Can you tell us about your educational background?"

"I'm a local boy. Undergrad at Cal-Berkeley, med school at Stanford and residency at UCSF. Board certified two years later. I did a year of rheumatology after the Army, and I sort of specialized for a while when I started practice. But over the thirty-two years it's been basically bread-and-butter general medicine."

"Harry, would you say that you are a fairly typical private internist in our community?"

"I'm not sure I understand what you're asking."

"Well, would you say that you are much smarter, or I guess much dumber, than the internists around you in practice?"

"No, I think I'm probably pretty typical."

"Do you think that there is anything about your style of practice that is atypical?"

"I don't think so."

Jensen flipped to the next page of his legal pad.

"Harry, you said that you spend about ten percent of your time caring for patients in the hospital. Is that about right?"

"About."

"From your exposure to other internists in the hospital setting, while cross-covering and so forth, do you think that your style of practice in the hospital is typical for our community?"

"Yes, I think so."

"Harry, have you treated many patients over the years with diabetic keto-acidosis?"

"Of course."

"Do you have any idea how many?"

"Not really."

"Well, could you estimate?"

"I guess over the years twenty or thirty cases."

"Harry, now I'm going to ask you what I hope are three straightforward questions about DKA. First, where in the hospital do you put your DKA patients?"

"Well, until they're well out of the woods, you know eating and on subcutaneous insulin, I keep them in the ICU."

"Okay. Secondly, do you routinely seek consultation on DKA patients?"

"It varies. If they're fairly simple and doing well in the ICU, I usually don't. If they're atypical or things start to not go well, I'll call an endocrinologist."

"Harry, are you aware of special considerations regarding serum potassium in DKA?"

"Well sure. These patients always need more potassium than you think they need from their blood tests. Their acidosis falsely elevates the measured serum levels."

"Would you say that that is widely known by internists?"

"Sure. I remember them grilling that into us when I was an intern."

"Carol, I think that's it."

Richard Reynolds intervened. "Excuse me, Doctor Jensen, Doctor Tessler. May I ask a few questions?"

Carol Tessler nodded her assent.

"Real brief, Doctor Rice. Sir, I presume you know Doctor Hill."

"Yes sir. We've had intermittent contact for decades."

"Doctor, have you ever had any kind of conflict, personal or professional, with Doctor Hill?"

"No sir. We've had contact at grand rounds, Medical Staff meetings, charity events. You know. I'm certainly not aware of any difficulty between us."

"Doctor, can you think of any reason that anyone could conclude that you would want to harm Doctor Hill in any way?"

Harry Rice looked directly at Walton Hill. "Certainly not."

"Thanks doctor. Okay, Doctor Tessler. That's it."

"Well folks, let's take one hour for lunch. Doctor Hill, we'll start at 12:30 sharp and you'll have the opportunity to question any of this morning's witnesses."

Dan generally didn't have a real lunch, except at catered meetings where he ate because the food was in front of him. As he tried to catch up at his desk during the break, he quickly went through a medium size bag of peanut M&M's and a Diet Barq's. He triaged his email and voicemail, discarding about half and saving the rest for the end of the day. There was nothing that couldn't wait.

As he reconstructed the morning, he thought that Jensen had been doing well. The information was presented clearly, and collectively it made a persuasive argument that Hill was negligent. He was surprised at Hill's calm demeanor throughout. Once Carol Tessler made it clear that Ferris was not going to be allowed to disrupt Jack's presentation, both Hill and Ferris settled into listening, Ferris taking copious notes and Hill quiet, hands folded, nearly expressionless.

He couldn't imagine that the Executive Committee would support Hill. In his mind the disciplinary choices were mandatory consultation for all admissions versus loss of admitting privileges altogether. In general, the Medical Staff tended to want to find a way to do the right thing without being overly harsh. In the end he thought that they would recommend mandatory consultation with some kind of augmented review by the Department of Medicine. He could live with that. Whether Hill could was another matter.

At 12:30, Hill and Ferris were in their places. The room settled down and Tessler told Doctor Hill that he and his attorney were free to question any of the morning's witnesses.

Ferris spoke. "Doctor Jensen, in your review of the details of the case this morning, you made no mention of any verbal orders given by Doctor Hill."

"That's correct. To my knowledge there were none involving potassium."

The room began to buzz. Tessler asked for quiet. Dan wrote on his legal pad, "Ask Tessler for a thirty minute break. Get the Two Center telephone logs for the two overlapping days of the admission and get the medical records of every patient where the log indicates a verbal order was made." He tore the paper off the pad, folded it, walked over to Jack and handed it to him.

"Doctor Jensen, if Doctor Hill, when the initial blood work came back, had given a telephone order for 80 milli-equivalents per liter of potassium chloride in the IV, would that change your opinion of his care in this case?"

Jack turned to Carol Tessler. "Carol, in view of this line of questioning, can we have a short break to collect the telephone log from Two Center?"

She nodded as though she had already thought of it. "Okay, everybody back in fifteen minutes."

Dan, Jack, and Richard made it to the Two Center nurses station in less than a minute. The telephone log had three entries from Hill. One was the initial call for the admission and two were related to insulin doses, each with clear and specific quantitative documentation. There were no verbal orders related to potassium. The log for the time period of Barber's admission had twenty-two verbal orders for nine different patients. None involved intravenous potassium. Dan called the Director of Medical Records, explained the circumstances, and asked her to immediately pull the records of the nine patients and have them sent to the first floor conference room. They made twenty photocopies of the telephone log and headed back to the hearing.

Ferris resumed. "Doctor Jensen, let me ask you again. If Doctor Hill, upon getting the results of the initial blood work, had given a telephone order for 80 milli-equivalents per liter of potassium chloride in the IV, would you change your opinion of his care in this case?"

"Yes I would, but in this case—"

"That's fine. You answered the question."

Tessler intervened, "Mr. Ferris, let Doctor Jensen say what he has to say."

"I asked him a hypothetical. He answered it."

"Mr. Ferris, this isn't a criminal trial. I want to hear what Jack has to say and I imagine that the rest of the Executive Committee does also. Jack?"

"There is simply no documentation that such a telephone order was given. Not in the telephone log, which I have here, not in the nurses' notes, not on the order sheet."

Ferris excused Jensen and called the consultant from UC-Davis, and then Doctor Rice. He asked the same hypotheticals and got essentially the same answers. Ferris then told Doctor Tessler that he thought that brief testimony by Doctor Hill could wrap up the afternoon.

"Go right ahead, Mr. Ferris."

"Doctor Hill, did you bring any materials, testimonials, with you today?"

"I did."

"Could you show them to us?"

Hill pulled a black three-ring binder from his briefcase.

"Can you describe the contents of your binder?"

"Yes. These are a collection of letters from my patients and their relatives, community awards, service acknowledgements from health care organizations, and letters of support from dozens of colleagues."

"Doctor Tessler, we would like to have copies made, and we ask that the members of the Executive Committee review these prior to making any decisions on the appeal."

"That's fine."

"Doctor Hill, how many patients with DKA have you cared for in your career?"

"I don't know. Maybe fifty."

"Have any of them ever had a serious complication while in the hospital under your care?"

"No."

"Then obviously none of them died under your care in the hospital."

"That's correct."

"Doctor Hill, would you say that you have a clear understanding of the management of fluids and electrolytes in DKA?"

"Yes I would."

"Is that something you've learned recently, or have you had that knowledge for a long time, say years?"

"For decades."

"Okay. Would you say, specifically, that you have a good understanding of what happens to body potassium levels in DKA?"

"Certainly."

"Could you concisely review that?"

"Yes," Hill said. "In the metabolic acidosis of DKA, the body raises the blood pH by pushing hydrogen ions into cells in exchange for potassium ions coming out of cells. The result is buffering of the pH, which is what the body needs to do, and a falsely elevated serum potassium relative to intracellular and total body potassium. It's crucial to realize that the patient needs more potassium than the serum levels would indicate."

Dan was dazzled. *Christ, the bastard's been to school since he killed this guy.*

The room was quiet enough to hear the ventilation. Ferris continued. "Doctor Hill, can you tell us why Dennis Barber got in trouble with his potassium?"

Everybody knew what was coming.

"The nurses failed to respond to my telephone order to raise the IV potassium."

"Doctor Hill, do you know which nurse you spoke to?"

"I don't, but it was at the same time that I changed the insulin dosage after the electrolyte results came back from the lab."

"Why do you think the order wasn't followed?"

"I have no idea."

"Doctor Hill, you've reviewed the chart and you are aware that there is no record of that verbal order. Is that right?"

"Yes. Obviously it never got recorded. If it had, I presume it would have been followed."

"Doctor, do you have any doubt whatsoever about your recollection?"

"None."

"Thank you. That's all I have, Doctor Tessler."

"Jack, do you have any questions for Doctor Hill?

"I do. Doctor Hill, did I understand you to say that you gave the telephone order for potassium at the same time that you gave the first verbal order to change the insulin dose?"

"That's correct. I changed the insulin dose and I told the nurse to change the potassium to 80 milli-equivalents per liter in the IV fluid."

Jack picked up a packet of papers and passed them to his right and left for distribution around the room. "I'm passing out photocopies of the Two Center telephone log for the days that Dennis Barber was there. When you get yours, please look at the three entries with your name on them. They are circled."

Hill took the copy and tilted his head slightly to align his bifocals. "All right. I see them."

"Do you see any mention of IV potassium on any of them?"

"No. But I told you that I gave the verbal order here. At the second one. At the first insulin change."

"Are you talking about the insulin order at 8:35 p.m.? The one signed S. Flynn, RN?"

"Yes, that's the one."

Jensen pivoted toward Tessler. "Carol, can we get someone to call Two Center to see if Ms. Flynn is working today?"

"I think we need to hear from Ms. Flynn, whether she's working today or not. And by the way, you know it could be a Mr. Flynn."

Unexpectedly, Clare came in the conference room and, without speaking, handed Dan a note. "Mr. Corbett called. Says it's very important that you call back ASAP." The message included C.J.'s private phone number.

He excused himself and quickly went to his office. He needed to talk to Marty. The Board was her domain and he wanted to be careful not to work at cross-purposes to her, especially concerning damage control in the Hill matter. He could get only her voicemail and he left a message for her to call as soon as she could. He was nervous about calling Corbett. His presumption was that Hill had gotten to C.J. through his son-in-law, and that he was calling to lobby. At the same time, he thought that it wasn't a particularly good idea to stiff C.J. Corbett. He dialed.

The Redwood CEO picked up and got right to the point. "Look, I know that this is very short notice, but I think that it's very important that we meet in my office today. Can you possibly manage it?"

"Well, I guess. Can you tell me what it's about?"

"This is something I'd rather not talk about on the phone. In fact, for now I'd like to keep this absolutely confidential. Can you trust me on this?"

"Is 5:30 too late?"

"Actually, that'll be perfect. Just come to the administrative suites. I'll make sure that someone's in the reception area."

By the time Dan got back to the hearing, Jack was questioning a young nurse, presumably Ms. Flynn. "Are you certain that you have a specific recollection of the phone call that took place at 8:35 p.m.?"

The woman seemed anxious, but was attentive and focused on Jack. "Yes, I'm certain. I'm sorry to say this, but Doctor Hill can be very harsh on the telephone. I am, we all are, very careful about getting everything exactly right with him. And writing everything down."

Dan tracked Jensen's effort to expose Hill for an exchange or two, and then was overtaken by his concerns about Corbett, and about his inability to contact Marty. The surprising and enigmatic call had derailed him. It felt like the quasi-legal process unfolding in front of him was about to be overtaken by the politics of power and connection, at a level that was beyond his ken.

"...once again, you have no recollection of Doctor Hill giving you a verbal order for potassium. Is that right?"

"Yes, that's absolutely right."

"If Doctor Hill was claiming that he gave you a verbal order to raise the IV potassium, would he be lying?"

Tessler intervened, "Jack, I think that's improper. We have her statement. We don't need to do that."

"You're right. I'm sorry."

"Any other questions, Doctor Jensen?" Jack shook his head.

"Doctor Hill? Mr. Ferris? Members of the Executive Committee?"

Ferris started to speak, hesitated, and after several beats said no.

Carol wrapped up the hearing, announcing that the transcripts would be distributed to the parties and to the Executive Committee members, and that they would vote on the appeal in approximately one week. In the meantime, Hill's suspension remained in effect.

The Lion's Den

H ELLO, THIS IS MARTY. PLEASE LEAVE A MESSAGE AFTER…"
Dan had once more tried her at the office, then on
her cellular, and finally at her home. As he worked his
way down 680 past Alamo and Danville, his anxiety mounted the
closer he got to the Redwood Solutions complex. He picked up
his cell again and speed-dialed.

"Hi, Tone."

"Hi, Danny. Where are you?"

"Well, I wish I could say I was coming through the Tunnel and
home in ten, but I'm headed toward Pleasanton for a visit with
C.J. Corbett."

"What's going on?"

"That's a very good question. I get this mysterious call from
him about an hour ago. Says he wants to see me today. Won't tell
me why, says it's confidential. I'm thinking it must have something to do with Walton Hill. You know, the guy who lost the diabetic patient."

"The father of the Board member?"

"He's actually the father of the Board member's wife."

"So what do you think he wants?"

"I don't know. It's hard to imagine that a Board member is going to try to interfere with a medical staff suspension. In a fatal case no less. But this is C.J. Corbett, a guy who's accustomed to having his way. This thing with Hill is coming to a head right now. I don't have the faintest fucking idea about the relationships among the Board members."

"What does Marty have to say?"

"I don't know. I've been trying to get a hold of her for the past hour. Left voicemails everywhere."

"Look, Danny. Obviously you're not gonna give up your principles because some rich jerk wants to protect one of his golf buddies. What the hell's Corbett gonna do? I mean do you honestly think he's gonna ask Marty to come down on you because a Board member's father-in-law got in trouble for killing a patient, and you didn't cover for him?"

"Well, when you put it like that, it does sound pretty farfetched."

"Look, this sounds corny, but just be who you are. You're not a member of the old boy's club. You know what you stand for. If he's disappointed, he's disappointed. Fuck 'em."

"Right, fuck 'em. That's my girl."

The guard at the security gate told him to drive through, that Mr. Corbett was expecting him. The Redwood Solutions complex was built on the western slope above Interstate 680 on what the San Ramon Valley locals called the Pleasanton Ridge. Corbett's enclave consisted of fourteen two-story steel and tinted glass buildings clustered among hillside stands of live oak, madrone, and eucalyptus. That these gorgeous acres were zoned for industry was stark evidence of the pragmatism of local politics. The stereotype of tree-hugging Northern California ecotopia existed far more in the bombast of talk radio than in the real world.

Corbett's receptionist pre-empted his self-introduction. "Please have a seat, Doctor Fazen. Mr. Corbett will just be a few minutes." She offered him an impressive choice of beverages.

"Nothing, thanks."

He was not accustomed to feeling viscerally afraid. It was one thing to obsess, to work and rework a disturbing thought. It was something else again to have a pounding heart and cold, clammy hands, something just before nausea. That was for stage-frightened speakers and singers and stand-up comics, not for grownup executives. For Dan, being in control of his circumstances was so routine, had been so routine for decades, that he was without awareness of it. Like water to a fish. Now his body was telling him that something was wrong, that this was a dangerous moment in a dangerous place. "Fuck 'em" third person from the car phone was one thing. "Fuck 'em" to his face was quite another. He wanted to leave. Just flee.

Jesus, calm down.

In the aftermath of the meeting, he would hours later remember the last thing he thought about before being beckoned into C.J.'s office. "Let me give you a little advice, Daniel. A little wisdom from an old Buddhist Jew." It was a few years earlier at one of their regular Thursday lunches. Dan had been going on about Carly, her dark moods and her fragility, the scariness of the junior high and high school scene in Berkeley. After listening to every fear from alcohol to heroin to unsafe sex to body piercing, Ben interrupted. "You know, Daniel, the stuff we worry about almost never happens. And the stuff that really gets us we almost never see coming. Relax a little."

"Mr. Corbett can see you now. Just go on in."

As Dan walked in, C.J. rose from a conference table to his left and strode toward him. It took a few moments to digest that it was Mark Rader, the Olympia Pacific Chief Medical Officer, who had come to his feet behind Corbett. A third man, a stranger, remained seated.

"Dan, thanks for coming right over. Sorry for the ambush but we had to get you here discreetly. You'll understand in just a moment. Of course you know Mark Rader."

They shook hands. Too firmly, Dan thought.

"Hello Mark. This is certainly a surprise."

"It's good to see you, Dan."

Corbett guided him to the other man who was now standing. He was at least six foot six, balding, slightly stout, in his fifties. "Dan, I'd like you to meet Beau Thurmond. Beau is Vice-President for the Western Region of Olympia Healthcare. He's visiting us from Athens. Beau, this is Doctor Dan Fazen, Memorial's Vice-President for Medical Affairs."

"Nice to meet you, doctor. I've heard a lot of good things about you." The way the man said *nahss* reminded him of Jimmy Carter. Thurmond handed him a business card.

"How do you do." Dan's mind raced as he tried to connect the dots without giving away his disorientation. "That's Athens, Georgia I presume?" Like Beau, the peanut farmer VP was from Greece. He felt like an idiot.

"That's right. You know Olympia's corporate is in Athens. I'll tell you though, I spend about half my life in California these days."

C.J. corralled the three of them. "Gentleman, let's take our seats. I think Dan's going to want to be sitting down for what he's about to hear. Beau, you've got the floor."

"Dan...do you mind if I call you Dan?"

"That's fine."

"Dan, as the head of OHC for the western U.S., and the guy mainly responsible for the acquisitions, I'm happy to tell you that we're dottin' the i's and crossin' the t's on Olympia's purchase of Walnut Creek Memorial. Both Boards have voted in favor of the deal, the lawyers are workin' out the final language, and the FTC has provisionally given it a clean bill of health. I'd say we're about thirty days from actual transfer of management. We've asked you to come here today to personally give you the news well ahead of any public announcements, to answer any questions y'all might have, and to discuss the future, at least the immediate future, of the new organization at Memorial."

From decades of doctoring, of listening to patients' embarrassing and frightening experiences, of absorbing the responses to the most devastating of medical pronouncements, Dan had developed the capacity to maintain a calm and pleasant demeanor in painful and disturbing circumstances. That, along with attentiveness and the air of competence, was after all what bedside manner was about. As his mind raced through algorithms of consequences and survival, what Thurmond and Corbett and Rader saw was a composed and engaged professional thoughtfully focused on their corporate bombshell. It was obvious to him that this had been carefully choreographed, and he quite consciously chose to simply listen, and think, until he was asked to respond.

They were seated at an oval conference table, he and C.J. facing Rader and Thurmond. The big southerner continued. "First let me tell y'all a little about the acquisition itself. Memorial will stay Memorial. We have no plans to change the name of an already prestigious institution with its own outstanding brand identity. The governance of course will change. The governing body will be Olympia's corporate board. And there's no reason not to tell you that we couldn't be more thrilled that C.J. here is the newest Director on the Olympia board."

From distant memory, movie memory, he retrieved an image and a sound. A view of the tumblers inside the door of a bank vault. Each flawless, polished tumbler falling into place, a perfect fit, with an elegant and deep, resonant "thunk." These were the pros—the board room, New York Stock Exchange, billion dollar big boys, and they knew what they were doing.

"Dan, we are certain that Memorial will be a great asset for OHC. As you know, we have Pacific in the city and Methodist in San Jose. Add Memorial in the East Bay and we can rationalize our specialty care in the region and deal from a position of real strength with the HMOs. We're of course aware that Memorial's had a tough year and a half financially. But, as I'm sure you also know, we have the cash to get hospitals through tough competitive transitions. Y'all have a terrific hospital here. Great care. Loyal docs and patients. We consider this a very low risk deal."

Dan's awareness shifted to Marty. If she knew about all of this, which surely she must, she had been keeping her own counsel. As CEO, she would have been dealt with prior to him. With abrupt clarity Dan understood that Marty's absence from this room meant that she was not going to be Memorial's CEO, and that meant she was going to be gone. He felt his heart in his chest again. He realized that Mark Rader had started to speak.

"…to talk frankly about Olympia and the dark side of its reputation. When I was asked to go to Olympia Pacific as CMO, I was initially reluctant. I was aware of the same media stereotype as everyone else. Olympia, the malevolent, for-profit, down-sized, quality-be-damned money machine. And some of that reputation may have been deserved by OHC's behavior in the early years. But I can tell you, Dan, that it's nothing like that now. Yes, we've re-engineered and down-sized somewhat. But I'll put our hospital up against any in the region in terms of quality. OHC now has numerous teaching hospitals with missions every bit as community-minded as Memorial. When OHC acquired Pacific, they set up a multimillion dollar foundation for the subsidy of care for uninsured patients. I'm quite certain that will be done at Memorial as well. Isn't that right, Beau?"

Thurmond nodded and Rader continued. "I think that it's very important, Dan, that you know that the Olympia of the nineties, which I don't think got a very fair shake in the media anyway, is not the Olympia of today. I've really been delighted with my experiences at Pacific."

He now felt certain that at least he wasn't going to be fired.

Thurmond again. "Dan, I'd like to reinforce what Mark has been sayin'. The company made some serious mistakes in the early years and paid dearly for them. Not the least of the costs has been the reputation that we're all well aware of. As I'm sure you know, all the top management was changed, and a philosophy of quality and service is now drivin' the organization. I'm damned proud of Olympia. We don't just do well, we do good." The big man paused and smiled. "By now you've probably figured out that we want you to remain as part of the team at Memorial. Maybe we should stop and give you a chance to respond. We're dumpin' a hell of a piece of news on you."

As was true nearly a year earlier with Marty, he understood that, whether he was emotionally and intellectually ready or not, he was in the opening phase of a negotiation.

"Well, gentlemen. I have to admit that you've taken me by surprise. I actually thought that C.J. was asking me here to talk about another matter entirely. I would like to ask you about Marty Sullivan. She is conspicuously absent."

"Fair enough." Thurmond was clearly in charge. "Dan, OHC has a hell of a lot of experience with acquisitions. Obviously. That experience has taught us that the CEO is critical to the successful transition. Time and again, when we've tried to go with the prior CEO, the hospitals have just struggled like hell to make the cultural shift to our style of management. At this point, as a matter of policy, we routinely put an experienced OHC person in the CEO spot."

Now the man reminded him of Fred Thompson, the actor/politician.

"It's nothin' against Marty. In fact we think she's a terrific person. I can't disclose the details to you, but let me assure you that her severance agreement is more than fair. By the way, part of her agreement is that she will not disclose the acquisition to anyone until we go public. My guess is that you've probably not seen or heard much of her in the past week."

He knew that the remaining item on the agenda was his job. Presuming that they were quite clear about what they wanted to do, he was not going to initiate. He expected Thurmond to continue, but it was Corbett.

"Dan, I sat in on all the Board deliberations about this. To a person, the Board members felt that it was crucial that you stay on as VPMA."

Dan interrupted, "Even Walt Hill's son-in-law?"

"What?"

"Never mind. I'm sorry. Go ahead." C.J. didn't seem to have the slightest idea of what Dan was talking about.

Corbett continued, "Particularly with a new CEO, we need continuity in the other senior positions. We understand that some of the docs may recoil because of the old OHC reputation. You have terrific relationships with the practicing community. It's our view that you'll be a crucial person in the transition."

Thurmond pulled an envelope from a manila folder on the table and handed it to him. "Dan, this is a formal written offer for you to remain as VPMA at Memorial. We'd like you to take it home, take the time to think about it, and get back to us within a week. Since Mark is already doing basically the same job at Pacific, I think he could be very helpful to you."

"Absolutely," Rader said. He wrote his home phone number on his business card and handed it across the table. "If you have any questions, anything you want to talk about, anything at all, don't hesitate to call. At work or at home."

Thurmond signaled the end of the meeting. "Dan, it's been an absolute pleasure meetin' you. I truly hope that you'll choose to stay with us. By the way, this deal is still confidential for the time being. Obviously you'll be talkin' to your family. But please limit your discussions to us and to your immediate family members, and please ask them to not discuss it with any other people."

"I will respect that." He knew damn well that he would not.

—

Uncomfortable reading the letter in full sight at Redwood, Dan took the interstate north to the next exit and the big well-lit parking lot at the Stoneridge Shopping Mall. He was surprised at its brevity.

Dear Doctor Fazen:

It is our hope that you will remain at Walnut Creek Memorial Hospital in your role as Vice-President for Medical Affairs. Your talent, experience and superb relationships in the community will be invaluable. Effective the date of the Olympia acquisition, your salary will be increased from your current $290,000 per year to $400,000 per year and there will be 10%

increases annually for two years tied to mutually established utilization management goals. As is traditional for senior executives at Olympia, you will receive an additional one-fourth of your starting salary, or $100,000, as a signing incentive. You will receive Olympia's executive fringe benefit package, which includes health insurance, life and disability insurance, a deferred compensation plan, and, if you remain two years, our executive stock options program. Under separate cover, we are mailing detailed descriptions of the benefit package.

If you have any questions, please feel free to contact me. I am hopeful that you will remain at Memorial and look forward to a long, enriching working relationship. Best wishes.

Sincerely,

Beauregard M. Thurmond
Vice-President, Western Regional Operations
Olympia Healthcare Corporation

It was 6:48 p.m.
"Hi, Tone."
"Hey, where are you?"
"Well, actually I'm still in Pleasanton. About to head home."
"So, how did it go with Corbett?"
"You're not gonna believe it."

Part 2

Six weeks later

In the Dark

E ASTBOUND, SIX HOURS OUT OF SFO, IT WAS 5:34 A.M. IN PARIS.
At the front of business class the roar of the triple seven
was barely audible. Susan had slid enviably into sleep
after the meal and ten minutes into the movie. Despite his fully
reclined leather seat and extended footrest, two glasses of champagne, five milligrams of Ambien, and the full regalia of the air-
plane insomniac—the nifty self-expanding styrofoam ear plugs,
the blindfold, the neck cushion, the blanket, the terry slippers—
Dan was awake. His unguided attention moved through conversations, remembered and rehearsed, to something like agitated
prayers for sleep, to attempts at attentional breathing he had
learned at places like Green Gulch and Esalen, and then without
apprehending the shift until after it had begun, back into another
cycle of obsessional inner dialogue. Since the revelations in
Corbett's office, he had found and consolidated the ethical ground
upon which he could stand, his justification for staying at
Memorial. In the dark, his awareness was invaded by the conversations of the past six weeks, and by the language of his defense.

"Marty, what are you gonna do?"

They were at Vernazza, a quiet trattoria in the shadow of the elevated BART tracks in Walnut Creek. She had responded to his messages after three days of laying low.

"I don't know. Nothing for a while, I think. I've never been in this situation before. Without work and not having to work. Not needing money. It's weird. You'd think that I'd feel this big sense of loss, but I'm feeling mostly a kind of relief. It's surprising, I guess. I don't know."

She was relaxed, soft, entirely lateral. No profanity, no cracking wise.

"You're the one on the razor's edge, doc. What are *you* gonna do?"

"I haven't decided," he said. Technically, it wasn't a lie. "I haven't seen the details of the offer yet." Short of refinements to the fringe benefit package, he knew exactly what was being offered.

"Well, the details of the offer are certainly none of my business. I was just curious about what you thought about working in an Olympia Hospital."

"You know, the new Memorial CEO evidently hasn't been appointed. I thought that it might be Mark, but nobody said anything. I suppose it could still be Mark. They're asking me to stay and I don't even know who I'll be working for. That's a little disconcerting."

"Why don't you just ask?" she said.

"Yeah."

"Dan, you didn't answer my question."

"Which question?"

"About working for Olympia?"

"Ah, that question."

"Look," she said, "if you don't want to talk about it, that's okay. I'm not going to give you a hard time."

"No, actually I do want to talk about it." He went through a few forkfuls of his calzone and sipped the Pellegrino. "Do you think Olympia has really changed?"

"I don't know. Who's Olympia? Each hospital has its own history, its own culture. Presumably Athens influences everyone, but there's bound to be at least some operational variation. Hospital to hospital, CEO to CEO. What with all the bad press and top management turnover, they probably have changed. They'd have to. Really, I don't have any inside information. I read the same *Wall Street Journal* and *New York Times* as everyone else."

He read neither, but kept it to himself. "I guess I thought that a long-time CEO like you would hear about this stuff. You know, through personal contacts, the buzz at conferences. There's certainly plenty of gossip in the doctor world."

"Well, among hospital administrators Olympia-bashing is definitely in vogue. They're such an easy target. They've down-sized harder than anybody, and for-profit governance from a distance can be plenty ruthless. But there's probably a lot of hyperbole too. You know, 'Exaggerate—it makes life more interesting.' I go back to my original premise. Each hospital has its own culture and cast of characters. For what it's worth, Mark tells me he's happy at Pacific. He says they haven't overdone it on staff cutbacks or stingy utilization management. And he says that their foundation for uninsured care is working."

"Can you tell me anything about that?" he said.

"Well, you probably know that when a for-profit takes over a non-profit, the tax savings they've accumulated over the years need to be paid back in some way. At least that's the law in California. Typically this is done by setting up a foundation which provides some kind of health-related service to the community. The foundation at Olympia Pacific provides care for unsponsored patients, usually working poor who have no health insurance but aren't poor enough to qualify for Medi-Cal. Mark thinks it works pretty well. I assume they'll do the same thing at Memorial."

"They mentioned it."

"They've got to do it, Dan. And it's a lot of money. As much as fifty million."

"Five-oh?"

"Yep. Course they can try to screw with it. But like I said, Mark thinks they're playing it straight. I have no idea." Marty held her water glass up to the sunlight coming through the window. "Meanwhile, I'm still doing all the talking."

He squinted at her. "Okay." Pushing his plate to the side, he put his elbows on the table and leaned forward. "Other than Susan, you're the first person I've talked to about this. Realistically, I have two choices. I continue as VPMA under Olympia or I go back into practice. Financially, I'm nowhere near being able to retire. And geographically I'm not going anywhere. Carly and Susan are locked in to the East Bay, and I love living here. I don't want to leave."

He could tell from her relaxed eye contact, her cheek cradled in her hand, that she wasn't waiting to talk.

"It seems to me that I could play an important role in the new organization. You know, I seriously doubt that they're as evil as their stereotype. Like you said, people love to exaggerate. As VPMA I would be in the role that you talked about months ago, the institutional protector of quality in the face of aggressive cost-containment. If it was important then, it's even more important now. It seems to me that the more bottom-line the CEO and the governing body are, the more the patients need an advocate high up in the organization. I'm not saying it wouldn't be hard, but don't you think it could be worthwhile?"

"It's hard to argue with that. But you know, Dan, it could also be pretty lonely."

He swapped his earplugs for his iPod, hoping that a continuous cycle of George Winston would mesmerize him into slumber. This resulted not in sleep, but with the thought after several minutes that the *Pachelbel Canon* should be outlawed by the Geneva Convention.

"I'm telling you, kid. Calling the Olympia executives a bunch of callous entrepreneurs is an insult to callous entrepreneurs."

"Oh come on, Ben. That's hyperbolic bullshit."

"Look, I asked if you wanted me to tell you what I really thought, and you said yes. For chrissakes, two of the original senior execs were convicted of Medicare fraud. The CFO actually served time."

"That was nearly ten years ago," Dan said. "They're barely the same organization."

This was their first lunch since the Olympia takeover went public. The media had given it minimal shrift. Of the majors, only the San Jose Mercury News treated it as a significant event, the lead story in their business section and a cautionary editorial. The acquisition of San Jose's Methodist Medical Center four years earlier had been Olympia's first foray into Northern California.

"They're the same organization," Ben said. "Just smoother."

Their banter was almost always good-natured. Now Dan was getting annoyed. "And when did you become such an expert on the Olympia Healthcare Corporation?"

"I read the newspapers. And even though I'm quite old, I actually use the Internet. Did you know that there's a website devoted entirely to the mischief of these Georgia assholes? Stop-Olympia-dot-com, see for yourself."

"Look, I'm in a real life situation here. This is no time for caricatures. Right now I do not have an acceptable job alternative. And I can't just pick up and go anywhere I happen to find one." He hesitated. "Yes, I want you to tell me what you think. I'd just prefer that you'd think before you tell me what you think."

They were in Ben's kitchen, sitting over the remains of lunch at the distressed oak table. Ben downed the last of his Corona and took a fresh cigar from his shirt pocket. "Do you mind if I smoke?"

Dan couldn't resist. "Do you mind if I fart?" The Steve Martin shtick was one of their standing gags.

Ben chewed on the unlit stogie. "Okay. You talk. I'll think."

He began his brief, hands in his pockets, slowly pacing the kitchen's terra cotta tiles. "I'm not naive. I understand that Olympia's number one priority is making money for its stockholders. And that a lot of their hype about quality and service is just that. I know that they buy and sell health care organizations like monopoly pieces. But I also know that they continue to get accredited by the Joint Commission, they continue to keep their licenses and, at least in the Bay Area, they seem to be staying out of trouble."

Ben was paying attention. No antics.

"Look, whether I like it or not, whether you like it or not, Olympia has acquired Memorial. They are who they are, which in fact is probably not as nasty as their reputation. If I leave now, they won't miss a beat. They'll recruit someone else and go right on about their business. And I'll be out there trying to find work and get my kids through school. Because I leave in protest, do you honestly believe that some cracker in Athens, Georgia is going to have an epiphany and transform Olympia Healthcare into America's most beloved corporation?"

Ben took the cigar out of his mouth. "So what makes you think they're not as bad as their reputation?"

If Dan heard the question, there was no evidence of it. "I think I've got a fair amount of leverage right now. They want me to stay. I'm sure I could further strengthen my hold on quality management in the hospital. I really believe that it could be worthwhile—you know, right livelihood—to be the principal patient advocate in that organization. I don't have any illusions about it being easy. But I do think it's worthwhile work."

"Do you really think they give a shit about any of that?"

"If it's in their interest, yes. And to the extent that they don't, all the more reason to have a strong VPMA."

"You sound pretty clear, Daniel. Whaddaya asking me for? I'm not your father."

"Thank God."

⟶

The dry and drafty chill of the cabin increased as the hours wore on. He shifted in his seat and pulled the blanket up around his neck.

⟶

"The meeting today with Mark Rader was pretty reassuring," Dan said. Carly had disappeared upstairs and he and Susan were in the kitchen cleaning up after dinner. "If anything, he was even more upbeat and encouraging than he was last week at C.J.'s."

"What'd he say?"

"Well, he basically said that, at least from his experience, Olympia's evil reputation was bullshit. He said that yes they were good at business and interested in the bottom line, but not at the expense of patient care. He says that he's enjoying himself and he says that he doesn't feel a bit compromised."

"Hmm."

"Could you try to contain your enthusiasm?"

"I'm sorry," Susan said, "but I just worry about these guys. I'm a Berkeley babe. I have a natural distrust of white southern businessmen."

"Well, so do I, I guess. But there's a little problem here. A bunch of white southern businessmen now own and operate the hospital I work at. I need to either make the most of the situation or find something else to do. And that something else would be to go back into practice, which I not very long ago left because I was bored and burned out." He wasn't concealing his irritation.

"Hey look, I don't mean to sound unsupportive." She faced him and took his hand in both of hers. "It scares me, Danny. I admit it. I'm cynical about big corporations in the health care business. It worries me."

"It worries me too, but it's what's real in the hospital business today. I'm being reassured that Olympia is maturing as an organization and that it's possible to work for them without being compromised. And I could have a meaningful role in assuring that the patients at Memorial don't get screwed by bottom line priorities." He continued without apology, but barely. "Look, $400,000 a year with a $100,000 signing bonus is a ton of money. And I might even be able to negotiate for more. That's easily enough to take care of everyone's education. And solidify retirement." His expression softened. "That's even Grizzly money."

—

I should have taken more Ambien. It probably wouldn't matter anyway. I can never sleep on these fucking trips.

—

Dan's first thought about Thomas Frost was that he had the kind of hairstyle that would remain undisturbed in a NASA wind tunnel. He looked like a televangelist—parted, puffed, and lacquered. Frost had been the Chief Financial Officer at the Olympia Greater Tampa Medical Center for the past six years. Athens decided he was ready to run something and sent him to Walnut Creek to be the CEO of its newest acquisition.

Dan had been summoned to Marty's old office to meet Frost. C.J. was there, still shepherding the transition. There'd been barely more than a two week hiatus between chief executive officers. Compared to an aggressive outfit like Olympia, non-profit academic hospitals made leadership changes in geologic time.

"Doctor Fazen, I'm Tom Frost. It's a pleasure to meet you."

He was five foot six, skinny and bespectacled. And he wore a high tab collar a la Orrin Hatch and Tom Wolfe.

"Please call me Dan." They shook hands. He turned to Corbett, "Hi, C.J., how are you?"

"I'm fine. Just so you know, Beau's done his thing and is back in Georgia. Tom's got the ball now."

As he and C.J. walked toward the conference table, Frost started to position himself behind his desk and awkwardly changed course toward the more egalitarian seating arrangement.

"Dan, I'm going to need your support and your insight as I find my way into this new position." Seated next to C.J., the man looked like a flyweight. "I'm an accountant by training. I entered the hospital world as an assistant controller about twenty years ago and have been a CFO at Olympia or one of its progenitors for the last fifteen. Greater Tampa was good preparation for Walnut Creek. Similar size, mission, demography."

Despite the well-tailored clothes, Frost had an essential nerdiness that reminded Dan of the math majors who hung out at Kepler Hall at Northwestern. Geek Central.

"One of the first things I need to do here is begin to learn about our medical staff and about the world of medical practice in Contra Costa County. I'll be relying heavily upon you to get me up to speed."

"I'll help any way I can," Dan said.

"Great. I'll set up a series of meetings specifically for you to educate me about the medical staff. Is there anything that I can do for you? Anything that needs my input right now?"

It seemed that Frost was proceeding as though Dan were on board, as though the details of his position had been resolved. He wondered if the man was intentional in his neglect or just spacey.

"Well, I have some questions that are related to my job offer. I presume you've seen a copy of my offer letter from Mr. Thurmond."

"Yes, I have it."

"Well, my preference would be to complete that process, hopefully reach an agreement, so that we can get on with the business of the medical center."

The chemistry of the room shifted. C.J. sat up straight and made direct eye contact with Dan. Frost leaned back and waited.

He took their silence as consent. "Can we talk a little about the Hospital Foundation?"

Frost seemed surprised. "I thought you'd be pushing us for a higher salary."

"We'll get there."

"Well, the Board has voted to set up a foundation to administer funds for patients without health insurance."

Dan asked, "How much are we talking about?"

"We're not sure. We think it may be as much as twenty or thirty million."

He interpreted Frost's first person plural not as hubris, but as evidence of his attachment to corporate, to Athens.

"Just so you know that that's a high priority for me." Now Dan left a space for Frost.

"So, I take it that you do want to talk about salary."

"Well, I don't know that we need to get into too much detail right now," Dan said. "I've done a little benchmarking, some calling around for comparables for senior medical execs at similar institutions in California, New York, Boston. Other high cost-of-living areas. What I would like to do is give you a counterproposal in writing."

C.J. was smiling. Frost had no choice but to agree. He told Dan that he looked forward to it.

Four days later, he received a new offer letter from Frost. His starting salary would be $450,000 a year, his signing bonus $150,000.

—

"Mesdames et messieurs, le Capitaine a illuminé le signe de ceinture de sécurité. Nous sommes dans notre approche finale de l'Aéroport de Charles De Gaulle. Veuillez vous assurer. . ."

Susan stirred.

A Samaritan in Paris

HOTEL MILLÉSIME ON THE SOUTH SIDE OF RUE JACOB HAD A tiny elevator traversing its six stories. When they were alone, which was nearly every ride, Dan delighted in coming on to Susan with uncamouflaged you're-gonna-get-it kissing, pressing her up against the mirrored walls of the little compartment. She made her faux objections and accused him of incurable adolescence. He took this as encouragement.

They had the hotel's only suite, a bedroom and a terraced parlor on the top floor. From the balcony they could see the river and the bulk of the Louvre straight ahead to the north, the long elegant roof of the Musée D'Orsay to the west, and to the right the sharp point of Ile de la Cité bisecting the Seine. With the windows and terrace doors buttoned up, the street was almost inaudible. The outbursts of the unmistakably European claxons of the police cars and the ambulances were perfect, especially at night. They reminded him of the Fellini and Truffaut films that he first saw at the Wildcat, the funky art house in Evanston, Illinois.

One energetic afternoon foray per day seemed about right. They did a long ramble through the Marais, the Musée Picasso, and Place des Vosges. Though they had sworn off the crowds, the D'Orsay was too close by foot to resist. So they navigated through the crush for glimpses of the haystacks and the lilies and the rosy cheeks, and fled in less than an hour.

Each afternoon was punctuated by some kind of confection, gouter, a stop at one of the fetching patisseries that seemed to be everywhere. Typically they ordered three to share, swooning in self-congratulatory pleasure for just being there. Susan, a hot chocolate aficionado, sampled her passion daily and declared that the astonishingly thick and dark version at Ladurée on Rue Royale made her ears ring.

They sat side by side through leisurely dinners, replaying the highlights of each day and shaping the next. Unwinding, the quiet conversations softened into their feelings for each other, their kids, their gratitude. After nearly twenty-five years of marriage, with their fair share of tedium and paroxysms of alienation, they could still tap into the sweetness that persisted beneath the tumult of their everyday life.

➤

Dan was shaking his head. "I didn't think that there could be a work of art more violent than Guernica."

The sun was out for their last full day in Paris. By their standards they had gotten an early start—out the front door of the Millésime by 11:15. They were shoulder to shoulder in the garden of the Musée Rodin looking up at The Gates of Hell.

"It almost looks like they're melting," he said.

"I don't need to look at this any longer." Susan pivoted and headed toward The Thinker. They circled the famous sculpture and settled on a bench facing west. Above the ecru garden wall was the dome of Invalides, and beyond that the upper half of the Eiffel Tower.

A few minutes passed before he spoke. "A week's not enough. I'm just getting over the jet lag." They had found Donormyl, a powerful over-the-counter French sedative, and were sleeping well. "I hate to tell you this, but I woke up obsessing about the damn hospital this morning."

"That sucks."

"Yeah."

He had a brief caucus with himself. She had not invited him to continue. It was a gorgeous day. They were in this remarkable sculpture garden sharing the *trois étoile* view and the perfect blue sky. Why spoil it? He indulged himself anyway.

"I was thinking about Marty. How different it feels with her gone. Nothing else has really changed, not yet anyway." She looped her arm through his and leaned in. "She taught me a lot. How to work the budgets, the regulators, the board. All that stuff. And with a few exceptions, she was always a pleasure to work with. It was fun. This guy Frost's an alien. Wait'll you meet him. They've sent a humorless Sun Belt bean counter to run our fucking hospital. In a hundred years I couldn't riff with this guy." He interrupted himself. "Hey, I'm sorry. This is a real intrusion. I'll stop."

"It's okay. Talk to me." She tucked herself in closer.

A group of noisy teenage girls in their tight blue jeans and precarious platform shoes walked past. He waited for them to get some distance.

"Tell me the truth, Toni. What do you think about what I'm doing? Really."

"I think, given the circumstances, you're doing the logical thing. There's no satisfactory alternative right now. If it's intolerable, you can always bail out. What have you got to lose?"

"Oh, I don't know. My integrity, my soul."

"Oh come on, Danny."

"Whaddaya mean, come on?"

"You're not going to sell out, for chrissakes."

"Maybe I already have."

"Oh please. Look, you said yourself that Olympia's made a lot of changes. You said that they're doing charity care, that they don't really resemble their reputation. You said that Mark Rader, a guy you respect, is happy with his choice. Don't you think you're being a little hard on yourself?"

"It sounds like you're colluding with my denial."

"Jesus, who's the shrink here?"

"Look, I want to know what you think about this. About me. I'm feeling really defensive. The guys in practice don't say anything but I'm feeling embarrassed around them. You know, it was one thing to be the patient advocate, the quality champion, working for Marty. This could be a whole other deal. These guys don't give a shit about any of that. I could be a pariah in that organization."

She sat up straight and faced him. "Do you know the jack story?"

"The what?"

"The jack story."

"What the hell is that?"

"It's a very old joke. Danny Thomas, I think."

"This has something to do with something?"

Like a stand-up, her hands went into motion as she told it. "This guy's driving his car out on a country road. Pretty deserted. Suddenly he gets a blowout. He pulls over and discovers that there's no jack in the trunk. He can see off in the distance, maybe four or five miles away, a sign for a gas station. So he sets out on foot for help. As he's walking, he's wondering what this is going to cost him. 'What, maybe ten bucks for a lift and the use of the jack? Shouldn't be much more than that. Then again, they could charge me pretty much anything they want. I don't have much of a choice. They could charge me fifty dollars, a hundred dollars. I could really get screwed. I'm completely at their mercy. And they're damned likely to take advantage of me. Those sonofabitches.' Exhausted and agitated he finally gets to the gas station and a courteous, well-groomed young man greets him with a smile. 'Good afternoon, sir. Can I help you?' 'Yeah, you can keep your fucking jack.' "

He smiled, shaking his head. "It's not exactly the same."

"I know. But it's a good joke."

"I guess it's not entirely irrelevant. I was getting a little apocalyptic."

"Yeah, I think so."

He took her hand. "Let's drop it. We've got a whole half-day left in Paris. I won't contaminate it any more."

From the Rodin garden they took a long circular walk past Invalides, down the Champs-de-Mars, through a quiet little park in the shadow of the Eiffel Tower, and then homeward via the side streets of the seventh *arrondissement*, stopping for the last *gouter* before the last nap before the last dinner.

Muniche, around the corner from their hotel on Rue Bonaparte, was, despite its Bavarian name, pure French bistro. Multi-tiered, brass railed, and wood paneled, it resembled the more famous Bofinger, with less noise and more linen. They had picked it out of expediency on their travel-worn first evening in Paris. Deciding it was terrific, they vowed to return fully awake. The maitre d' gave them a crescent-shaped booth on the top tier. They were thigh to thigh nursing a split of champagne.

Susan spoke quietly, "Carly sounded pretty good this morning." They had made a six a.m. call to catch her before bedtime. "She's always happy with Serge and his family."

"It's a good thing for us."

"You bet," she said. "Although she did give me a hard time about being away for more than a week."

"So what else is new?"

It had only been in the last few years that they felt comfortable about traveling alone. Carly's intolerance of separations had been relentless. When she was eight, Susan's sister came down from Sacramento to stay with her and her older brother while Dan and Susan went to the Oregon Coast for a week. Carly's tantrums and bedwetting brought them home after two days.

The waiter was headed their way. They had already negotiated that English was acceptable. "*Madame, Messieur.* Would you like to order?"

Dan did his franglais anyway. "Yes, *s'il vous plait*. Could we have one *steak tartare*, one order of *carré d'agneau*, rare, *saignant*, and one order of *pommes frites*. And one large bottle of Evian, *s'il vous plait*."

They savored their last supper, eating slowly and quietly, Dan splitting the portions in half and Susan pushing a little extra his way. For dessert, they ordered the mandatory *creme brulée* and added a piece of *gateau chocolat et framboise* because it was, well, the last dessert. In typical French style, the waiter was taking his time between courses. They punctuated comfortable silences with small talk about their day in the Seventh.

She said, "Wasn't that a great spot next to the Tower?"

"It's hard to believe that those huge lines of people waiting for the elevators were so close by. It felt like a neighborhood park."

"How about those houses with the big picture windows—"

"Help! Please! *M'aider!*" They were jolted, wrenched from their little conversation. One tier below and to the right. At first he thought the woman in the chair was having a seizure. The man who was shouting was kneeling in front of her, holding her by the shoulders.

Dan was on the move. As he approached the woman, he told a waiter on his left to call an ambulance and asked him if he understood. The waiter said that he did and moved away. He reached the man and crouched next to him. "I'm a doctor." The man looked bewildered. He pointed to himself. "Doctor. Physician. *Medécin.*"

"Yes. Doctor. Please help. Please." The man was panic-stricken.

He saw another waiter. "Ambulance. Call an ambulance. Do you understand?"

"*Oui*. Yes."

He turned his attention to the woman. The man was still holding her by the shoulders. Her appearance was grotesque. She sat straight, rigid in her chair. Her neck was extended and her face was turned toward the ceiling and about thirty degrees to the left.

Her eyelids were wide open and the globes of her eyes were rolled high in their sockets, ghoulishly revealing mostly white with a crescent of iris above. He gently removed the man's hands from her shoulders and moved directly in front of her for a closer look. He took her pulse at the wrist and neck. Then he closed her eyelids and re-opened them to attempt to check the pupils' reactions to light. The pupils were hidden behind her upper lids. Leaning to her right ear, he loudly asked her to speak. There was no response. With one hand on her shoulder and another to the back of her head, he attempted to bring her neck to its normal position. He was surprised by the rigidity and backed off. He quickly checked the range of motion of her elbows and knees and found those to be limited, but not as dramatically as the neck.

He turned to the man. "Is she taking any medicine, any drugs?"

"*Drogue?*"

"Yes, *drogue*. Drugs."

"Yes."

"What drugs? What *drogue?*"

The man tapped his temple with two fingers. "For the head."

The tables around them had emptied. From a safer distance the diners stared with curiosity and horror at this poor woman who looked, as much as anything, like she was possessed.

Susan crouched down next to Dan. "Is she having a seizure?"

"No, I don't think so."

"Is there anything I can do?"

"I think I know what this is. I'm gonna go with her to the hospital. If they let me."

"What do you want me to do?"

He was retrieving a memory from his emergency medicine days.

"Dan."

"What? I'm sorry. What did you say?"

"What should I do?" Susan said. "What do you want me to do?"

"You'd better go back to the hotel. I've gotta go with this woman. I think I know what's going on. They may not figure it out. I'll explain later."

He decided to get her out of the chair. With one forearm behind her knees and the other across her back, he lifted then lowered her to the carpeted floor. She felt like a mannequin adjusted for the sitting position. On his knees to her right, he placed her purse under her head and her coat across her body. The man with her knelt at her left shoulder. He was crying. The woman's bizarre countenance had not changed.

Dan met the man's eyes and spoke slowly. "She's going to be all right. This is not as bad as it looks. They will be able to help her at the hospital. She is not going to die. Do you understand?"

"You can do something, please? You can help?"

"At the hospital. They'll help her at the hospital. It's going to be all right." He extended his hand. "My name is Daniel."

"Nick. Nicholas." They shook hands.

Dan pointed to the woman. "What is her name?"

"Irene."

"I'm an American, from California."

"We are from Athens."

＞

They spilled out of the ambulance and into the fluorescent glare of the emergency department corridor. Though Dan had anticipated some resistance, he'd gotten a casual *"certainement"* from the paramedic when he identified himself and said that he wanted to accompany the woman. What with mid-evening Paris traffic, the ride to the hospital was the vehicular equivalent of running under water. Siren insisting but low speed bumper-to-bumper most of the way. With jostled penmanship, he wrote out a message and handed it to the paramedic. He didn't know if its content was radioed ahead. Then he wrote out a second identical message, folded it around his business card, and placed it in his own shirt pocket. "Not a seizure. This is a drug reaction. Probably a reaction to a phenothiazine, maybe haloperidol. Give diphenhydramine, 50 milligrams, IV push."

"*Excusez-moi.*" He attempted to get the attention of the receiving physician. "*Excusez-moi.*" He didn't understand the woman's rapid-fire response. "*Je ne parle pas bien francais. Parlez-vous anglais?*"

"Yes. Are you the doctor who sent the message?" Her English was flawless.

"Yes, Daniel Fazen."

"Sylvie Rigaud. I need to examine her. Will you please stay?"

"Yes, *oui.* Of course."

The patient was now on a gurney in a treatment room. Nicholas was at her side. As Dan followed the doctor in, Irene was simultaneously being connected to a cardiopulmonary monitor, having blood drawn from her left arm and having an IV started in her right. Her strange facial contortion was unchanged. Rigaud did a rapid physical exam while eliciting a medical history. Nothing like this had occurred before; Irene had no history of a seizure disorder; she was on multiple medications for some type of a psychiatric condition. Nicholas did not know the names of the medications. Upon request but to no avail he went through Irene's purse in search of pills. There was a rapid exchange in French between Rigaud and the treating nurse.

Rigaud led Dan into the corridor and out of earshot. "I have never seen this before. How certain are you?"

"She's on psychiatric meds," he said. "These neurologic reactions are known to occur with phenothiazines, especially haloperidol. She could easily be on at least one of the phenothiazines. The findings are classic for oculogyric crisis. Neurotoxicity, extrapyramidal. It's not a seizure. I don't believe she's seizing, do you?"

"I don't think so," she said. "I'm not sure."

"The IV diphenhydramine won't hurt her. If it's going to work, you'll know right away. I mean within a minute or two. If it doesn't work, you haven't lost anything."

"All right, we'll try," she said. "You just push it IV?"

"Yeah. I'd push it in over maybe five or ten seconds. Then flush the IV."

As it turned out, they had taken his message seriously. The filled syringe was already on a stainless steel tray next to the patient. Rigaud pushed the drug through a needle port in the IV line, increased the IV flow rate, took a few steps back and watched. Dan was just behind her. Nick, at the edge of the bed holding Irene's right hand, gazed back and forth between the faces of Irene and Doctor Rigaud. Riguad was alternating between Irene and the second hand of the wall clock. For thirty seconds nothing happened. Then Irene's chin gradually began to lower and move to the midline as the muscles of her neck relaxed. The arching of her back subsided and she sank into the gurney. Seconds later her eyelids closed and her face softened. It was over in less than a minute.

———

Nick was profusely thanking Doctor Rigaud as she finished a repeat physical examination. Dan could see from the cardiorespiratory monitor that Irene's vital signs were normal. Looking at her, he realized she was younger than he had thought, perhaps mid-twenties. And uncontorted, she was quite pretty.

Rigaud approached him, grinning. "Wow. Thank you."

"What can I say? What an adventure."

"Is there anything we can do for you?"

"I don't know what. I'd just like to get back to my hotel. I abandoned my wife at the restaurant."

"Maybe someone here can give you a ride. Where are you staying?"

"Hotel Millésime. Rue Jacob."

"Just wait here."

"I can take a taxi."

"I insist." She headed toward the nurses station.

"Doctor Daniel." It was Nick. He walked up and gave him a bear hug. Dan thought that the man didn't really smell that good. "I don't know how to thank you. You are, ah, wonderful."

"It's okay, really," Dan said. "It's my pleasure. She looks like she's going to be fine."

"I would like to somehow thank you in some better way."

"No, really. You don't have to do anything. I was happy to help."

"Can we write to you to thank you? Irene would want to. I know."

"Sure. That would be nice." He extricated the business card from the folded message in his shirt pocket and handed it to Nick. "Yes. Please write. That would be nice."

Rigaud returned. "If you go right now, one of our clerks can take you."

"That's great. Thank you for your kindness."

"Thank you for your help."

A young woman with no English drove him through the still busy late evening streets to Rue Jacob. Unencumbered by conversation, he was thinking mostly about how good it felt to directly and individually make a difference for a patient.

———

Navigating through the half-packed suitcases on the parlor floor, he got to the phone by the fourth ring. He was in his sweats. The airport limo was coming in two hours. The receptionist told him that there was a man in the lobby who wanted to speak to him.

"Hello, Doctor Daniel Fazen?"

"Yes."

"This is Nicholas. Nick. From last night."

"Oh yes. What a surprise."

"I am here and Irene is here. We want to thank you. I hope this is not trouble. We bring something for you."

He looked at his watch. "That's very nice. We're, uh, we're getting ready to go to the airport. We're flying home today."

"Oh, it is trouble?"

"No, no. Can you hold on? Just a moment, okay?"

"Yes. I understand."

He found Susan packing toiletries in the bathroom. "Toni, we've got company."

"We've got company?"

"The woman from the restaurant. She and her husband, I guess husband, are here. They want to thank me and I think give me something. Do you mind if I invite them up for a few minutes?"

"Sure. I suppose. Do you think they'll be able to stand the glamour?" She struck a pose in her tattered UC-Berkeley sweatshirt and red plaid boxers. "I'll put on pants."

When he opened the door, there was Nicholas holding a crystal vase containing an enormous bouquet of fresh cut flowers. He was beaming. Irene stood at his side clinging to his arm. She smiled nervously and then diverted her gaze like a child.

Dan took the flowers and placed them on a table. "These are wonderful. Thank you very much."

"It is a little thank you." Nicholas bowed slightly from the waist as he said it.

Introductions made, the four of them sat in the parlor. He asked Nicholas how he knew they were at the Millésime.

"The doctor. Doctor Rigaud. She told me. I hope this is okay."

The visit became ten minutes of dueling thank yous. At one point, while Irene was in the bathroom, Nicholas said he felt bad that she wasn't saying much. "She doesn't have English. And she is very shy."

Susan joined in. "She seems okay this morning. She's completely back to normal?"

"Yes, because of the doctor here," gesturing to Dan. "They said this at the Emergency."

"Well, I don't know about that," Dan said, "but I was glad to help. And I got to take an ambulance ride through the streets of Paris. An adventure. The important thing is that she is better." Irene returned to the parlor and Dan continued, "Did they tell you that the attack last night was caused by her medication, her *drogue?*"

"Yes. Yes, they did. We see her doctor at home. Immediate."

"Good."

Susan walked over to the bouquet. "You know, you should take these with you. We are leaving and the flowers will go to waste."

"We leave also. Tonight."

"Well, we'll take the vase. It's lovely. The next guest will get to enjoy the flowers."

Just as Dan was getting edgy about the time, Nick took the initiative. "We must let you make your trip."

After one last round of appreciation and bon voyage, they were gone.

"Danny, that was sweet," Susan said. "You did a good thing."

"It's been a long time since I made a difference as a real doc."

She stepped into his embrace. After several seconds she whispered, "We'd better get our butts in gear."

———

"Honey, is my watch out there?" They were in jeans, sneakers and sweat shirts for the flight home. A bellman was moving their luggage to a trolley outside their door.

Dan did a quick scan around the parlor. "I don't see it, Tone."

"Are you sure? Could you look around carefully?" She sounded anxious.

He canvassed the room again and then went into the bedroom. He found her yanking the bed away from the wall. She was obviously agitated.

"It's not out there."

"Danny, I can't find it. I've looked in every drawer three times. Please look around in here. Maybe I'm looking right at it and not seeing it."

She was on her knees between the head of the bed and the wall. Dan started in the bathroom and methodically looked at every surface and every drawer. Nothing.

She rose from the floor, her eyes thick with tears. "I can't leave here without that watch."

The engraved little timepiece—the Hamilton Watch Company had named it *Nightingale*—was a Giuliani heirloom, from grandmother to mother to Susan on the morning of her college graduation. An art deco design with tiny diamond scraps around an alabaster face and lacey black hands, it was worth maybe three hundred dollars on the open market. But Susan treasured it—for herself, and someday for Carly.

"You know what I think?" Susan said. "I think that woman took my watch. She was in here alone. I don't know exactly where I put it, but it was probably on the dresser or the night table or in the bathroom. It was here. And she was alone in here. Fuck!"

The telephone rang. He answered and listened for a moment. "Hold on." He cupped his hand over the handset. "It's the limo. They're here."

"Shit."

He uncovered the phone. "Can they wait five minutes? ... Yes, I'll hold ... Thank you."

He sat on the bed next to Susan. "They'll wait."

"I can't believe that fucking woman stole my watch. She's on major meds. She's probably fucking schizophrenic."

"Toni, look. If you want to stay, we'll stay. But I don't think we're going to be able to find these people. I don't know where they're staying. I don't even know their last name. We could probably get it from the Emergency Room. We'd have to do that, get the police, find them. And they're leaving for Athens tonight. It just seems impossible."

She was staring straight ahead, livid.

"If you want, I'll ask the desk to call and find out when we can get on a flight if we miss this one. I don't want to make—"

"I can't fucking believe this. I love that watch and I loved this trip. And that fucking crazy woman just comes in here and takes it. I'd like to fucking kill her."

He didn't know what to say. "I'm sorry. I wish I could do something."

She visibly steeled herself. "Let's just go. Carly wants us back. We both have to go to work. And you're right, we'll never find them anyway. And if we did, they'd deny it and we'd never know if she took it or not. Come on, let's just get the hell outta here."

"Are you sure?"

"I wanna go home. I hate this."

"On the way out I'll tell the desk what happened," he said. "Maybe we'll get lucky and they'll find it and send it to us."

"Yeah right."

—

He was staring at the rivets on the near surface of the wing. Susan was napping, maybe. They had spoken little since leaving the hotel, and each had unenthusiastically picked at the business class cuisine. The sweetness of the trip was tainted. His big medical coup was now just the prologue to a miserable memory. And he knew that he had no way to console Susan, at least not for the time being. The theft was creepy, somehow ominous. Still, up until the last moments, it had been a wonderful vacation. His thoughts flowed through fragments of Memorial and the Paris ER and the charm of their left bank neighborhood and Susan heartbroken and furious on the bedroom floor. And about their little talk on the bench at the Rodin. He exhaled and closed his eyes and told himself that everything was going to be all right. Twice.

The Olympia Way

—

J ACK JENSEN WAS BRINGING HIM UP TO SPEED WHILE THEY WAITED
for Frost, or perhaps C.J., to begin. With Marty gone, the
Chief of Medicine was Dan's closest approxima-
tion to a hospital confidante.

"Apparently Hill's decided to let it go," Jack said.

Before he left for Paris, the Medical Staff Executive
Committee had voted unanimously to require mandatory consultation for any patient that Walt Hill admitted to the hospital.
What they didn't know was what Hill and his attorney might try
to do about it. Dan was surprised by the news.

"He missed the appeal deadline?"

"Right. You know, he's been reported to Sacramento. He's
already embarrassed. There's nothing he can do about that.
Overall, it's pretty damn lenient. He's still got his privileges, he
can still admit. He just can't hide."

Dan was shaking his head. "Not exactly the mother of inter-
ventions."

"I think he'll just fade away," Jack said, "cut his malpractice exposure, admit to other people's services. I don't think we're gonna to be seeing very much of Doctor Hill."

"That's fine with me," Dan said.

"Good Morning, everyone." It was Frost. Despite the fact that Corbett was now an Olympia Director, and that they were in the cavernous Redwood Solutions Board Room for the retreat, C.J. was not going to do anything to upstage the fledgling CEO.

Listening to the introductions, Dan thought about how dramatically his professional life had changed. After three decades among doctors, nurses, and patients, he was now surrounded by accountants, lawyers, and marketing consultants. Of the thirty people there to determine the future of Memorial Medical Center, exactly two, he and Jack, were medical professionals.

In front of each participant on the big round conference table were two gifts. A teal knit shirt with the company logo, a caduceus overlying three interlinked Olympic rings, embroidered neatly in black. And a Cross pen. Not the ordinary skinny one, but a chunky gold and silver beauty with the OHC logo on the clip. Dan calculated that the pens cost them about a month of an intensive care nurse.

Frost was wearing the teal shirt. In his nasal voice, he began by paying homage to quality of care and community responsibility. Dan thought about hand-over-heart rituals preceding professional athletic bloodbaths. As if it were a simple, high-minded statement, Frost said, "It is crucial that we create the perception out there that we care about the patients and the community." He spent nearly three quarters of an hour on an overview of the Olympia approach to hospital turnarounds, and to his expectations for the retreat. He spoke rapidly, his demeanor stiff, out of synch with a dress casual, off-campus, big picture conversation.

Dan knew that Olympia had done this hundreds of times. Their takeover targets were financially strapped hospitals that were either long established, or were in an unstable marketplace. They rarely built new hospitals. That was too expensive and took way too long for a company that moved at their pace.

In the era of managed care, a for-profit hospital made money for its shareholders by controlling costs. The days of "the more you do, the more you make" were over. The hospital that did the least amount of care for the maximum number of patients made the most money. Olympia was notorious for ruthless cost reductions and containment. Fewer staff, lower levels of training, cheaper supplies and equipment, rapid hospital discharges, reduced ordering of everything—drugs, lab tests, x-rays. Olympia's critics liked to say that this was an organization that specialized in doing less with less.

Their strategy depended heavily on developing and maintaining a loyal network of physicians who admitted patients to their hospitals. It is illegal for a hospital to financially compensate a doctor for admitting patients—strictly speaking. So Olympia offered physicians lucrative partnerships in outpatient surgery centers or home health care businesses. While these deals did not directly assure the physicians' hospital admissions, they created relationships and loyalty, which indirectly paid off time and time again. Dan remembered reading that Olympia executives talked about having "happy captives" on the medical staff.

And when they came to town, they went deep into their pockets to saturate the area with intensive marketing and advertising campaigns. Only weeks after the Walnut Creek acquisition, half the buses in Contra Costa County had twelve foot ads on their sides for "The New Memorial." On the lowest road, Olympia was notorious for portraying non-profit hospitals as unpatriotic, as non-taxpaying parasites.

Dan had heard it all, especially from Ben. Yet Rader and Thurmond and C.J. were telling him that things had changed. That the acquisitive, ruthless organization of a decade earlier no longer existed.

On the second day of the retreat, late in the afternoon, there was a two-hour session entitled "Staff Ratios and Skill Mix: Applying the Tampa Model." Dan wondered how he could possibly stay awake. When he realized that Tom Frost was going to make the presentation, he poured some coffee, unusual after his early morning dose, got himself fully upright in the executive swivel rocker, and attempted to focus.

Frost brought the lights down, lowered a projection screen, and punched up a title slide using a laptop. It read "Willie Sutton, Nursing Care and the Financial Health of Your Hospital." He at least had the subtlety to not actually talk about Sutton, letting the reference incubate. He spoke as a financial fundamentalist, without a nuance of doubt about the truth of his message.

"Hospitals spend the majority of their money on labor. True, pharmaceuticals are going through the roof. But services and supplies and equipment don't hold a candle to personnel costs. That's where the money is."

Frost went through a series of projected spreadsheets, methodically building the layers of his case. Slide after slide depicting the relative costs of registered nurses, licensed vocational nurses, and medical assistants, and detailing the actual tasks performed by these people. All leading up to his fundamental approach to cost-containment.

"As you can see, registered nurses spend approximately seventy percent of their time doing tasks that are at the skill level of vocational nurses and medical assistants. And that's on the inpatient side. In the outpatient setting it goes up as high as ninety percent. We've demonstrated that this is clearly the area where we can reduce expenses without any threat to quality or service. We're not talking here about reducing staff. In fact, we'll probably end up with more folks taking care of patients, people doing what they were trained to do."

Despite Dan's liberal biases, his antipathy for these waspy business types, he admitted to himself that Frost's approach had undeniable merit. Nurses did spend much of their time doing clerical work—answering phones, filling out forms, chasing down doctors for signatures. And giving family members directions to the cafeteria, and transporting patients, and filling supply shelves, and wiping up spills. Even in critical units like intensive care and coronary care, where the nurses were dealing with very sick patients needing skilled observation and procedures, they wasted their talent and training doing tasks that could be done by clerks, transportation aides, and janitors.

Frost projected a title slide, "The Olympia Templates." Dan had heard about these, OHC's controversial mathematical staffing models for which they had been scalded by their critics. They had been accused of reducing hospital care to number-crunching, of approaching patients' needs with spreadsheets instead of individualized professional judgments. A much circulated editorial cartoon had depicted a physician with the Olympia logo on his white coat, green eyeshades, calculator and clipboard in hand, and a stethoscope discarded at his feet.

Dan felt a vibration on his right hip, his pager in silent mode. He responded from C.J.'s reception area.

"Clare, it's Dan. What's up?"

"A reporter from the Contra Costa Daily News called and said that they're about to run a piece on Memorial and Olympia. He wants to interview you this afternoon. He said he wants to give you a chance to respond."

"All right. Call him and tell him six-thirty. My office. And tell him no more than ten minutes, okay?"

When he returned, Frost was running through pro formas, projections of cost savings accomplished by different staffing scenarios. The range of annual cost savings varied from four million to nearly twenty million dollars. As he spoke, "with no consequence to quality" was the recurrent parenthetical.

Late afternoon tired, numbed by the cool numbers, and distracted by fragments of rehearsal for the local journalist, Dan lost his focus.

—

He waited for the reporter in full physician. White coat and stethoscope adangle. Even tongue depressors and a flashlight in his breast pocket. He was nervous. As a private practitioner, he had never been interviewed by the media. In the early months at Memorial, he'd had some contact with the press. A few aggrandizing puff pieces choreographed by the Public Relations

Department, and a series of press conferences chronicling the progress of an Oakland A's outfielder who'd been in a high speed wreck in his Mercedes SUV.

"Doctor Fazen?"

Clare had gone home. He walked out to the reception area to greet his visitor, who could have passed for a well-dressed college freshman.

"Mr. Colburn, I presume."

He gave his visitor a firm, brief handshake, led him into his office, and sat down at his desk. No first name, no business card, no cordial seating.

The young man gestured to the chair opposite Dan. "Is this okay?"

"Please sit down."

"Doctor Fazen, I appreciate you seeing me on such short notice. I'm sure you must be busy."

This was hardly the grisly adversary that he was anticipating, some Lee Cobb type with chewn cigar, fedora, and pot belly. James Colburn had the hip monotone look of his generation. Black, narrow, three-button jacket, buttoned only at the top, almost matching black slacks, and a dark gray shirt and solid tie. He was lean and handsome, his blue eyes striking against his café-au-lait skin. Dan thought of Derek Jeter.

"As I told your assistant on the phone, we're preparing a story on Memorial. Specifically on the implications of the acquisition of Memorial by Olympia. It'll probably run the day after tomorrow. I was hoping to get your responses to some of our material."

Intending to control the pace of the conversation, Dan let a few seconds lapse before speaking. "I'll answer whatever I can. I'm as new to Olympia as everyone else here."

"Sir, you understand that we're on the record, that what you say may be quoted in the articles?"

He wondered if veteran reporters reminded their subjects of such things. "I assumed."

Colburn took a small electronic device from his pocket and placed it on the desk. "Sir, this is a tape recorder. I want to make sure that I get exactly what you say. You know, not misquote you. Is that all right?"

"If you're gonna print it, I'd prefer that you get it right."

"Doctor Fazen, the medical director at the county hospital has said, and let me quote, 'the Olympia takeover is a threat to the health of the public in Contra Costa County.' Would you like to respond?"

"Well, that's pretty apocalyptic. You know, the medical staff at Memorial hasn't changed. We have a long history of superb care, and of very successful surveys by the Joint Commission and the State Department of Health Services. There is no prospect that that is going to change."

"Sir, if I understand correctly, the medical staff is private, it doesn't work for Olympia. What about the nursing staff? Is it not true that Olympia has a track record of dramatically reducing the number of nurses when they take over a hospital?"

"Well, I don't know about *dramatically*. Any smart hospital tries to match its staffing to the actual work that needs to be done. For a given portion of a hospital, say a general inpatient floor, there's an appropriate combination of registered nurses, lower skilled nursing staff, clerks, and so forth. Many hospitals, including this one, are still using some very expensive staff to do work that's appropriate for people at a lower salary level with a different set of skills. That just raises the cost of health care. It may turn out that Memorial will change its staffing patterns somewhat. My guess is we'll end up with as many staff, maybe even more staff, than prior to the acquisition."

"Doctor Fazen, are you saying that Memorial is going to increase the number of nurses?"

"No, that's not what I said. Likely somewhat fewer registered nurses but without a reduction in overall staff. Perhaps an increase in overall staff. And with a better match of workers to tasks."

Colburn flipped a page in his hand-held notes. "Doctor, I'd like to ask you a few questions about the community foundation that Olympia's created."

Dan waited. No sociable nod, no "uh huh."

"There's a state watchdog group that's claiming that Olympia's debt to the foundation is much greater than the eighteen million they've set aside. Do you have a comment on that?"

"You know, this is really beyond my expertise. This is something the accountants or actuaries do. I just can't comment."

Colburn's manner was polite and diligent, more like a conscientious journalism student than a street-wise investigative reporter. Dan watched him as he leafed ahead through his notes.

"Doctor Fazen, you're probably aware that some Olympia hospitals have been found guilty of illegal billing practices. Overcharging Medicare and so forth. There have been indictments and convictions of Olympia executives. With the acquisition in place, are you concerned about the billing practices at Memorial?"

"Mister Colburn, that was a long time ago. Almost ten years ago. And the parties involved are long gone from OHC. I am certainly not concerned about it." Dan wondered if he sounded as defensive to the reporter as he did to himself.

"Would you say you were in a position to be able to know if the billing practices were appropriate?"

"Well, if you mean do I keep tabs day to day on the billing process, then of course no. But if there were a problem in the institution, I'd know about it."

"How, sir?"

"Well, if the Feds find you in violation, it's no secret. Certified mail, site visits, threats to reimbursement for all your Medicare and Medicaid patients. You can't miss it." He realized he was riffing. "Mister Colburn, it's time for me to go home for dinner."

"I understand, sir. I appreciate your time. I really do."

Dan stood and extended his hand across the desk. "It was nice to meet you."

"It was good to meet you too, doctor." He held Dan's gaze for a few extra seconds. "Doctor, off the record. I want you to know that I'm not trying to harm Memorial. I just want to get the story right. There's a lot of fine people here. And from what I hear, you're one of the good guys."

I wonder.

"That's kind of you, Mister Colburn. But I have to tell you: I think you may be wrong about your bad guys."

⟶

He was at the Starbuck's on Mount Diablo Boulevard in Lafayette when they unlocked the doors at five thirty-two. He paid for his Vente, a hazelnut bun, and the morning edition of the Contra Costa paper which he extracted from the wooden bin next to the pastry counter. Sitting at his usual table, he paged straight to Colburn's piece. It was the lead story in the Community section. He read it twice. The young reporter had done his homework. He laid out Olympia's history chronologically, the spectacular successes in acquisitions and corporate growth, the early tumult of revelations, investigations and resignations, the recent aggressive strategy in the Bay Area. He described Olympia's approach to taking over a marketplace and establishing itself with the local physicians. And he wrote in detail about the jeopardy to the staff and the patients of the acquired hospital. Dan wasn't misquoted but he hated the copy.

to the Joint Commission. Olympia executive Fazen countered that there was no prospect that the quality of care at Memorial was going to change. He predicted that, rather than reductions in staff, there might actually be increased numbers of staff, and that there will be "a better match of workers to tasks." When asked about Olympia's history of fraudulent billing practices, Fazen pointed out that those practices had occurred nearly a decade earlier by individuals who were no longer in the organization. He said, "I am certainly not concerned about it." The civil attorney

He was enough of a private citizen that he still experienced a sizzle when he saw his name in print. But despite his fifteen microseconds of pleasure at his newsworthiness, he felt, physically felt, rising in him a deep and unfamiliar nervousness. He was re-reading rapidly, going in and out of focus. His left leg was in fine agitation at a few hundred beats a minute. His belly was queasy and he could feel his heart. Dan knew caffeine intimately and this wasn't it. He closed his eyes and took a few slow breaths.

His thoughts went not to the hospital. Nor to the patients or the staff. He thought about how he could not have been more intentional about his appearance at the interview with Colburn. If he had placed a sign on his chest reading "I am a doctor," it would have added nothing. Yet what the young reporter saw was a corporate bureaucrat, a suit. An Olympia man.

The Rainmaker

MARVIN SELDES WAS A GYNECOLOGIC ONCOLOGIST AND the pre-eminent cancer surgeon in Contra Costa County. Each year he and his partners brought eighteen to twenty million dollars of business to Memorial. And ask anyone, Marv Seldes was also a hot-tempered, abusive son of a bitch. Feared and tolerated at the hospital for nearly three decades, Seldes was minimally congenial only to the primary care physicians. Just cordial enough to the internists and family practitioners and general gynecologists who referred patients to his practice. For that reason Dan had over the years managed to stay out of conflict with him. As he sat at his desk late in the afternoon re-reading the scrupulously documented confidential memorandum from the Operating Room Nursing Supervisor, he was thinking that his long history of peaceful coexistence with Doctor Seldes was coming to an end.

"Hello Dan." Carol Tessler, the Ob-Gyn department chair and Medical Staff president, was striding in.

He steered her to his conference table. "Thanks for coming right over. I know it's late."

"I can't believe Seldes," she said. "He's obnoxious, but this is off the goddamn radar screen."

"No shit."

"What do we know?"

Using the memo, Dan punctuated his description with direct quotes. "What we know with certainty is that he walked out of the OR this morning with an anesthetized patient on the table, a forty-six year old woman with recurrent uterine bleeding who was here for hysteroscopy. Evidently, Seldes typically calls in from the road and gives them an ETA."

"That's right," she said. "And he's incredibly punctual. And really irritated if they're not."

"Well, 'really irritated' doesn't quite capture it. He shows up and the patient is not only not ready to go under, but is not even in the OR suite. At which point he starts shouting, 'Where's the goddamn fucking patient? I can't believe you fucking people are wasting my time.' The scrub nurse tells him that he has no right to talk to them that way. And he shouts, 'I will talk to you any way I damn please. I'll be in Medical Records. Page me when you have your fucking act together.' And leaves."

Tessler asked, "Do we know why the patient wasn't there on time?"

"Something about staffing in pre-op and difficulty with another patient. I don't know. Anyway, about twenty minutes later the patient's there, the nurse anesthetist is there, the gynecology chief resident's there. Seldes comes in, they put her to sleep, and things seem to be back on track. Now the real explosion comes when he asks for the distension fluid for the uterus and they don't have what he wants. He wants mannitol and they give him glycine. Does it matter that much?"

Carol didn't actually do hysteroscopies herself, but she knew what was involved. "Well, you know in order to spread out the uterine lining so you can see clearly with the scope, you have to distend the uterus, fill it with fluid. The fluid used for years by most gynecologists is glycine. It's been the standard. All the urologists use it in the bladder for cystoscopy. There have been a few reports of serum electrolyte problems with it. And possibly, I say possibly, CNS complications. Brain swelling. So some of the docs are switching to mannitol, which can actually have some of its own complications. The majority still use glycine."

"You're sure that glycine is well within the standard of care?"

"Absolutely," she said.

"Anyway, Seldes asks for mannitol and they tell him that they only have glycine. That mannitol has been removed from their inventory and that glycine is now the standard distension solution for gynecology and urology procedures. And Seldes goes apeshit. He's screaming, 'I can't fucking believe this. Do you want me to kill the fucking patient?' The scrub nurse tells him that she thinks he should calm down. He's yelling, 'You don't fucking tell me what to do or how to be. If we kill this woman, it'll be my ass on the line, not yours.' "

Dan set the memo aside. "The scrub nurse described him as completely out of control. She tried to convince him to use the glycine this one time and then get the policy changed for subsequent cases. He keeps bellowing and swearing at them and after a minute or two more he takes off his gloves, throws them on the floor, and walks out of the OR."

Tessler covered her face with both hands. "Great."

"So they wake the patient up, tell her there was a technical problem and that the procedure would be re-scheduled."

He slid the memo across the table to Carol. Slouched in his chair, legs extended and hands folded in his lap, he closed his eyes while she read. He was tired, and thinking that the really crappy stuff always seemed to happen late in the day.

Tessler skimmed it quickly. "What now?"

"I think we'd better talk with Richard Reynolds. Maybe we can still get him."

He sat up straight and entered a short sequence on the telephone keypad. The tinny speaker amplified the rings. He tapped down the volume. "Richard, I'm here with Carol Tessler, on the speaker phone. We've got a situation here. Do you know who Marv Seldes is?"

"Sure. He was in the group that worked on developing the radiation therapy contract. He's a little grumpy."

"Yes, well, that is a creative way to describe him. It seems Doctor Seldes abandoned an anesthetized patient in our OR. For sure, one of the things I'm going to need to know is what actually constitutes abandonment. There was another surgeon left behind in the room, the Ob-Gyn chief resident. And he is licensed, but he's not an attending physician on our medical staff."

"Dan, give me a little detail here," Reynolds said. "What actually happened?"

Carol interrupted. "Actually, the chief resident is a member of the medical staff. His board requirements are complete and he occasionally moonlights as an attending here and at a few other hospitals." Then Tessler mostly listened as Dan went through it. She responded to a few questions from Reynolds about how hysteroscopy was done and about the distension fluids.

Reynolds was a quick study. In the Walt Hill business, he had absorbed the complex information about the intricacies of diabetic management on the first pass. When Dan finished the description of the event, he circled back to his opening question.

"So Richard, aside from all the incivility stuff, which I really do want to deal with, did he abandon this patient? I mean technically, legally."

"Well, he obviously caused her to have an unnecessary general anesthetic, which was apparently without complication. And presumably he was the surgeon of record on the OR schedule. Carol, was the chief resident capable of doing the procedure without him?"

"Absolutely not. He has never done one independently. And he doesn't have privileges for it anyway."

Reynolds gave himself some wiggle room. "Well, strictly on the abandonment issue, the patient was still attended by OR staff that could be considered complete after Seldes left. A licensed gynecologist who was a member of the medical staff, an anesthetist, and the nurses. She was not abandoned to no care at all. I want to review the Medical Board regs and maybe some case law. As far as his behavior is concerned, there's more than enough there to justify disciplinary action. Have there been any formal actions against him in the past?"

"Lots of complaints about his tantrums and his language. But to my knowledge, no medical staff action. Carol?"

"No, just the obnoxious behavior. He's a very good clinician. And a spectacular cutter."

Dan pressed his eyes with his left thumb and index finger. He was tired. And disappointed that he was going to be at least an hour late for his dinner date with Susan.

"Richard, I need to hear more from you on the abandonment issue," Dan said. "And I need to think about this a little. I mean I'm pretty sure there'll be a disciplinary action. I'm just not sure right now what it's gonna look like. I don't see how we can let it go. Call me as soon as you have something."

As he drove toward the restaurant in Oakland, he imagined Seldes screaming at him, threatening him. The volume and texture of rage, no particular words. He didn't like to think of himself as cowardly, but he had all his adult life avoided conflict, navigating safe passages steps ahead of projected confrontation or danger. And while he had been told for years that he was a peaceful person, he thought himself less still at his center than tactically good at controlling his circumstances. Had he a choice, he would never engage the Marvin Seldeses of this world.

➤

They'd been going to Bay Wolf for years. The food and service were wonderful. And what they especially liked were the quiet acoustics and the little extra distance between the tables. It was a place where you could have a conversation. Even if you weren't sitting side by side, which they were.

"I'm sorry about the last minute re-schedule. I hate doing that," he said.

Susan brushed it off. "It's no big deal. I got a little extra time with Carly. Which I'll tell you is a scarce commodity these days." She was genuinely not upset. "What's going on?"

As usual, he initially balked at churning through the aggravation du jour, then relented to Susan's receptivity and his desire to debrief. He went through the facts.

"He actually walked out on her while she was anesthetized?"

"Yes, that's exactly what he did."

Shocked by little, she looked persuasively incredulous. "Jesus Christ."

"And I'm going to have to deal with this imperious asshole."

"Is there any way you can deflect it?"

He explained that the Operating Room and Medical Executive Committees would review the quality of care considerations. "But assuring compliance with Sacramento is mine. And I've got to respond to his behavior with the nurses. It's gonna be ugly. This guy's a load. Everyone's been tip-toeing around him for decades."

"What's he gonna do if he's told to cut the crap? Take his ball and go play somewhere else?"

"Well, I doubt it," he said. "Memorial's the only place in the county with radiation therapy and a real medical oncology program. And Ob-Gyn residents, who he relies on plenty. I suppose he could wave his book of business under the nose of one of the other hospitals. It'd be pretty hard and damned expensive for them to put together a real cancer capability from scratch. One that would satisfy Seldes. I don't see it. Plus his office is right there. He'd have to undo the whole thing. No, I don't think so."

"So what's really likely to happen? A couple of tantrums and back to status quo?"

"I guess. I don't know. Let's talk about something else."

Having some reality out loud with Susan, even briefly, quieted the inner hum of worse-case scenarios. He was feeling that the stakes were lower than they seemed just minutes earlier. He remembered, how could he forget, what they had planned to talk about over the best food on Piedmont Avenue.

"So what did Harriet have to say?" he asked. Harriet Gomberg was the agent for the Grizzly Peak house.

"It looks like it's available."

"No shit?"

"She said there was a buyer, a contract, and the deal, the financing, fell apart. It's available."

"What'd you tell her?"

"I told her we'd talk about it tonight. Probably get back to her tomorrow."

They sat there, eye to eye. This was one of those decisive moments, changing home and community after decades. Leaving the principal setting of their life together, where their kids had grown up. All of the memories and meaning invoked by the look and feel and smell of a place.

He broke the silence. "Whether a teenager should decide such things or not, I think it rises and falls with Carly. If she's reasonably happy about it, or at least not completely resistant, I think we should go for it. We both love it. And with the new income, we need the tax shelter. If we don't put it in the mortgage, then a huge amount is just going to go to the IRS. At least in the house, it'll be doing something. Eventually we'll cash out for retirement. That house is an incredible asset."

"Well," she said, "I don't think we should decide just on the basis of finances."

"I'm not saying that. We're not doing that. The place is fabulous. We've been salivating over it for three years."

Susan executed a long pause and then did a Groucho thing with her eyebrows. "Wouldn't it be just unbelievable to live there?"

⟶

It was hard to pay attention to Frost describing the long run-up to the survey by the Joint Commission. Despite his specific responsibilities for such visits, Dan was bored by the regulatory trivia, and distracted by his thoughts about the Seldes incident. It had been five days since he sent him a certified letter formally requesting that Seldes come in without delay to discuss it. He'd heard nothing. And oddly, he'd been unable to have a follow-up conversation with Richard Reynolds.

Frost sat at the head of his office conference table, wrapping up. "We've got almost exactly one year before they're here. I know that sounds like a long time, but it isn't. Memorial's done very well in the past. Very few serious recommendations. I see no reason why the surveyors should be coming with negative expectations. I'd like each of you to develop a work plan with timelines for your departments by the first of next month. We'll meet monthly to assure that we're hitting our own expectations, then more frequently, say, starting in January. Any questions?"

The Chief Financial Officer asked something about the fixed asset budget and the power plant. Dan stared at the bridge of the man's nose.

Frost had another agenda. "Let's deal with that off-line. Thanks, everyone. Dan, could you please stick around." It wasn't a question. Frost moved behind his desk and waited for the room to clear and for Dan to seat himself across from him. To the trailing executive, "Please close the door."

It had been only seven months since Frost's arrival. But in that short time he had implemented a radical cost-containment program and re-organized the hospital's administrative structure. And he had become comfortable with command. He had the bearing of a CEO.

"Dan, Marv Seldes paid me a visit."

He felt his autonomic nervous system go on alert. "When?"

"Three days ago. With his lawyer."

He waited.

"He said that problems with our OR supplies are endangering his patients. That he had to cancel a surgery because of it. That his patient, a Mrs. Barbara Lassiter, got an unnecessary general anesthetic that caused him considerable embarrassment and he thinks malpractice exposure. And that he got a certified letter from you calling *him* on the carpet. He's very angry and he's threatening to take his practice out of here. Now, what the hell is going on?"

Dan constructed his response presuming that two things were true. That Frost had already concluded that Seldes was in the right, or at least that he was the wronged party. And that this was a vertical conversation. He was going to be talking up to his boss.

"Tom, I think that there's some additional information that you may want to look at. Have you seen the formal complaint from the OR Supervisor?"

"No, I haven't."

"Let me get you a copy. It'll just take a minute."

"Fine."

He called Clare, who had a copy to Frost in three minutes. Then he sat with his hands folded in his lap while the CEO read.

As Frost finished, he was shaking his head. "What I get from this is that Seldes is a vulgar egotist whose patient was mistreated because we didn't have what he medically needed in our OR. He told me that he's been using mannitol in our OR for years. That nobody talked to him about changing fluids. He showed me a copy of his preference list for that procedure. It clearly stated 'mannitol.' It was properly updated and turned in to the OR Committee only two months ago."

Though it wasn't his intention, Dan's agitation was obvious. "His Department Chair told me that glycine is perfectly good for that purpose, the choice of most gynecologists doing that procedure. That this was not important enough to cancel the procedure. Much less after the anesthesia had been given. Much less by storming out of the OR."

Frost fired back. "Are you telling me that he isn't entitled to get the equipment and supplies that he needs to do his work in our OR?"

"Standardizing equipment and supplies is a money saver. It's a specific project within re-engineering. Huge custom inventories for every individual surgeon cost a fortune. I hardly need to tell you that."

"That's off point," the CEO said. "Nobody communicated with him about the change. His preference list was ignored. In this case, not stocking mannitol, which I guess is fancy sugar water, is penny wise and multimillion dollar idiotic."

He was not going to get anywhere on this tack. Frost, now the principal driver of the re-engineering process, was declaring it counterproductive in this instance. And he was right.

"We do have to deal with the issue of patient abandonment," Dan said. "I spoke to Richard Reynolds and he was—"

"Reynolds assures me that this was not technically or legally abandonment. Fully trained and qualified staff were left behind in the OR with the patient."

Frost had done more homework than he suspected. That Reynolds had responded to Frost instead of him was unnerving, but he couldn't deal with the implications in the moment. He tried again. "Don't you find his behavior with our nurses disturbing? He's the worst offender on the whole surgical staff."

"There'll always be obnoxious surgeons. They can't help themselves. I don't like it, but it's part of their culture. Let the nurses try to deal with him directly. I don't want the hospital leadership, and that includes you, scolding Marv Seldes. We can't afford to lose him. If some nurses quit, then they quit. We'll hire new nurses to replace them. At entry level, at lower salaries. I can live with it, easily. You need to contact Seldes. Call him, write him, however you want to do it. Tell him that there is no need for a meeting, and that his beloved mannitol will be back in the OR immediately. I've already instructed the OR people to re-stock it. We're not going to risk losing twenty million a year to save a few cents on supplies or to protect some thin-skinned nurses. It's not going to happen."

It was the first time in his professional life, at least since finishing internship and residency, that Dan had been instructed by anyone to shut up and do what he was told. Sitting at his desk at the end of the day, he wondered how Marty would have handled it.

Probably with a softer touch and the same outcome. And he didn't know what to think about Richard Reynolds. His initial perception of Frost as nerdy was gone. The man now seemed somehow larger. Decisive, ruthless if necessary. And he had not been remotely interested in his VPMA's counsel.

Feeling weak and embarrassed, he wondered what he was going to say to Carol Tessler, or for that matter to Susan. Sharing it with Ben was out of the question. His relief at not having to confront Seldes was little consolation. He was nearly alone with it, and wanted to be.

Grizzly Peak

T O THE MAILBOX POST WHERE THEY HAD CHAINED THEIR BICYCLES on their first foray three years earlier, a cluster of six large black and white balloons were string-tied, straining upward toward a made-to-order afternoon sky. Dan and Susan had started talking about a housewarming, CD release, Fourth of July, invite-everybody party even before they finished negotiating for the house. They figured that if they called it for six o'clock— everyone shows about an hour late in Berkeley—the timing would be just right to finish with the fireworks which began in synchrony around the Bay at exactly nine-thirty.

Other than the work and exhaustion of the physical move itself, the transition had been surprisingly smooth. Upon re-visiting the Grizzly Peak house and learning that she would not have to change anything else of importance, Carly was not only not resistant—her basic black modus operandi of late—she couldn't wait to go. She thought that the view from her new room was "absolutely bad." The seller was motivated. Of course the real estate agents always say this, but this seller actually was, and they got nearly ten percent off the ask. The sale was contingent on the sale of the Elmwood house, which turned out to be a breeze. Great old East Bay brown shingles were a hot commodity and they exceeded their asking price when, after only three days on the market, Harriet Gomberg maneuvered two excited prospects into what amounted to an auction. Alan Greenspan was no longer conducting the money supply like George Solti, but they got a fixed mortgage under six. Within eight weeks of Susan's eyebrow shtick at Bay Wolf, their worldly goods were in a moving van.

The Fazens were in the same place at the same time for the first time in over two years. Ben was in from New Haven for a few weeks before hitting the road in Europe for the summer with some of his Yale buddies. Sarah, who typically came across the Bay about once a month for a meal, actually did an overnight. Generally in agreement that the empty nest was vastly under-rated, Dan and Susan were enjoying the packed house. Carly, caught up in the family exuberance, even offered to play a few cello pieces as part of the festivities.

The band members showed up early to set up and do a sound check. Avram Goldbloom, the banjo player, especially compulsive about the mixes, had over the years become the resident audio engineer. Susan called him the "sound nazi." He was wiring the microphones while she and the others, in separate little zones around the big first floor deck, made minute adjustments to string tensions while staring intently at their electronic tuners. When they were ready, they would warm up with *a cappela* har-monies and then do a full run-through of their set opener. Noah Sampson, the bass player, was alone in the far northwest corner tuning the big instrument. Dan, in sandals, cutoffs, and an ancient denim shirt, approached him with a beer can in each hand.

Though he would deny it, Dan got a buzz out of being around celebrities. When the A's or the Raiders came to the hospital to visit the pediatric ward, he always made a point of showing up. He met Mark McGwire before he defected to the Cardinals and shot the moon in the summer of '98. Dan loved to tell how he once had dinner with Michael Douglas. The two of them had been each vacationing alone at a small hotel on the south shore of Bermuda. He complimented him on *One Flew over the Cuckoo's Nest,* which Douglas had produced. One thing led to another and they shared a meal. Dan had been telling the story for thirty years.

Noah Sampson was a Bay Area celebrity. Virtually everyone recognized the tall, handsome broadcaster with the James Earl Jones larynx. The morning news anchor for over ten years on Oakland's KTVU, he was committed to his hometown and he rarely turned down any of the large number of invitations that came his way to host awards ceremonies, charity events, and the like. Though he was the least featured singer or player in Heart to Heart, the audiences loved seeing the local star up close. Dan never missed a chance to chat him up.

"Hey, Noah. How the hell are you?"

Noah accepted the beer. "I'm fine, Dan. Congratulations on this fabulous house. What a spot." He shaded his eyes with his left hand and, squinting, panned left to right across the glare of San Francisco Bay. "It's gonna be a hell of a sunset."

What a voice.

"We really appreciate that you and the guys were willing to play for this. It adds a lot. Really."

"Hey man, it's a pleasure. I wouldn't miss it."

"So how's the career?" Dan asked. "Anything new?"

"Nah. I'm locked into the morning spot. We give the national morning shows a good run for the ratings. The station's happy just like it is. I can't complain. They treat me very well. We're talking about maybe adding an occasional evening special. Doing selected local human interest stuff or possibly an investigative thing. It could happen. It's pretty much up to me."

"Sounds interesting."

"It's more work but that's fine. The variety is appealing and, you know, it'd be fun to be Ed Bradley. How's *your* new gig? Do you like the big chair?"

"Well," Dan said, "the big chair's not quite as big as it appears to be. But it's fine. It's different but it's really okay. Practice was getting old." Hardly convincing, he thought.

Noah nodded. "Hey, I better tune this thing. It looks like my mates are waiting for me."

—

When Carly played the cello seriously, it made Susan cry. From the side, the setting sunlight glistened through her tears.

Knees akimbo and back to the Bay, Carly balanced the beautiful instrument on its end pin, lightly making and unmaking contact at the left knee and collarbone. Her arched left hand shortened and vibrated the strings against the ebony, while her right arm, as a mechanism oiled at the shoulder and elbow, drove the piston of the forearm, hand and bow as a unit.

Moments earlier, all attitude in her black jeans and T-shirt, Doc Martens above the ankle, faux tattoos, and real piercings at the nostril and eyebrow, the kid was eyes down a goth vision. Carly did not transform as she played, she transformed the instant she played. As her bow initiated the opening groan of the "Sarabande" from Bach's Third Cello Suite, her eyelids fell, her chin rose, and a just-like-that serene countenance began its subtle oscillation, side to side in unison with her right arm. Repeatedly, the slow meditative piece slid off the deep introductory note of the C string to one gorgeous harmony or another on the second and third strings. And with each ascension, her chin and eyebrows extended slightly and returned in time. You can hear the music and even appreciate the hands from most seats in a concert hall. But for the facial choreography, you've got to get ringside.

With the exception of a few buzzy clusters at the far sides of the deck, the crowd was rapt, focused on Carly against an orange-going western sky and the San Francisco monuments in profile. She was at ease. These two pieces from Bach's Third had been in her repertoire for years. Compared to an audition or a competition—facing a jury and moving from piece to piece, ten measures from one, then forty measures from another, jumping styles, composers, tempos—this little recital was a confection. The second piece, the "Bourre," is sixteen to a measure da-ba-da-ba-da-ba Bach, light and airy and loaded with toe-tapping exclamation points. She nailed it in three minutes flat and for her pleasure got a raucous ovation.

Dan, standing alone at the back of the deck's north rail, watched Carly rise from her chair and elegantly bow in her incongruous get-up. He was remembering her at nine and ten wowing them at recitals in her flowered dresses and perfect hair and silk ribbons.

"Olympia executive Fazen."

Since reading James Colburn's piece in the Contra Costa paper, Ben had been needling him. Dan waited before turning.

"Gimme a break."

"Will you look at me if I rave about your daughter?"

Dan pivoted, smiling. "Isn't she something?"

"That she is. It's the first time I've heard her play in over a year. She's wonderful. And it's not just the music, which is remarkable enough. It's her presence."

"I know," Dan said. "She's terrific. Now if we could do something about the wardrobe."

Ben's shrugged shoulders and cocked expression were articulate. No big deal.

Dan swept his arm theatrically across the western horizon. "So whaddaya think?"

"What do I think? I think you've got the best view in the neighborhood. You're on the top of the mountain, kid."

Dan's visits with Ben had become sporadic. When he was in practice, he'd regarded their weekly lunches as inviolate. His office staff had been instructed to never schedule a patient that would interfere. Even with emergencies, Dan would have the Memorial ER docs fill the gap to protect their time together. In the past four months he had cancelled seven times. Each to attend a meeting that he could have declined. Each of just enough gravity to provide a plausible justification for avoiding his dear friend.

Truth be told, Dan thought that most of these meetings were a waste of his time, corporate rituals where his attendance mattered not in the least.

Their lunches of late, when they occurred, were mostly as they had always been. Good natured, funny, pimping. Lots of banter about politics and current events. Keeping up with family news. Ben didn't overtly complain about Dan's truancy, and Dan felt sheepish about bringing it up. What was absent was detail about his experiences at Memorial. Dan would allow that there was an abundance of "boring, bureaucratic bullshit" and he would talk about institutional and regulatory and marketplace matters. But he scrupulously avoided discussing specific disturbing cases. For example, the Seldes episode. He and Ben had had lunch the day after Dan was cowed by Frost. He knew that he couldn't tolerate Ben's ethical laser, his certain outrage. As upset as he was, he chose not to confide. He wasn't precisely embarrassed, he was ashamed.

"I'll tell you, Ben, it was hard to move. I mean physically. But on a night like this, I have no doubts about whether we did the right thing. We miss The Elmwood, the neighborhood. There's no village to walk to up here. That was always nice. But we can drive down to Shattuck and Vine in five minutes. It's fine."

"It's beautiful. Especially this time of day."

The descended sun lit an intense red-orange highlight along the edge of Mount Tamalpais, north of the Golden Gate. The Bay was a particular luminous steely gray that happened about ten minutes an evening if it wasn't too cloudy.

"So, how are you, Ben?"

"Me, I'm fine. You know, the same. I feel good. I'm happy in the greenhouse. My hands bother me after long sessions, but what else is new?" He paused, sharpening his eye contact. "How are you, kid? Really."

Dan understood what he was being asked. He felt chilled. His long sleeved denim shirt wasn't enough for the East Bay cliffs now that the sun was down. Arms folded across his chest, he embraced himself. His fifteen second pause seemed longer.

"All we talk about is money. Everything is money. If a doc calls about a patient, it's never to talk about an interesting case, or 'whaddaya think?' He's calling to say there's a problem with a treatment authorization from a payer, the HMO, the IPA, whoever. Once the patient is in the hospital, all we talk about is controlling what we spend. And measuring and analyzing what we spend. And if it's in our financial interest, which it usually is, getting them the hell out as fast as possible. For every conversation about quality, there are a hundred about money. Something bad happens, it's risk management. Work the family. Strategize with the liability carrier. Hope the media doesn't get it. We could give a fuck about the patient."

They were side by side at the redwood railing, their backs to the crowd. Dan had taken two beers, three glasses of wine, and leave of his defenses. He was gazing north at nothing in particular.

"Last week we sent a guy out of the ER who nearly fucking died right on the front lawn of the hospital. Drunk, no insurance. Not exactly an Olympia kinda guy. He supposedly got triaged, a decent medical screening exam, and was told to go up to the county hospital. Called him a taxi. Ten minutes later the cabbie is looking for him at the triage desk. They find the poor sonofabitch face down on the lawn out by the flagpole. Cyanotic, coughing up fucking blood clots. He ended up in the ICU with bilateral pneumonia and esophageal bleeding. Now do you think he had a normal fucking screening exam in the ER? And do we focus on the triage nurses? Do we critically look at the quality of their training? Do we ask ourselves if maybe the docs should do the triage instead? Please. We ask the lawyers to look at the paperwork to see if maybe our Medicare reimbursement is at risk because of an anti-dumping violation. I'll tell you, man. We are really a bunch of fine upstanding motherfuckers."

While Ben Berman was inarguably an irrepressible gadfly, he was not a sadist. "Do you think that's maybe a little harsh? I mean, wouldn't any hospital try to protect itself after an event like that? They need to—"

"That's not the point, Ben. That's all we do. Protect ourselves and our financial interests. That poor bastard out there coughing up a lung is a problem all right. A regulatory problem. Bad PR. A threat to our revenue stream. Nobody gives a shit about quality. I mean, I say the right things and they patronize me. But nobody really gives a fuck."

Ben let it lie. Dan looked directly at him and took a deep breath, exhaling loudly. He began shaking his head as he slowly spoke. "I don't know, Ben. I just don't know."

"Anything I can do?"

Dan thought about it for several seconds. "Yeah. Don't beat me up, okay?"

"It seems like you're taking care of that quite well all by yourself."

"Okay. So don't pile on, all right?"

"You hear me doing that?"

"No, you're not doing that. Just don't, okay?"

The first pyrotechnic came from the left, from the direction of the Oakland Coliseum. A thump from a mortar followed three seconds later by a single aerial, a momentary golden too-many-legged spider. And light hurtling ahead of sound, a single crack a moment after that. Then nothing. It must have been a test shot. Dan and Susan, holding hands, stood among the crowd at the west rail of the deck. They waited and watched.

Heart to Heart had followed Carly with a half hour set, all from their new CD. As usual, the audience of friends and family, utterly biased and uncritical, ate them up. They cheered, stomped, whistled, and demanded two encores, which of course they got. Dan was predictably slayed by Susan's performance, and not just a little by the way she looked. She had slipped upstairs when Carly finished, changed out of her Second Harvest T-shirt, baggy chino shorts and Birkenstocks, and strutted out with the band in painted-on blue jeans tucked Emmy Lou style into her boots, and a gossamer white silk blouse that luffed in the wind. Her dark brown eyes were just visible beneath the brim of her black Stetson. She had most of the leads and was in great voice. For about forty minutes Dan wasn't preoccupied with the Walnut Creek Memorial Hospital.

Two red bursts, exploding flowers side by side with yet another pair of white bursts from inside them, lit up over the San Francisco shoreline midway between the bridges. From the East Bay Hills they looked like they were next to each other. They were actually over a mile apart, electronically synchronized duplicate displays over Maritime Park and Pier 39. And within a few seconds, blue linear bursts and golden arcs, like the leaves of a palm tree, north of the Golden Gate over Sausalito. The muffled explosions began to arrive from across the water. In the right foreground the sky over the Berkeley Marina erupted, booming and crackling, red then gold then white. And to their left, the Oakland Coliseum began in earnest. An amazing vision, five locations at once hurling pyrotechnics skyward. Across the Bay, the twin San Francisco shows gathered momentum, rocketing pair after pair of exploding sound and light. Not to be outdone, the East Bay displays thundered back. The crowd on the deck oohed and laughed and cheered.

Dan felt detached. He watched the fireworks and heard the jubilation around him. But the child in him wasn't available. Holding Susan's hand, he closed his eyes. Listening to the percussive reports, he found himself thinking about war, wondering what it sounded like at night in Baghdad and Fallujah. He felt nauseous. He opened his eyes and, letting go of Susan's hand, steadied himself with both hands on the railing. He took two deep breaths of the night air. It was sulfurous. He realized that Susan had been talking to him.

"Danny, are you all right?"

"Yeah, I'm okay."

"You don't seem okay."

"I think maybe I drank a little too much. Maybe I should go inside and sit down."

"I'll come with you."

"No no, it's all right. I'll just go in for a few minutes. Maybe have a cup of coffee."

"Are you sure?"

"Yeah, really. It's okay."

"You're making me nervous."

"Please, I'm all right. Just let me be."

He made his way to the master bedroom. Sitting upright at the head of the bed, he had an unobstructed view of the colored lights over San Francisco. The double-paned glass of the oversized windows blocked out the sound. He watched for several minutes, unmoved, and then saw what he imagined was the finale. Dozens of aerials of every color bursting within moments of one another. And then the sky was overtaken by a dense gray cloud. He watched it enlarge for a few minutes. It seemed to extend from bridge to bridge over the city's eastern shoreline. Eyes closed now, he thought about the fireworks shows at Soldier Field in Chicago. He couldn't remember how old he was when his parents first took him. Maybe seven or eight. At the end, all 100,000 people simultaneously lit their sparklers on cue. He remembered thinking that the place looked like the world's biggest birthday cake.

"I'm sorry. I don't mean to disturb you, but I got worried." Susan sat down next to him and ran her hand through his hair. "Are you okay?"

"I'm fine. Really. I just needed a little time to myself."

Though her concerned expression didn't ease, she let it go. "Folks are starting to leave. Do you want to come down with me?"

It was about the last thing he felt like doing. "Sure."

Sentinel Event

A SATURDAY AFTERNOON, HE HAD NOT PLANNED ON GOING IN. Even after getting off the phone with Jack Jensen, it was not clear that he needed to. For most physicians the obligatory impulse is deeply embedded, typically erring on the side of showing up, whether necessary for patient care or not. This expectation, to always respond if beckoned, is pounded in through medical school, internship, residency, and persists as a moral imperative. It's not that Dan never said no. It's that he couldn't do it without feeling guilty. And his superego could not tolerate much more of that these days.

Jack had not even asked. Dan just said, "I'll come right in." He was not officially on call for anything. Even with minimal information, he had no doubt that the incident Jensen had described constituted a "sentinel event," regulatory jargon for something very bad, and preventable, happening to a patient. As arranged, he found the Chairman of the Department of Medicine in the nurses station of the Intensive Care Unit.

"Hey Jack. How's she doing?"

"Unchanged, comatose, flaccid on her right side. She's gonna go back for another CT in about a half an hour. Her vitals are stable. Maggie's still with her."

Dan had gotten the highlights over the phone. Every nurse's nightmare, a massive medication error with a dangerous drug. An otherwise healthy seventy-eight year old woman living alone in an upscale retirement complex in the nearby suburb of San Ramon had developed DVT, deep vein thrombosis. Her local doctor immediately recognized the seriousness of the pain and swelling of her left leg and sent her up to Memorial for admission. An x-ray study showed complete obstruction by a blood clot of the femoral vein, the large vein of the upper part of the leg. She was in danger not only of damage to her limb, but also of dislodging a piece of the clot to her lungs. A serious, even lethal complication. She started out on the general Med/Surg floor where she was immediately treated with heparin, a potent IV anticoagulant. She should have never needed the Intensive Care Unit, at least not for the reason she was there.

The twelve patient rooms in the ICU—actually they were large glass-doored stalls—were arranged in a circle around the nurses' station. The staff had both line-of-sight to each of the patients, and remote telemetry of their monitor readings at the desktop. Dan walked slowly counterclockwise past each endangered patient, past the panoply of machines, until he saw the familiar face at the bedside of an unconscious elderly woman. Sitting motionless in white, kleenex in her clenched hand, she stared through swollen eyelids at the face of her patient. Dan had known this nurse for a third of a century.

Maggie Herrmann was hardly a saint. She rarely smiled, not even for the patients. She had terrorized Dan when he was an intern, and decades later the trainees were still afraid of her. She was one of those people that did her job, actually quite well, kept her own counsel, and could not care less what other people thought. She was that particularly prickly kind of person who would be said to *brook* no this or that, the Professor Kingsfield of nurses. But Dan could not recall her making a mistake. In fact, over the years she had saved him and countless other docs, catching their commissions and omissions. Never failing condescension, but nonetheless protecting the patients, and them. If you had a sick patient, and no time or inclination for social protocol, then Maggie Herrmann, in her joyless way, was a welcome antidote to perky nursiness.

He could only imagine what Maggie was feeling. She had pushed 50,000 units of heparin, ten times the correct dose. The treatment of DVT was bed rest and anticoagulation. Heparin, the anticoagulant, was given intravenously. First as a bolus, a substantial dose all at once to begin the effort to dissolve the clot, and then as a continuous infusion. The attending physician had ordered an initial IV push of 5,000 units, a typical and correct loading dose. This was not an uncommon therapy. Over the years Maggie had given this drug in this fashion dozens of times. In a blur of tasks professional and menial, moving from patient to patient, falling behind the clock, detail upon detail, she apprehended her mistake thirty seconds too late.

"Hello Maggie."

She glanced up at him and returned her gaze to the patient. "Doctor Fazen." He had never heard her address a physician by their first name. She even called the medical students "Doctor." Perhaps some utterly dull M.D.-to-be could have confused her intimidating formality with respect.

Dan took a chair from the corner, placed it opposite and sat down. "Do you feel like talking?"

"What's there to talk about? I made a terrible mistake. This woman had a stroke because of me. What is there to say?"

Her mistake was simple. Instead of 0.5 cc., she had given 5.0 cc. Instead of filling half of a 1 cc. syringe, she had filled half of a 10 cc. syringe. Her attention had failed her. As she placed the just emptied syringe on the stainless steel tray of the medication cart, she was stunned by the sudden awareness. That syringe was impossibly big. She had never given heparin in anything other than the skinny 1 cc. syringe, or in a small fixed-dose cartridge.

"Come on, Maggie. You don't know that."

"I don't know what? I know I gave her 50,000 units of heparin all at once. And I know that she bled into her brain. It seems straightforward to me."

"Look, she has a deep vein thrombosis. She could have thrown a clot to her head. It's not impossible." Dan knew that this was a real stretch. "And she got the antidote, the IV protamine, evidently before the bleed. At least some of the heparin activity was reversed before anything happened. You can't be absolutely sure that the events were related."

She stared in silence at the comatose woman.

Once Maggie had recognized the overdose, the professional response was flawless. She immediately notified the charge nurse, who called the attending physician and then the nursing supervisor. In less than five minutes, the woman had coagulation studies drawn, the antidote was given, and she was transferred to intensive care for observation. The brain hemorrhage occurred quietly within the first two hours. The senior medical resident, summoned when the ICU nurse couldn't rouse the patient from apparent sleep, was unable to elicit neurologic reflexes of her right arm and leg. She was rushed to Radiology where an emergency head CT demonstrated a large acute hemorrhage in the left cerebral cortex. This was the expected finding, since the left side of the brain controls the neurologic activity of the right side of the body. To make matters worse, in most people the left side of the brain also controls speech. If this woman survived, she would be at least partially paralyzed, and would likely have impairment of her ability to speak.

Dan tried again. "Old people have strokes. It happens. You can't really be certain that the heparin did this. She almost assuredly has cerebral atherosclerotic disease and she could have even had an underlying—"

"Doctor Fazen, I appreciate what you're trying to do. No disrespect, sir, but would you mind just leaving me alone. You're not helping. Just let me be."

The concept of a sentinel event was championed by the Joint Commission on the Accreditation Of Healthcare Organizations, abbreviated JCAHO and pronounced by everyone, oddly enough, as *jay-koh* with the accent on the *jay*. The idea is that these bad things, these sentinel events, happen because of failures of complex processes, not simply because of lapses by individuals. Hospital care is supposed to be designed so that patients are protected from mistakes by individuals. The institution and its leadership are accountable for patient outcomes, good and bad. This made sense to Dan, and was overtly endorsed by hospital administration. Which explains, at least in part, why he was stunned to learn that Maggie Herrmann had been suspended without pay prior to any formal evaluation of the case. And had that been the extent of the bad news, it would have been disturbing enough.

As networks go, even in the age of the Internet, the nursing grapevine in a hospital is something to behold. The medication error had occurred on Saturday, the suspension on Monday morning, and by mid-afternoon on Tuesday the news had burned through the nursing staff and six veteran nurses had met with their union representative and a local attorney and submitted a joint letter of resignation.

We, the undersigned, resign effective immediately from the nursing staff of Walnut Creek Memorial Hospital. As loyal long-term professionals committed to the care of our patients, we deplore the administrative policies and practices that have been inflicted on our hospital and patients since the takeover by Olympia. The reductions in staffing and the conversion of registered nurse positions to slots for unlicensed people with lower levels of skill and knowledge have reduced the quality of care and increased the danger to the patients, and have placed undue and intolerable stress on the front-line nurses. The recent suspension of our colleague Maggie Herrmann following a medication error, without any analysis of the intolerable working conditions on that shift, was disgraceful treatment of a superb experienced nurse, and was an utter abandonment of your responsibilities as hospital administrators. If this is where health care is going in America, then God help us all.

It was addressed to Frost, signed by the six—two from ICU, two from Med/Surg and one each from Pediatrics and Rehab— and copied to everybody in the place with a title, including the Olympia Board of Directors.

Dan re-read the letter as he waited for Maggie. He didn't think she would return his phone call, much less agree to meet with him. But she was emphatic about not meeting at the hospital. She chose the little park at the George Miller Community Center near her apartment in Concord. From a secluded bench on this unseasonably warm winter day, he saw her walking toward him from fifty yards away. She was wearing a dark blue pantsuit with matching pumps, a bright floral silk scarf bunched at the neck, and pearls.

He rose and closed the distance. "Hello Maggie. Thank you for taking the time to talk with me."

"You're welcome, Doctor Fazen. I have no reason not to speak with you."

"You know, it would be just fine if you called me Dan."

"That's quite all right. That's not my way. It would make me uncomfortable."

He had never seen her with makeup. Lipstick, eye liner, mascara, powder and rouge. Her short brown-gray hair looked like it had just been blown and set in a beauty shop. He imagined her in a solitary life. Maybe church. Probably. He realized that this meeting was, for her, an occasion. They settled on a nearby shaded bench.

"You know your patient is doing a little better. She's out of the ICU. She's awake and starting to eat. But it's way too early to tell about her neurologic status."

"I know. The nurses call me everyday. Every shift, actually." She sat upright with her hands folded in her lap, legs crossed at the ankles.

"Maggie, I'd like to understand the circumstances on the ward during that shift. Try to see what factors contributed—"

"Doctor Fazen, I'm responsible for that overdose. I make no excuses."

"Look, I admire your sense of accountability, and I suppose that sometimes accidents just happen. But other experienced nurses at Memorial think that way too many accidents have been happening lately. That there are not only more medication errors, but more patient falls, more accidental needle sticks, more back injuries from unassisted lifting, more people just blowing up, losing it."

"I can't argue with any of that. But I'm still the one who gave that overdose."

"How many patients did you have on that shift?"

"I'm not exactly certain."

"About how many do you think?"

"I don't know. Maybe twelve."

"It was fourteen. I spoke with the charge nurse."

"Okay, fourteen."

"Do you really think that's okay? One nurse for fourteen patients?"

"In the old days we had five or six," she said, "but that was a long time ago. These days, it's often ten or more. On Saturday, an RN called in sick. The shift managers weren't allowed to use the registry for backfill other than on critical care units. That's how we had what we had." She had been unfocussed on the green field in front of them as she spoke. Now she shifted her gaze back to him. "But it's still my mistake. It doesn't change anything."

"You're aware that six nurses have resigned in protest of your suspension?"

"Of course. But I'm just the last straw. If it wasn't this, it would have been something else."

"Do you agree with their criticism? Do you think they're right?"

"Well, about what's happened to nursing I think they're right. But I don't agree with their quitting. That's not going to help anything. They'll just be replaced by less skilled people and we'll be worse off. Their leaving won't help Memorial."

"Well, I certainly agree with you about that." He felt tired. Several seconds passed in silence. "What about you? Do you want to stay? You haven't exactly been treated well."

Her eyes welled with tears as she started to speak. "Doctor Fazen, maybe you don't understand. Memorial's patients are my life. And they have been my entire adult life. They are what I care about. I have relationships with them. It's what I know how to do. I'm not a manager and I never wanted to be. I just want to do what I do." She took a tissue from her purse and meticulously dried each eye. "If I'm allowed, of course I'll stay. Someone's got to keep the doctors in line."

Dan anticipated a smile, mistakenly.

⟶

Even though there had been several months of peaceful co-existence since the dress-down over Seldes, Dan was keeping his contact alone with Frost to a minimum. He knew they had little common ground, ethically or professionally, and it seemed to him that private proximity was likely to be hazardous. Nevertheless, after the conversation with Maggie, there he was at the end of a long day waiting to speak his mind.

"Hi, Dan. Sorry to keep you waiting."

He was surprised. First by the fact that Frost came out to the waiting area to greet him. He typically had his secretary lead visitors in while he remained seated behind his desk. And secondly by his appearance, shirtsleeves rolled to mid-forearm, tie undone, collar open.

"Come on in." Frost led him to the conference table and sat in a neutral chair. "What's up?"

"I wanted to talk with you about Maggie Herrmann's suspension and about the nursing resignations. By now you probably know about Maggie's history at Memorial. I've known her and worked with her for decades. This is a terrific nurse, incredibly dedicated to the place, and she wants more than anything to stay. And believe me, she's harder on herself than we are. She does more for upholding quality around here than most of the doctors."

He was digesting Frost's body language, his apparent receptivity. As he continued, he was thinking that he was going to get what he wanted.

"I spent some time with her yesterday and there's absolutely no question about her commitment. We need to quickly restore her status. Not because of the actions of the other nurses, but because she's earned the right to work here. Everybody makes mistakes and hers was a bad one. But there were, in fact, mitigating circumstances on that shift. She had way too many patients. You do that to a nurse, no matter how talented and experienced, and eventually they're gonna screw up. We need to put her back on duty."

"I really have no quarrel with that," Frost said. "If you think she's a terrific nurse, then that's good enough for me. She did make a serious mistake and it's been documented. If there's a recurring problem, we'll be able to deal with it."

Dan had not expected this to be so easy. "So she's unsuspended?"

"Yes, I'll make sure of it. And we'll undock her pay as well. But you understand that if it turns out that this is the beginning of a decline in her performance, then we'll have to do something about it."

"Fair enough."

"Good. Is there anything else I can do for you? You mentioned the nursing resignations."

"Well, you know together that's a lot of talent and experience to lose. We won't easily replace them."

"That may be," Frost said. "But they're gone and I'm afraid they're going to stay gone. You know, I'm not going to be bullied by a bunch of angry nurses. We'll just have to find first-rate people to replace them. We'll do whatever it takes."

"I'm just saying that it won't be easy"

"I understand. Look, I'll be sure that Ms. Herrmann is notified immediately. And I promise you we'll do whatever we have to do to replace those nurses. Okay?"

"All right. Well, thanks for your time."

When it came to self-delusion about OHC—the everyday trickery of denial and rationalization—Dan could hardly be accused of swallowing them whole. He had no admiration for the corporation or its head man in Walnut Creek. He didn't lose sight of the fact that Olympia's overwhelming focus was to make money. Though so stated at the bottom center of every piece of OHC stationery, he knew that their actual mission was surely not about quality and accessibility of healthcare. From the moment he learned about the takeover, Dan was never sanguine, never better than gnawingly ambivalent about what he was doing and who he was doing it with. And yet, out of an optimism and naiveté that were an essential part of who he was, and at the same time an undeniable attachment to the big salary and benefits, he could choose to believe, or at least try to believe, unbelievable things. On a large scale, that Olympia's cost-containment would not be ruthless, that they would not deny patients essential services. And in this instance, that Frost would do "whatever it takes" to replace a group of high-priced veteran nurses.

At dinner he told Susan about the CEO's promise. She surprised him. Not with her opinion, but with her edge.

"I don't think the man can be trusted. I hope I'm wrong, okay? Now, can we talk about something else?"

At lunch the next day, Ben was succinct.

"Danny, don't be a schmuck."

Mason Kanzler

—

Though four days had passed since the Herrmann business, and Maggie had already been reinstated, Dan was still off balance. Irritable, out of synch with his own temperament. And now he had to contend with an attorney who presumably was suing on behalf of Barbara Lassiter, the woman who had been abandoned by Marvin Seldes.

"Doctor Fazen, he's here."

He was not about to give this lawyer the courtesy of a greeting in his waiting area. He had refreshed himself on the facts of the case and was annoyed at the intrusion. Seldes may have behaved like an abusive jerk with the operating room staff, but there was no evidence that his patient had been harmed. The OR Committee had concluded that, yes, she underwent unnecessary anesthesia, but that it was without complication.

"Give me a minute, Clare."

He had no particular thing to do, he just felt like letting the lawyer wait. In his few minutes of self-indulgence he rehearsed his rebuttal. He thought that *frivolous* and *mischievous* didn't capture it. Too light-hearted, whimsical. He mused over *opportunistic* and *wasteful*, and then decided that *groundless* was best.

He conjured his adversary in pinstripes. Early forties, tall, clean shaven, athlete lean. His parted hair pristine. The suit the deepest of blues, two buttons with faint white piping. A mostly dark burgundy silk tie precisely knotted into an intensely white straight collar. His slender attaché, belt and tasseled loafers, each of a low finish black leather whose feel would evoke specifically the word "buttery." Just showing at his left cuff, the gold Rolex.

If Dan Fazen were accused of an affinity for stereotypes, he would strenuously object but his defense would be shaky. He would not want to acknowledge the extent to which his expectations were shaped by advance intelligence on career, geography, age, even oh Jesus gender, religion, and race. This the product of an organized mind trying to render something predictable out of the blur of humanity. Surely more taxonomic than misanthropic, but not infrequently dead wrong.

His initial experience of this lawyer turned out to be the click of wooden clogs traversing the parquet of his outer office.

"Hi, I'm Mason Kanzler."

He couldn't help noticing first the hair. Straight blond and gray in roughly equal proportions starting at a receding hairline and progressing rearward to a six inch ponytail secured by a black rubber band.

Half rising from his desk chair, Dan gestured him to sit opposite and shook his hand in transit. "Daniel Fazen."

"It's nice to meet you." Kanzler withdrew a business card from his shirt pocket and placed it on the desk blotter between them.

Dan let it lie. As he surveyed the oval wire-rim spectacles and the diamond stud in Kanzler's left earlobe, he wondered how Seldes' patient, a suburban bank manager, had found this particular attorney. He folded his hands in his lap, leaned back in his chair and waited.

"Doctor Fazen, I'm here to ask you a few questions about the care of Mrs. Barbara Lassiter. As I presume you know, she was here under the care of Doctor Marvin Seldes. I need to specifically ask—"

"Excuse me, Mr. Kanzler. You must know that I can't share medical information without a consent."

"Of course." At his side was a weathered, accordion-pleated brown leather briefcase. With some effort he hoisted it to his lap and rifled the bulging contents. More quickly than Dan expected, Kanzler extracted a single document and handed it across to him. "A signed release. It's a copy. You can keep it."

He read it quickly, placed it on his desk and again waited.

"As I was saying, Doctor Fazen, I need to ask you some specific questions about Mrs. Lassiter's care here at Memorial. I hope you don't mind."

Dan removed the woman's medical record from his desk drawer. "I'll answer what I can."

"Sir, I'd like to focus on what actually happened in the operating room." Kanzler was working off hand-written notes on a yellow legal pad. "According to the medical record, she was scheduled for the procedure because of uterine bleeding. Is that right?"

"Multiple episodes of abnormal uterine bleeding."

"And the intended procedure was a hysteroscopy?"

Dan corrected Kanzler's pronunciation, accenting the "os."

"Can you tell me, please, just briefly, about the procedure, the equipment, how it's done?"

He went through it. The scope, the distension fluid, the biopsy technique.

As Kanzler paused to frame the next question, Dan surveyed the rest of his attire. Blue jeans, a not recently pressed tan corduroy blazer with suede patches at the elbows, and a solid navy tie at three quarter mast. He entertained the idea that this man owned one tie, and it exclusively for public lawyering.

"Now, Mrs. Lassiter did get general anesthesia?" Quiet and conversational, Kanzler's was not a courtroom voice.

"That's correct."

"And Doctor Seldes chose not to continue the procedure because he wanted mannitol as the distension fluid and they didn't have it."

"That's right."

"Do you mind if I ask you a few questions about these distension fluids?"

Dan leaned back again. "Well, you can ask but I'm no gynecologist."

After navigating through the mannitol/glycine controversy, Kanzler made his way to his first probative question. "Sir, shouldn't the hospital have had the mannitol, the fluid that Doctor Seldes wanted?"

"Hospitals simply cannot stock every single thing that every doctor wants. Every other surgeon, gynecologist and urologist here uses glycine. They feel it's perfectly safe."

"I see. But Doctor Seldes did specifically list mannitol on his preference list. That is right, isn't it?"

"That is correct."

He could see that Kanzler was about to change direction. He had checked off a series of items on the yellow pad, flipped to a new page, and seemed to be collecting his thoughts. Aside from Dan's surprise at the man's appearance, he had likewise not anticipated his demeanor. Kanzler struck him as more professorial then lawyerly. Not so much in the questioning as in the way that he listened to the answers. More curious than aggressive, as though he were actually trying to find out what was true.

"Sir, because Mrs. Lassiter did not get the procedure done, is it fair to say, in retrospect, that she experienced unnecessary general anesthesia?"

"It would be hard to argue with that."

"Sir, could we talk about complications of general anesthesia?"

"Well, we could. But this patient had none."

"Do we know if she was tested for any complications?"

"Mr. Kanzler, to my knowledge she had absolutely no signs or symptoms of anything after she woke up. Just to do whatever it is you're thinking of, I don't know, laboratory studies, x-rays, would make no sense at all. Particularly these days."

If it were physically possible to gather the words with his hands and shove them back down his throat, Dan would have done it.

"Why particularly these days?"

It wasn't that he couldn't contend with the question. There was simply no need to take the conversation down the economic path, to entertain, even for the purpose of dismissal, the extent to which financial considerations drove the decision to do or not do a diagnostic study. He did his best, which was pretty good.

"I'm sure that it's no surprise to you that physicians and hospitals are expected to not waste money on unnecessary care. Health care costs spiraled out of control through the last two decades. That's why we've had a managed care revolution in this country. Everybody's conscious of trying to not waste money. It's certainly not in the individual patient's interest to do unnecessary studies."

Kanzler brought it back to the patient. "Forgive me, but if, say, a chest x-ray had been done, is it possible that it would have been abnormal?"

"Is it possible? Yes. Probable? No. Indicated? No. Standard of care? No." He felt agitated and self-conscious in the presence of this lawyer's placid exterior.

Kanzler again checked off a few items and moved to a new page. "Doctor Fazen, I'd just like to ask you one more thing and then we'll be done."

Watch out.

"After Doctor Seldes walked out on the patient, the doctor left behind was a resident, is that right?"

"Actually, he is the chief resident. He's fully trained and a member of our medical staff. Therefore, officially an attending physician."

"And was he capable of independently performing the scheduled procedure on Mrs. Lassiter?"

"If he had been capable, he would have done it. Under the circumstances, the choice to wake her up was correct."

The lawyer paused for a few moments. "Sir, I think I'm done. Would you mind giving me a second?"

As he methodically went back through his notes, Dan couldn't help himself.

"May I ask *you* a question?"

Kanzler looked up, unperturbed at the interruption. "Sure."

"We had no notice of a negligence action being filed in this case. Is there actually a law suit?"

"On behalf of Mrs. Lassiter? No, not now." Kanzler was shaking his head. "Probably won't be."

Dan pressed it. "Well, I certainly don't think there should be. But would you mind telling me why you don't think so."

"Well, there's no evidence of residual damage from the anesthetic. In the law, no harm no foul."

"But you knew that before you walked in here. Why did you bother to come?"

Kanzler squinted at him, as though he was making a decision. "Doctor Fazen, have you ever heard of CCHL, the California Center for Health and the Law?"

"No, I don't think so."

"I'm afraid that's about to change, sir."

Dan waited.

"CCHL is in the process of defining and aggregating a group of plaintiffs for a joined action against Olympia Hospitals in California, Jameson v. Olympia. Today I was doing due diligence on the Lassiter case. My guess is she won't qualify. But believe me, there's no shortage of injured parties."

"Well, this is news to me. And I'm right in the middle of medical risk management."

"I'm sorry." Kanzler said it like he meant it.

"Who's Jameson?"

"Kerry Jameson is a nine-year-old girl from Fresno. She's the heart and soul of this law suit. If you want to understand why we're targeting Olympia, what these people are doing to patients, go meet this little girl and her family. I'll be glad to arrange it, get you the medical records, whatever you need."

With a lawyer, of all people, Daniel dropped his corporate pretense.

"You know, I just might take you up on that."

⟶

He told Clare to cancel the day's remaining appointment, a performance evaluation that could easily wait. And so could Frost and Reynolds. Surely they knew all about Jameson v. Olympia. Dan guessed that among the Memorial executives, it was he alone who had been out of the loop. He had no plan other than to get away from the hospital.

Approaching his car, he saw a pale yellow business envelope tucked under the windshield wiper on the driver's side. He waited until he was seated behind the wheel to open it.

From: ███████████████████

To: frosttom@olympia.com

Subject: Nursing Resignations – reply

Strongly agree with you. Eliminate any positions possible. Then replace remainder with entry level or unlicensed. Re MH, drop suspension but then zero tolerance. DF will have to live with it. Good work.

On first reading, there was so much interference from the Kanzler conversation that he couldn't take it in. He closed his eyes, took a few deep breaths, and tried again. The realizations came in two waves. That Frost had lied to him about his intentions for the nursing replacements was infuriating, but not surprising. That someone was leaking sensitive Olympia corporate correspondence—stunning.

He didn't decide to drive, he just drove. Instead of west on 24 toward home he made his way south on 680 to a small road east in Alamo which left the town and worked its way through the horse ranches on the way to Mount Diablo. He punched up the volume on the CD player. Bruce Springsteen was singing a heartbreaking song about Mexican illegals and death in the methamphetamine labs of the San Joaquin. About the cruelty of El Norte. He switched to Bocelli's arias. The voice soothed and soared and there was nothing to comprehend.

Though it hadn't crystallized for him yet, months later he would say that it was on this afternoon, on the day of these revelations, that his course was irreversibly altered. He drove for over two hours, his thoughts churning, fragmented, through his experiences at Memorial, his career in practice, his family obligations. Finally he went home. For the time being, he made no decisions. There were miles to go.

Yosemite Valley

—

DAN HAD FOR YEARS ENCOURAGED SUSAN TO GET A NEW CAR. But Olympia money notwithstanding, she was sticking with the old one, which she regarded as one would an ill-behaved but beloved family pet. The thing about her 1990 navy blue 240DL was that it had this chime, actually a double-chime preceded by a loud metallic click. It would just start clicking and chiming, not to tell you that a door was ajar or that a brake light was out, but whimsically. And when it did this, the car stereo, the potential counter-measure, was entirely disabled. Susan liked to say that this was the work of a troubled person, a forlorn soul trapped in Volvo's design division in the interminable Scandinavian winter. It turned out that it had something to do with the fuses.

The fortress of a wagon, with its four-speed automatic and ballast over the rear wheels, was their vehicle of choice for the Sierras. Particularly for Old Priest Grade Road, the clutch-frying shortcut to Yosemite Valley.

It was the third week in March and they were returning to Yosemite for their umpteenth visit. It was a good time—almost spring, mid-week. The waterfalls were nearly full and the valley wasn't. A year earlier, Dan had reserved a cottage at The Ahwahnee, the ritzy old Arts and Crafts lodge, the best beds in the park.

They made it by mid-morning Tuesday, hours early for check-in. Swapping the Volvo for rented bikes, one speeds, they set out in the general direction of Half Dome, the sheared granite hemisphere hovering over the east end of the valley. The bicycle path with its faded yellow stripe meandered along and over the slow moving back tributaries of the Merced River. Just upstream of the runoff from the grand photo chutes, Yosemite and Bridalveil Falls.

They rode at a lazy pace over the stone bridges and along the sandy edges of the streams. The amateur botanist of the two, Susan offered a sparse tutorial as they pedaled. "Check out the dogwood." The little trees, dwarfed by the oaks, pines and cedars, stood mostly creekside with their creamy-white flowers in early blossom. She was scanning down and around at the still waters and the trees and the new wildflowers, while Dan opted for up, way up. What he loved about this place was the scale. The mass and the height of the granite, most of a mile straight up on both sides of the meadow between.

Geologically, Yosemite Valley was a razor cut, a mile wide and seven miles long, into the Sierra Nevada. The blade was ice, glacial penetration and withdrawal, leaving behind granite cliffs and an ancient lake below. The lake's sediment and vegetation outgrew its liquid container and became the valley floor, and this new grassland was in turn etched by fallen water, the Merced River. The native people, the Ahwahneechee, came, and much later John Muir and Teddy Roosevelt and Ansel Adams. By the turn of the millennium, four million people a year were showing up.

Dan and Susan rode as far east as you could on a bicycle, to the base of the foot path angling up to Mirror Lake, then re-traced their way west in the direction of the big falls. Tourist Central.

Even when the valley was unpopulated in general, there was always a centripetal crush at the base of Yosemite Falls.

Moving through a trail dense with trees and boulders, they knew they were getting close because they could hear the falling water and they could smell the diesel fuel. The path swung left and ended abruptly, disgorging them into a maelstrom of parked and moving cars and motor coaches. Every configuration of persons—singles, couples, small groups, schools of daytrippers clustered next to their buses and their guides. College sweatshirts, daypacks, baseball caps, serious backpacks, cameras, binoculars, videocams, elaborate walking sticks. With Dan in the lead, they took it like a gymkana, slowly weaving and darting past the vehicles and the people. He heard German, then French, probably Japanese, then something musical and guttural, maybe Danish,

They cleared the parking lot and locked the bikes to a sign cautioning "Slippery Surfaces." It took six minutes to hike to the weathered wooden bridge, *the* viewpoint for the Lower Falls. By minute four they could feel the vibration in their feet. Stepping up onto the bridge and into the microclimate, Dan barely saved his Cubs cap from a trip down Yosemite Creek to the Merced. They went to the left rail and leaned into the wet, gusting wind, wholly created by the thirty-two story cascade right in front of them. The dense white plume, fluorescent against brown-black lichenified granite, was an uninterrupted freefall for three quarters of its length and then it rebounded and boiled the rest of the way. The runoff, abruptly cowed by the barricade of jumbled rock in the immediate creek bed, ran below and behind them, riverbound. They suffered the little monsoon long enough to snap one picture each, and headed for their spot.

Crossing the remainder of the bridge, they took a hard right and within twenty yards were working their way downcreek, navigating over and between the boulders at the water's edge. They passed dozens of people who alone or in little groups had settled into their granite seating arrangements. They kept going, fifty yards beyond the last settler, got briefly disoriented, and then found what they were looking for.

The big boulder was about five feet high and eight feet wide, its upright concave surface facing the departing water. It sat on a smooth, slightly hollowed out flat rock which met a pile of smaller rocks directly at the waterline. He had glowingly embellished it, more than once. "It's like a reclining bucket seat in paradise. With footrests." Their promise to return was kept.

He eased down closest to the water and she tucked herself in on his left. By trial and error, slightly altering their positions and using their daypacks and jackets for contour, they tried to perfect their little encampment.

Dan started laughing. "You know, this isn't quite as comfortable as I remember it."

Susan smiled. "Yeah, but it's still damn nice." She interlocked her hand with his. "I love it here."

"I love it too," he said. "And I need it."

They mostly watched the water. The creek was a downhill thoroughfare of stone. Granite specimens, no two alike, awash in the foamy snowmelt. Shifting with the sunlight, the water was a kinetic patchwork of black-green gradients. Inky in the shadows and green like a martini olive in the shallows.

"Look over your shoulder." He turned in her direction. "No, the other way."

He came around over his right shoulder and saw—he could not recall seeing one before—a vertical rainbow. The sun was refracting just so through the wall of mist created by the falls. He extracted his daypack, his lumbar support, and fished for the pocket Nikon. By the time he pulled it from its case, powered it up, and pivoted, a cloud had covered the sun and the rainbow was gone. Feeling chilled, he traded the camera for his sweatshirt, and sat back. Susan put on a jacket and snuggled under his arm.

After a few minutes, he felt warm again. He was noticing how the foam shifted from silver to gray and back to silver with the movement of the clouds. And how the granite blackened and blanched at the water line. That in one particular spot, the eddy was slightly different each time it recurred. For nearly two minutes his attention was on a small half-submerged boulder just to his right, its porosity and variety of color. Sitting entirely still, he closed his eyes and listened. At first to everything, and then to each thing. The creek, the falls, the birds, the wind, Susan's breath. For a little while, fully awake, he had stopped thinking. There was plenty to not think about.

The dining room at The Ahwahnee Hotel was part cathedral, part log cabin. Columned and raftered by the improbably linear trunks of debarked sugar pine, the famous refectory had the dimensions of a serious nave. Racks of electric candles were suspended from the thirty-four foot ceiling, each candelabra floating twelve feet above the diners. The long south wall had ten full-length vertical windows facing across the valley toward Glacier Point. Dan and Susan had gotten lucky, a deuce with a view.

"How about this?" He asked it as though he were personally responsible for the late-winter dusk lighting the Ahwahnee Meadow.

She hoisted her chardonnay with a flourish. "You've done a fine job, honey."

They'd had a good Wednesday—room service breakfast in the cottage, out of the white hotel robes a little before noon for a drive up to Glacier Point and the view from the top. It had grown colder than the day before, but in full sun they were able to shed their jackets. They descended, driving to the bases of Bridalveil and El Capitan for brief walks at these holy places. Nothing too energetic. Then back to the hotel where, after chocolate sundaes, they napped and showered and crossword puzzled and dressed and strolled (fifty yards, if that) to this extraordinary dining room for another slow and pampered meal.

Dan interrupted their assault on a platter of scallops and shrimp. "So what do you want to do tomorrow?"

They discussed the merits of this and that hiking itinerary, and which falls was the fullest, and how early morning exuberance was out of the question. They agreed to a midday trek to Vernal Falls, actual exercise.

"Tentatively, right?" she said.

"Of course tentatively."

They were holding their lightness as though it were a fragile thing. As if their playfulness wouldn't withstand the gravity of a serious intrusion. They riffed and small-talked their way through dinner, and drank more than usual. Afterward they strolled the hotel's enormous public rooms, found a turquoise trinket for Carly in the gift shop, and headed outside.

Underdressed for the Sierra chill, they double-timed it, watching their vaporous breath against the unlit path to the cottage. His key in the door, Dan extended his neck to the limit, remembering at the last moment that the night sky in this elevated place could be as wondrous as the topography. Anticipating a show, a dense and glittery assemblage, maybe the distinct stripe of the Milky Way, he was disappointed. What he saw was a slow moving and starless matte, indistinct layers of dark and darker grays.

"The weather's turning," he said.

"No kidding, Willard. Can we get inside? I'm freezing my butt off here."

Probably because they were coastal Californians, and it was almost spring, neither of them entertained even a momentary consideration of snow.

⟶

It seemed like four or four-thirty. There were no clocks in the room and anyway his eyes were still closed. He wasn't sure how long he had napped. There was a pillow between the back of his head and Susan's right thigh. Her hand rested, palm down, over the center of his chest. He could feel and hear and smell the fire.

The day had started like the day before. Up well before Susan, unbrushed and uncombed, in sweats, sneakers and baseball cap, he was going to walk over to the Great Lounge in the main building to liberate a pot of coffee and a plate of pastry. He never got out the door. Twice so far the room service staff, for their care and feeding, had suffered the icy wind and the three feet of snow.

They were at right angles to one another, he outstretched on the couch, and she from the couch to the ottoman. He opened his eyes and inventoried the place. The interior of the cottage was, from the upholstery to the shades to the paintings to the soap dish, an ecru, teal and terra cotta coordinate. A southwestern package. The furniture was chunky yellow pine, and the walls were a pine laminate, something slightly darker. There was a recurrent native hieroglyph, an eight-pointed monogram, on everything. The fireplace, an elongated granite rhomboid, gradually narrowed from the floor of the hearth to the ceiling. Seeing that it needed attention, he got up, jostled the embers with an andiron, added two hunks of oak and jostled again. When he slid back into position, Susan, her book in her left hand, began slowly massaging his scalp with her right.

"You slept a little?" she said.

"Yeah, a little bit." He closed his eyes again. "I, uh, I was thinking about the hospital." Now there was only her breathing. Normally, of course, the client does not have his head in the analyst's lap, but otherwise they were in the traditional configuration. He didn't know how to take her silence. "Did you hear me?"

She spoke quietly, almost a whisper, "I thought we were gonna have a couple of Olympia-free days. That we weren't going to talk about it."

"Yeah, well." He was waiting. "Do you mind?" he finally asked.

"The truth?"

"No, lie to me."

Her voice rose as she spoke. "The truth is that I'm sick to death of Olympia this and Olympia that. Day after day." She hesitated. "Danny, I really don't feel like talking about it. Can we just take a break?"

He sat up and rummaged through the magazines on the coffee table until he found a *National Geographic Traveler*. He paged through the ads and the articles, looking at the pictures. When he looked up, Susan was staring at the ceiling. In all their years together, they had mercifully little practice at this sort of thing. Finally, she had a solution for at least the silence.

"Do you mind if I play?"

"I always like it when you play."

She took the hard-shell case from the closet and extracted her guitar, the same one that she was playing the first time he ever saw her. At the Brick in 1973.

The Brick n' Board Coffee House and Used Bookstore was a Berkeley landmark. In the fifties the Beats, even Alan Ginsburg, would come, dressed black on black, to read their poetry. In the sixties, while most of the Bay Area clubs transitioned to rock and psychedelia, the Brick became the acoustic folk mecca. Styles ranged from protest songs to delta blues to Irish jigs to bluegrass. On Friday and Saturday nights, big name folkies would draw the crowds. During the week it was open mikes and local favorites. On this Wednesday night, and most Wednesday nights, the chalkboard on the sidewalk read "Toni Giuliani."

Inside, the setting was untheatrical with no stage and no special lighting, just a space against a brick wall at the back of the bookstore. About a third of the twenty or so tables were occupied. Dan was alone at a table against the side wall, and she sat on a wooden stool behind a vocal microphone and a second mike for her Martin. She was wearing an oversized white linen top which looked East Indian, a silver and turquoise necklace, bell bottom blue jeans and ropy sandals. He noticed that she wore no rings. Her straight dark blond hair reached almost to her waist. She had flawless fair skin apparently covered by no make-up, and eyes the color of black coffee. He thought she was gorgeous.

She spoke little, heralding each song by title and writer, sometimes mentioning the artist she was covering if it was someone other than the songwriter. Resting on her musical laurels, she made no effort to be witty or entertaining in her introductions. He recognized a few of the songs: Thirsty Boots, Hickory Wind, The Dutchman. She played simply and cleanly. Her voice was lovely, a rich, comfortably phrasing, vibrating alto that went into the upper registers without loss of pitch or resonance. Daniel was rapt. He came back the following two Wednesdays, and he was thinking about her each of the days between.

—

"Doctor Fazen?" The voice was barely audible.

He was seated at the nurses' station composing a consultation note on a surgical patient. It was the beginning of his three month rotation at Sumner Hospital in Oakland, a primary teaching hospital for UC-San Francisco School of Medicine. This also marked the beginning of his last year in training. His new role as senior resident was largely supervisory, overseeing the internal medicine ward team, the junior residents, interns and medical students. He was the principal liaison to the faculty and to the private attending physicians, and he had a good deal of latitude in the management of their patients.

"Doctor Fazen?" she repeated from behind, this time louder.

He swiveled 180 degrees, looked up, and stared. Toni Giuliani was smiling at him. She looked different, but it was her. There was eye makeup and lipstick, her hair was piled and pinned, she wore a skirt and a blue blazer and a mannish, blue button-down shirt closed at the neck. It had been five days since he last saw her at the Brick.

"Excuse me, Doctor Fazen. My name is Susan Giuliani. I'm a social work intern and I'd like to ask you about Mrs. Wahlberg. I'm working on her nursing home placement, and I wonder if you could tell me when you think she'll be ready to go?"

"What?"

He was having trouble processing. The object of his obsession had materialized right in front of him. And he was sure that she had said her name was Susan. He was quite certain that she did not say that her name was Toni. He looked at the name tag that was pinned to her blazer. *Susan Giuliani, B.A., Social Work Intern.*

"Your patient, Mrs. Ann Wahlberg," she said. "Can you tell me when you're planning to discharge her?"

He had almost approached her after her last performance, but some people began talking with her and he decided to wait. He had been trying to figure out what he would say. Everything he could think of seemed lame. "Hi, my name is Dan. I think you're really terrific. I'd love to get to know you better." Please. He was planning on going back the next time she played, which was only two days away. He had no idea what he would say, that is if he got up the nerve to say anything.

"Uh, Susan? Is that right? Susan?"

"Right. Susan Giuliani," showing him her name tag.

"Um, I uh, I'm not certain yet. She'll probably be here at least another two or three days. Why?"

"As I said, I'm working on her nursing home placement."

"Okay, great. If there's any way I can help, just let me know."

"Right."

He imagined that she walked away thinking he was an idiot. She would later tell him how nervous she was about her new role, and how he had seemed to have no interest at all in what she was asking.

⌐

He was certain that she saw him during her second song. She was covering Bonnie Raitt's version of "Love Has No Pride," and she looked right at him, fixed her gaze for a few moments, and then didn't look in his direction for the rest of the set. He said to himself that this could not *not* be the social work intern that he spoke with two days earlier. Yet here she was with her different look and different name. Thinking about this the day before, he had imagined himself a dupe in a goofy sitcom about beautiful twin sisters and their unsuspecting suitors. At the end of the set, she put her guitar on its stand and walked straight to him.

"Doctor Fazen, what a surprise."

He stood up and extended his hand. "Hi. It's Daniel. Dan."

She shook his hand. "Hi. Susan."

"So who's Toni?"

"Oh, that's my nom de coffee house. Actually it's my middle name. The short version of my middle name. Some of my family call me Toni. I'm mostly Susan."

He lied a little, "I saw you here a few weeks ago. When I met you at the hospital, it really took me by surprise. I think you're a terrific singer."

"Well, thanks. I love it. I won't get rich doing it, which is partly why I'm becoming a social worker, but I love it."

"Well you're great at it."

"Thank you."

She was eighteen inches away, smiling broadly. His impulse was to kiss her. He stepped back and gestured toward the chair next to his. "Would you like to sit down?"

He saw her hesitate and look at her wristwatch. An old-lady watch, he thought.

"You know," she said, "I need to get something to drink and I have to tune the guitar for the next set. Are you gonna stay?"

"Yeah."

"Can I buy you a cup of coffee after I'm done?"

They talked until two in the morning, had a sixty hour date the following weekend, and were married exactly one year and three days later.

—

Susan didn't sing at all. She just noodled and finger-picked but it was a relief from the dead air. Later, restless and tired of confinement in the cottage, they hiked the shoveled footpath through the elements to the dining room. Near-empty in the storm, the space was cavernous, an echo chamber. You could hear the heel strikes of waiters fifty yards away. Dan thought of "The Shining." After dinner, they trudged back through the re-accumulated snow and retired early with nothing but civility.

—

Even with an early start the next morning, it took nearly seven hours to get to Berkeley. They could have remained an extra day and night, but Carly had an unmissable Saturday morning cello recital. And anyway, between the weather and the silent and sexless turn of events, their little vacation had gone sour. The description of the drive home, particularly the slippery switchbacks, would later have some entertainment value, invariably featuring the word *hairy*. In truth, it was more slow and irritating than frightening. The California Highway Patrol closed Old Priest Grade Road, which in the continuing storm would have been a demolition derby on the downhill run to the west. This left every car and truck and bus and camper creeping down the long way, the tedious serpentine descent on Highway 120. After three hours of braking and unbraking, of absorbing the blinking red glare of the vehicle ahead through the wet windshield, the view just distorted and obstructed enough to be annoying without being outright dangerous, the two-lane finally straightened and the snow turned to light rain. At least the Volvo didn't start chiming and clicking.

At the first opportunity, Dan yielded the driver's side, threw down 800 milligrams of Advil and closed his eyes. He just wanted to be home. In his own house without this murderous headache. On Monday, he would be right back in Central California.

Kerry Jameson

———

THE NEEDLE-NOSED TURBOPROP, ONE OF THOSE BEND-OVER-
and-walk-down-the-aisle commuter jobs, was the only
non-stop to Fresno. Dan used the time on board, all of it,
to read through Kerry's case summary. Left alone by the over-
whelmed Olympia-Fresno nurses, she had bled nearly to death
following a tonsillectomy, and was rescued by only the most des-
perate and invasive measures. The icy prose of the medical narra-
tives did nothing to diminish the horror of it.

After a brief misadventure in his Avis sedan, Dan found the
house, a stucco one-story in the southeast part of the city. The
driveways in both directions were packed, house to curb, with
SUV's and pick-ups.

"Well, thanks for letting me come down to talk with you," he
said. "You must be tired of going over this again and again." They
were in the living room, Dan in a flowered armchair and Ed and
Paula Jameson across on a matching sofa. She had just placed a
basket of warm muffins on the table between. Nine-year-old

Kerry was propped in a wheelchair to Dan's right. He was certain that she comprehended nothing.

"That's okay. Anything we can do for Mason Kanzler, we will do." Dan thought that Paula sounded Oklahoma or West Texas. He would learn later that she had spent her whole life in Bakersfield and Fresno.

"Well, I came down here basically to meet you and to learn more about Kerry. As much about her life now as about what happened four years ago. Mrs. Jameson, you're with Kerry most of the time?"

"Please call me Paula, okay?"

Dan smiled a half smile and nodded.

"Yeah, I'm with her most of the time. But I get some breaks. Ed'll take over for a while on the weekends. Gives me a chance to get out. Kerry's aunt, my baby sister, she'll watch her so we can go out to dinner, go to a movie. We've got a routine. But no question, I'm the main child care worker 'round here."

He repositioned himself so that he was facing Kerry. "Can you tell me a little bit about the daily routine?"

As they spoke, he dissected the details of her appearance. At nine, she looked five. To stabilize her in the chair, there were pillows stuffed at both flanks, and cloth straps, like seatbelts, across her chest and thighs. Her stocking feet were pigeon-toed on the metal foot plates. She was in a dark blue jogging suit, similar to the one her mother was wearing. A thick tube snaked from the bottom edge of her jacket to a plastic bag hung from the left armrest. It was one-third filled with dark yellow urine.

"Well bless her, she sleeps a lot. We put her down about eight. She'll fuss some during the night but usually sleeps 'til about seven or so. She'll be more fussy if she gets stuffed up or somethin'."

As Paula began, Dan grasped an essential part of this tragedy. She was describing her daughter in the specific language of mothers and their infants. Their school-age Kerry had died. Their new Kerry was an oversized, disabled infant, developmentally frozen.

"We do give her little tastes of baby food and pudding and sips of water by mouth," she said. "But most everything, her supplements and drugs and water, she gets by the G-Tube. She can't swallow too good."

"What medications is she getting now?"

"She's down to the Macrodantin, the Valium, and the Dilantin."

If Dan had never seen or heard of Kerry Jameson, one look would have told him she was on the anti-convulsant Dilantin, and had been for years. It was her thick, protuberant gums which had overgrown her teeth, covering nearly half their surface. She held her mouth partially open, exposing her tongue and those huge gums. As he watched, her head was in constant random motion. Her eyes, open and moving in unison, did not seem to fix on any particular thing.

"What's happening with her seizures?"

"Well, she gets the little ones all the time. On the right side. She hasn't had a big one, you know a grand mal, for maybe three weeks." She pronounced it as though it were the name of a shopping complex. "And that one lasted only about two minutes. Hell, I hate the way the damn Dilantin makes her look, but it works better than all that other stuff. Excuse my language."

The photograph had been in his peripheral vision, on the end table next to Ed. As Paula spoke, he realized it was Kerry. She was thigh-deep in a round inflatable swimming pool, smiling and waving at the photographer. He thought she looked four or five, and wondered how close in time this had been to her hospitalization. Her first hospitalization, the one that led to all this.

"What do you do when she has a grand mal?" Dan adopted Paula's pronunciation.

"Not much. We hold the padded blade between her teeth." As she said it she pointed to a metal jar on a bookshelf behind her daughter. In it was a cluster of wooden tongue blades, the kind used for routine throat exams, each wrapped with white gauze at one end. "If it keeps goin', you know five minutes or more, we'll call 911. Usually doesn't though."

"Do you keep those in more than one place?"

"Here and her bedroom."

On an impulse, unexpected and unwelcome, Dan began to construct an image of Carly, his own daughter's arching back and jerking extremities. He wrenched himself from the hideous vision. The thought, even the beginning of the thought, could not be held. Like swallowing broken glass. And here were these people, working their child's seizures into their daily routine.

So far, Kerry's father had been a spectator. In his late thirties, Ed Jameson looked like a man who had begun losing his hair at about the time he got his high school diploma. He was dressed for work. Solid black tie, gray cotton slacks and a white shirt with a red, white, and blue "All-Star Hardware" patch over one pocket.

"Mr. Jameson, uh Ed. May I call you Ed?" He consented, bemused, as though this was not the sort of thing that people asked him. "Ed, can you tell me a little about Kerry's abilities?"

"Her abilities? Like whaddaya mean?"

"Well, vision, hearing, recognition of things, pain responses, likes and dislikes, everyday things. Whatever you observe."

Ed hesitated, resting the side of his face against a calloused hand. Then he answered without looking up, "Paula, I think maybe you could tell him better than me."

She stared at her husband, expressionless. Then she turned, not just her head, toward Dan. "Well, she can tell a real bright light. She'll turn away from it. Maybe a year ago her doctor, her rehab doctor, was checkin' her eyes with the, uh, whatchamacallit. . ."

"Ophthalmoscope?"

"Right. And she sorta thrashed at it. She could see that light."

"Uh huh. Do you think she ever fixes, you know focuses, on anything?"

Paula smiled. "Well, I like to think that sometimes she sees my face. Her eyes'll line up with me for a few seconds. But I know she can't."

"How about her hearing? I mean I understand that she can hear, but can you tell me how she responds to sounds?"

"Well, she'll turn toward a loud noise. Sometimes she'll act like startled. And she likes music, I think it soothes her. There's times when she's like real agitated and I'll put on a CD—we've got a little stereo in her room—and she'll just calm right down."

Ed spoke up. "Yeah, she especially likes this one Vince Gill album Paula likes to play."

She looked at him and then turned back to Dan, as though she had something to say and reconsidered.

He wanted to acknowledge Ed, but came up short. The three of them sat there in the awkwardness for a few seconds, though it seemed longer. Dan pushed ahead, "Do you think Kerry recognizes your voice?"

"I do. If there's company over, you know a bunch of people talkin', she'll stop or slow down when it's me doing the talkin'. I can just tell. Or when I put her to bed and read to her, she'll just settle down. She knows me."

Dan wondered how this little girl could "know" anything. He had read the description of her resuscitation three times and yes, it was by the book and it had worked. The problem was that Kerry had been choking on her own blood clots, suffocating, for as long as nearly half an hour. Unobserved and unmonitored. Putting himself in the place of the physicians on the scene, he would have made the same choices. The actual period of asphyxiation and brain injury was unknown. Children can be resilient. This was a previously well child. If you can, you save the kid's life. Ethical ruminations are for the terminally ill and the ancient. And before or after the action.

He looked at the bag hanging from her wheelchair. "Tell me what's going on with her kidneys, and her infections."

"Oh, she's doin' good there. Since they put the catheter through her belly, the neurologic bladder hasn't been a problem." He knew she meant *neurogenic,* but he left it alone. "There's no new infections and they say her kidney function is stable."

"That's great. How about her bowel movements. Any problems there?" He knew there were.

"Well, yeah. She gets constipated real bad." She hesitated. "I hate it. Nothin' works. We've tried everything. All the stool softeners and all the special enemas. She gets like a rock, seems no matter what."

Dan had suffered more experience than he ever wanted with his constipated geriatric patients. "How often does she go?"

"She'll go two, even three weeks without a BM. Her belly swells up and you can feel it through her skin."

"So what happens when she just can't go?"

"I used to take her to the ER. She'd be there for hours. The nurses hated it. They'd give her the enemas and then dig her out with their gloved hands. Now I just do it myself. It ain't no fancy skill."

The matter-of-fact acceptance of particularly this task embedded itself into Dan's comprehension of Paula Jameson. Of her dreary adaptation to her losses.

"Well, I'm afraid I've got to get to work." Ed was on his feet, extending his hand across the coffee table. "It was nice to meet you, Doctor Fazen."

Dan was surprised. There had been no prelude to the departure. He rose and met his grip. "It was nice to meet you too, Ed. I'm sure I'll see you again." He remained standing as Ed went out the front door, then sat and waited for Paula.

She stood, walked over to Kerry, and pivoted toward Dan, her hand on her daughter's shoulder. She was looking at the carpet. "He's a good man, you know."

People talk to doctors. Not just to their doctor, but to doctors. Informal second opinions, settling arguments, scouting forbidden territory, just getting freebies. Throughout his career, Dan had been dumbfounded at the things that people, all but strangers, had said to him. An auto mechanic once asked him a question about his (the auto mechanic's!) testicles. The woman behind the counter at the dry cleaners wanted to know what he recommended for excessive farting. This in response to his asking if he could get his shirts by five o'clock. And they ask about deadly serious diseases in themselves and loved ones. Scary questions, too frightening to confront with their own doctors. And unsolicited, they talk about the most private things in their lives.

She looked up, directly at him. "He really is. He helps out in every way he can. Besides the SSI from the state, he provides all the money. I went back to work with the IRS when Kerry was four months, but since this happened I haven't worked a day. Ed does it all. He does all the shoppin'. He helps with the household chores, the cleanin', even fixes supper. He keeps the yard."

He watched her return to the sofa.

"Like I told you, he'll look after her so I can get out. Maybe once a week, but then he'll want me back soon. Like no more than say two hours. I know he hates it. He even doesn't want to look at her. Like watchin' TV, he'll angle his chair so he doesn't have to see her. He does it subtle, but I can tell."

She was speaking in her strong cowgirl voice without emotional hitches.

"This broke his heart. He was so close to her, she just lit him up. We used to talk about havin' two or three more. Now he won't hear of it. Says that with Kerry I wouldn't have time for a baby. That it wouldn't be fair. He'd never say it, but he's scared to death."

Though it wasn't something Dan had intended, Paula's plain-spoken defenseless soliloquy transformed the Jameson living room into a psychotherapy space. They were directly opposite, each with their legs crossed, she in her jogging outfit and he in his business suit.

"You know, we were high school sweethearts. Ed's the only man I've ever been with. You couldn't tell it now, but he was the happiest guy around. He loved to be with people and everybody just loved him. We were invited to everything. After we got the house, he'd always want to have a crowd over on Sundays. He'd invite everybody, his high school buddies and their wives and kids. Grill steaks and burgers and hot dogs. Buy a couple of cases of beer."

Dan kept quiet as she hesitated and then started again, more slowly and sadder, he thought.

"When Kerry got sick, it's like his light went out. He actually started workin' more, doin' overtime. He said it was for the money since I wasn't workin'. And that's true, but I also think he just didn't want to be here. Seein' her the way she was. He'd be real responsible about chores and stuff, but most of the time he'd just sit in front of the TV. He never wants to have company any more. Just lost his spark." She emitted a one syllable laugh, a nasal exhalation. "Lost his spark for me, I'll tell ya."

Dan was no shrink, but he knew when to talk and when to shut up. There was nothing that he could say that was going to improve this woman's life. What he could do was get in her way. For all he knew, he was the first person, stranger enough and by credentials trustworthy, that she could open up to. He gave her soft eye contact and she went a little further before retreating to the safety of Kerry's problems.

"He loves me, I know he does. But we haven't made love in over two years. And we don't talk about it. It's not the kinda thing we talk about. Never did." She was quiet for several seconds, eyes averted. "I don't think he's doin' anything. You know, with someone else. That's not his way. I think he's just lost his desire." She looked up and lightened. "Hey, I'm sorry. You don't need to hear this. You didn't come all the way down here to listen to me cryin' in my beer."

"It's okay, really."

She turned toward Kerry. "One thing that I think helps her is the physical therapy. Twice a day I do the range of motion on her arms and legs. Keeps her from tightenin' up too much. And it seems like she likes it."

They talked for another twenty-five minutes. About the passive range-of-motion treatments, the care of the suprapubic catheter, the gastrostomy feedings, the intranasal medication. As he was leaving, she offered him the muffins. "Here, for your family."

He knew it was risky to go there in March. About its weather, a local wrote that Fresno was more hospitable than, say, the moon. In the summer it's the relentless three-figure heat. In the winter it isn't the cold or the wind or the rain, it's the fog. Named after reeds that grow in the marshes of the Central Valley, they call it Tule fog. And when conditions are just so, it closes the airports and, for anyone with a scrap of sense, the roads.

It would take him almost four and a half hours to get home on the San Joaquin, Amtrak's clackety antidote to zero visibility. At the window there was no distinguishing night from fog except when they passed something bright and close, headlights or a street lamp. Then the energy diffused in the vapor, luminous, like isinglass.

After a few minutes of the ghostly show, Dan closed his eyes and listened to the wheels muffling along the railbed. He thought about Kerry and about his daughter Carly at Kerry's age, and about what life was supposed to be like when you're nine years old.

COBRA

DAN FELT LIKE HE WAS IN A WAR ROOM.

"Folks, we are in the crosshairs." Frost was making sure that everyone got the context. This was not going to be a lofty academic discussion. "We've got less than two weeks to get ready for our regular Joint Commission survey and a simultaneous visit by the Feds on this COBRA thing. Now that may seem unfair but that's the hand we've been dealt. We tried to get them to re-schedule the COBRA investigation and they wouldn't go for it. The Feds have not exactly been Olympia-friendly."

Even Samuel Shem, creator of the classic GOMER (Get Out Of My Emergency Room), never nailed an acronymous bon mot like the federal regulators themselves, of all people. COBRA, for short, was the dreaded government process monitoring hospital emergency care—full name COBRA/EMTALA (Consolidated Omnibus Budget Reconciliation Act of 1986 / The Emergency Medicine Treatment and Active Labor Act).

What started as a well-intentioned law against dumping patients from emergency rooms for financial reasons had become, if you were to ask hospital officials, a menacing regulatory reptile nearly paralyzing the movement of any patient who showed up at a health care facility with an acute medical complaint. An episode of non-compliance, widely referred to as a *COBRA violation*, is quite literally a federal case bringing formal investigators and the possibility of disqualification from the Medicare and Medicaid programs (read "financial death of your hospital"). Little wonder that Tom Frost was distraught over the Jackson debacle.

By appearances, the conference that had just begun in the office of the medical staff president was a routine review of a bad patient outcome—for the purpose of quality improvement and protected from legal scrutiny. The minutes would record only that the care of Thomas Jackson was discussed. Carol Tessler chaired, and Dan, Jack Jensen and Jim Swain, the ER Director, were the physician participants. Officially, Frost and attorney Richard Reynolds attended as guests. But not for a moment was there any doubt that this was the CEO's meeting.

Frost continued, "We need to figure out exactly what we have, and then figure out how we're going to defend it. I don't think I have to remind anyone here how much is at stake. Let's begin with the details of the medical care."

Jensen was there for technical expertise. With Tessler allegedly presiding and Swain on the block, it fell to Dan to present the case. His sources were the Memorial ER record, the ambulance notes, and the Contra Costa County ER record. And of course the coroner's report.

"Thomas Jackson, a fifty-eight year old African-American male, was evidently well until approximately one hour prior to his appearance in our ER when he fell off a ladder in his apartment. While the story is a little bit unclear, apparently he initially felt that he was okay and didn't think he needed any attention. In fact, he went back up the ladder. He had been installing a light fixture in his living room ceiling. Shortly thereafter, we're not certain exactly how long, he developed sharp left-sided chest pain and difficulty breathing. He called 911 and was brought to the ER."

As Dan spoke, his attention alternated between his notes and Frost. The man was scared, and that was scary.

"Upon arrival, Jackson was complaining of pain localized to the upper left lateral chest. It was worse when he took a breath. He told the docs that he'd had occasional chest pain in recent years, but never a heart attack. He said he'd been given pills for angina but had none now. He also had a history of hypertension but was likewise on no medication for that. No other past history is noted in the record."

"What did they do for him in transit?" Jensen asked.

"Oxygen, vital signs." Dan scanned the room for further questions. "His physical exam upon arrival was pretty much unremarkable except for his chest. He was alert and uncomfortable. His color was described as good. His pulse was ninety-six and regular, blood pressure one forty over ninety-two, respirations twenty and regular with wincing on inspiration. His head, eyes, ears, nose, and throat were fine. His neck was supple. On palpation of his chest, he had point tenderness over what were thought to be the fourth and fifth ribs on the left. No overlying bruising was noted. His breath sounds were described simply as symmetrical. One word."

Jensen interrupted, "That's all?"

"That's all. The heart had a regular rhythm. No murmurs. His abdomen was soft and non-tender with no masses. It says skin, extremities, and neuro unremarkable. The impression was chest trauma, rule out rib fracture, rule out cardiac pain. He got a chest x-ray, an EKG and cardiac enzymes. The EKG and the enzymes were okay. The chest x-ray was read as non-displaced fractures of the fifth and sixth ribs on the left. And as we all know, that's all."

Frost took the lead. "Now I want to get this straight. Who exactly looked at that chest x-ray?"

Swain answered, "The radiology tech and the ER attending."

"They were not seen by a radiologist?" This was the fourth time that Frost had asked this question in the past six days.

Dan confirmed it. "Not until later. I spoke to the radiology tech myself. The only physician who saw the film at that time was the ER doc." He pushed ahead. "Mr. Jackson was given Percocet and a rib binder, and a decision was made, just to be on the safe side, because he had chest pain and the history of angina, that he should be hospitalized for observation. Because he had no insurance, arrangements were made for an ambulance to take him to County. And off he went."

Jack Jensen couldn't resist. "Off he went, all right."

Frost snapped at his Chief of Medicine, "You think this is funny, doctor?"

Dan cut in, "Tom, a little gallows humor. That's all. Just us docs being docs." Jensen was glaring at the CEO.

Frost backed off. "Go on."

"Okay. Well, it seems Jackson got into trouble about halfway between the two hospitals. At exactly—let me check the log—at eleven minutes out, the EMT noted increased respiratory distress and couldn't hear breath sounds on the left side. He called base, which is of course County, and they suggested increasing the oxygen. Jackson seemed stable over the next few minutes. Then at twenty-one minutes out, his heart rate started to decrease and there were no breath sounds at all on the left side. So they talked the tech through the emergency procedure in the ambulance. According to the log he started to pull a substantial amount of air from the man's chest through a large bore needle and a fifty cc. syringe when Jackson went into cardiac arrest. Upon arrival at County, they were doing CPR. They had already shocked him twice. In the ER they put in a chest tube, and continued the resuscitation effort for nearly an hour. He was pronounced about an hour and a half after he left here."

"Do we have the final report on the post?" Jensen was asking about the autopsy.

Dan pulled a document from his stack. "We have the preliminary narrative on the post-mortem exam. Fractured ribs. Blood and air in the left chest. Some minor cardiac and cerebral findings. Provisional cause of death is cardiac arrest secondary to massive pneumothorax caused by accidental trauma and fractured ribs. Basically he fell a few feet off a ladder, broke two ribs, and died of a collapsed lung, a pneumothorax. And by all the evidence, a treatable pneumothorax that we missed. Has everyone seen the chest x-ray taken here?"

Carol Tessler spoke up. "I haven't."

Dan pulled it out of its folder and handed it to her. She held it up, using the fluorescent ceiling light.

Dan had been lucky. To his knowledge he had never through omission or commission killed anyone. But he knew that was to some extent simply a matter of chance. Over decades of practice and tens of thousands of diagnostic and therapeutic judgments, he had made his share of mistakes. And though most were inconsequential, there were a few that still haunted and embarrassed him. There was an elderly gentleman who had cancer of the colon which he mistook for evidence of constipation on repeated visits. In another, he erroneously diagnosed a complication of gonorrhea in a man who actually had a twisted testicle, a surgical emergency. By the time he made it to surgery, the testicle was not salvageable and it was removed. For that one, Dan had his one and only experience as a defendant in a malpractice action. As is commonly done, the parties agreed to have the hospital pay damages while the physician, Dan, was dropped from the suit. But he knew what it was like to be ashamed of his work.

Tessler handed the chest x-ray back to him. Roughly half of the left chest cavity, which should be entirely filled with expanded lung tissue, was pitch black air sharply outlining the edge of the collapsed left lung.

Dan looked across the table to his Emergency Department Director. "Jim, let's give you a chance here."

Frost cut him off. "Excuse me. The medical staff will have its chance to do its quality thing on this case. Doctor Swain, there'll plenty of opportunity for the ED to give its side of the story, to the extent that there is one. We're here today to talk about COBRA. The Feds are coming and we need to understand our exposure." The CEO turned to Reynolds, who was sitting immediately to his right. "Richard, are we clearly in violation?" Not that he didn't know the answer.

"It looks pretty bad," Reynolds said. "A hospital is clearly not supposed to transfer unstable patients. It doesn't really matter that someone thought Mr. Jackson was stable. What counts is whether he actually was. Not to be overly crass, but we put him in the ambulance on one end, and he came out dead on the other. I can't imagine that anyone thinks that a moving ambulance is a reasonable place for an emergency thoracentesis, or a full resuscitation for that matter. And...", Reynolds hesitated as he shifted context, "if we were a non-profit, and the patient had insurance, we'd still be in trouble. The fact that we're Olympia and the patient had no insurance—"

Frost finished it for him, "the Feds'll be salivating." He spoke uninterrupted for several minutes about Memorial's Medicare revenue, about the amount of money that was at risk in a worse case scenario, about the need for new policies in the ER, about intensive training of the nurses and doctors in the COBRA law. His speech was driven, more agitated as he went on. It wasn't really didactic, much less Socratic. It was a rant. He calmed enough to task Reynolds with a number of preparatory matters for the site visits. After one last tirade about the "goddamn Feds," he ended the meeting.

Walking back to his office, Dan was thinking about Frost's demeanor over the Maggie Herrmann incident. Utterly disingenuous but calm, even charming. Now the man seemed to be coming unglued. He imagined him being hammered by Athens and the Olympia Board over the COBRA threat. Dan was also thinking that the discussion of the Jackson case had accomplished little. He remembered something that Marty liked to say about hospital management. How most of the time was spent sitting around large tables "admiring the problems."

Coming into his outer office, Clare told him that Frost had just called and wanted him to come to his office right away.

"But I was just with him."

"What can I tell you? That's the message."

Frost had not calmed down. He sat Dan at his conference table, briefly took a chair opposite, and then immediately stood up and paced the big office as he spoke.

"This COBRA stuff is damn serious. The Feds might really hurt us, make an example of us. They hate Olympia. They hate all the for-profits. But they especially hate Olympia. When we got vulnerable in the nineties on the fraud and abuse stuff, it was a feeding frenzy."

Dan shifted in his chair, trying to keep contact with Frost as he changed direction with nearly every sentence.

"Tom, even with the most obvious violation, it seems to me we'll get cited, we'll get warned, they'll come back and visit again. But they're not going to take away our funding for a single incident."

The CEO was having none of Dan's reassurance. "You want to be on probationary status, one incident away from disaster? And we can't control these things. Hospital policy didn't do a damn thing in the Jackson case. And it won't in the next. An ER doc screws up one more time and we're out of business? Excuse me? Doctor, we are in trouble." Frost sat down and seemed to be collecting his thoughts. "We need to present this case in the most benign way that we can. Any way we can mitigate the damage, we need to do that."

"Look," Dan said, "the documentation here is very damaging. I don't know how we're going to make this look benign. The facts are the facts. We—"

"Dammit, the physician screwed up. The hospital shouldn't be punished for that."

Dan did it without premeditation. "You think the hospital isn't culpable? You think the atmosphere of hostility toward the uninsured patient doesn't contribute? Come on."

Frost recoiled. Staying seated, he dug his heels into the carpet and pushed his chair back from the table, increasing the distance from his medical executive. "How about we have a debate on the mission and philosophy of this hospital some other time. Right now we have a practical problem in front of us. And that's how do we sanitize the Jackson case so we can all continue to make a living. Okay?"

"Sanitize?"

"Do you have a better word?"

"I don't know how to do that," Dan said.

"You mean to tell me that there's no latitude in how a case is presented?"

"Around the edges, yes. But a collapsed lung is a collapsed lung. You can't sanitize an x-ray."

"Is there anything we can do about that?"

"What?"

Frost got up and started to pace again. "About the x-ray."

"What are you asking me?"

The fifteen seconds that the man took felt like an hour. Later, in retrospect, Dan would wonder if it was precisely then that Tom Frost decided to fire him.

"Nothing," Frost said. "Never mind."

⤚

"Doctor Fazen, this is James Colburn at the Contra Costa Daily News. Could you please call me? I'd like to ask you a few questions about a Mr. Thomas Jackson. He was seen in your emergency room last week and died shortly after transfer to County. I'm at 935-754-2000, extension 342. Thanks."

It was the last of eight voicemails that stood between him and a rare escape from the hospital before six o'clock. The others were innocuous, or at least not urgent. He listened to the reporter's message twice, dialed, and hung up after the first ring. Doing nothing was the easiest choice. No tortured conversation, no published comments to justify, no delay in his evening homecoming. And ruminating over the details, he could not imagine a quote about this case that would be less damaging than "Memorial officials were unavailable for comment." Though he might be accused of failing to defend the hospital or of passively colluding with Colburn, Dan made his decision without malice. At least consciously.

After several minutes in the dark, Dan and Susan were still awake. Dinner had been quiet and brief. Carly was off at a friend's house and Dan was distracted, his thoughts careening around the Jackson case, the mess with Frost, and whether he had made the right call with Colburn. They were in bed early after an evening of parallel routines. Susan watering plants, returning a few phone calls and reading *Going to the Sun* by James McManus, her book of the week. Dan doing some laundry and soothing himself with the two easy Chronicle crosswords while osmosing HBO. He was fetalized, on his right side.

"Danny, you're a thousand miles away. What is it now?"

He described the Jackson case briefly and then the aftermath with Frost in detail.

"What do *you* think he was going to ask you to do?" she asked.

"I don't know. Disappear the x-ray, get everyone who'd seen it to lie about it, claim the patient got his pneumothorax in transit. It's preposterous. I can't imagine what the little prick was thinking."

Even with Susan's sporadic reluctance to listen, Dan had shared basically everything since the Olympia takeover—the staffing cuts, the protection of Seldes, the guy with pneumonia who almost died on the front lawn, the duplicity around Maggie Herrmann, Kerry Jameson and her family, and now this preventable death and Frost's desperation. There was no concealing his growing sadness and anger and embarrassment. As bored as he had become when he was in private practice, he had never gone through his days and nights in doubt and shame about his choices and his integrity.

"What are you gonna do?" she said.

"Whaddaya mean?"

"I mean what are you gonna do about this job? I've never seen you so miserable."

He rolled onto his back and closed his eyes. Silently, and not for the first time, he waded into the implications of resigning.

"You hate working with these people. It seems like you're unhappy every day, and it's just getting worse."

"Have you thought about what it would mean if I quit? About the house, for example, about—"

"I could give a good goddamn about the house." Her voice broke but she pushed her words through. " I care about what's happening to you and to us. These people are assholes. You don't belong with them." Tears were streaming down her cheeks. "And it's all we ever talk about anymore. Do you know that? You come home practically every night pissed off or depressed or obsessing over the latest fucking Olympia atrocity. This… *thing*," she shouted it, "is taking over our life. I want it back."

Her ferocity pierced him. His self-involved professional drama was leaving his best friend and lover behind. At most he had been worrying about whether she approved of him ethically. He rolled to his left and pulled her in.

"Toni, I'm sorry. I am so caught up in this. I'm just taking you for granted. I—"

"You can take me for granted. I'm here for you, Danny. This job is making you miserable. You're a misplaced person. It's not your fault, it just happened. But it's not all right. You're unhappy all the time. You're not yourself and I miss you, goddammit." She laughed and sobbed at the same moment.

"I am so sorry." He cradled the back of her head with his hand and slowly brought her mouth up to his, giving her the chance to resist. She didn't.

He was whispering, "You know I can't just turn this around in a moment. There's a lot to handle. The house, another job, the cost of the kids. Don't think I haven't thought about it."

"Danny, you're too good for those people." She exhaled slowly and whispered back. "Let's not talk about it right now."

They made love for the first time in weeks.

The Longest Day

H E NO LONGER NEEDED TO SET HIS CLOCK RADIO. HIS SLEEP, always fragile anyway, had become even more elusive, and padding out of bed at four-thirty was most mornings a relief from waiting. At least his trip to the hospital brightened, if only visually. As the April days lengthened, the eastbound routine went day for night and the suburban hillsides morphed out of their flat black profiles. Driving past his mid-point marker, the Orinda BART station, the most clarity of purpose Dan could muster on this Monday was to be there when they unlocked the doors at Starbuck's in Lafayette.

He was expecting nothing less than an anticipatory frenzy at work. The Feds and the Joint Commission site visitors were three days away, and his calendar was bursting. Not just breakless, but overlapping. Today he would deal with one regulatory hot button after another. Absence of signatures on physicians' verbal orders, inappropriate physical restraint of psychiatric patients, excessive narcotics for the dying, high post-operative infection rates, the COBRA imperatives in the ER. And the anxiety of Hospital

Administration, particularly of Frost, had been contagious. An atmosphere of fear permeated a staff that had more than it could deal with, despite the outrageous hours they were working.

Three minutes early, Dan nodded to the two early morning regulars who waited a few feet away. They were there every Monday. Tan and fit, late forties, dress casual. The shorter preppie one drove a big white Lexus. The taller one, with the beard, a navy Porsche Carrera. They always took the same table, spoke quietly, laughed easily. Dan fantasized that they were post-workaholic, post-IPO Silicon Valley megawinners who'd gotten out before the bubble burst. Schmoozing about the weekend's golf scores.

Once in, he got his coffee and scone, went to his spot, the table in the corner furthest from the counter commotion, and began leafing through the Contra Costa paper. Going back to front in his usual order, he looked at the baseball scores and the standings, then the movie reviews. The op-ed page had point-counterpoint pieces on illegal immigration and border fences. Scanning the Local section, an article at the bottom of the first page obliterated the sanctity of his early morning routine.

East Bay Infant Dies
Doctors say probably abuse

By James Colburn
Daily News Staff Writer

A five month old Concord child with multiple injuries to his head and body died at Oakland Children's Hospital yesterday. A spokesman for the hospital said that the injuries "definitely appear to have been non-accidental." The infant, Robert

Michael Wittman, had been transferred
from Contra Costa County Hospital after

Reading it two more times, he could feel each contraction of his heart. Though there was no mention of it, this child had been discharged, and with some controversy, from Memorial's pediatric floor ten days earlier. His mind was racing, reconstructing the details. He needed to get outside. Gathering the newspaper sections, he struck the nearly full paper cup, and dark steaming liquid flooded the tabletop, cascading onto the floor. He leapt from his chair. "Shit!"

A woman at the next table glared at him.

"Sorry." He grabbed a handful of napkins and began spreading them on the table.

His hot shots gave him a moment's notice, and a young man came from behind the counter in his green apron and began mopping up with a large sponge. "It's okay, sir, we'll take care of it. Would you like another cup?"

"No. Thank you, no." Scattered, he reconsidered. "Wait. Yeah, I would." He got the fresh coffee and, newspaper under his arm, fled.

—

Even at six in the morning there was no problem getting to the Medical Records stacks. The night nursing supervisor let him in and, finding the Memorial patient number in the network terminal, he was able to locate Robbie Wittman's chart. He signed it out and went to his office.

Reading cover to cover through the details of Robbie's hospitalization, he nervously re-mapped the discharge decision. In retrospect, it was arguably all right. But only if you discounted the social worker's assessment. The admission diagnosis was "failure-to-thrive," meaning failure of an infant to gain weight. Carla Ricci, the Wittman's family doctor, had become concerned when

Robbie gained only a few ounces from three to four months of age. She did a few simple outpatient studies, a blood count and urinalysis, which were normal, and encouraged the mother to increase the amount of formula and start solid baby foods. After three more weeks of no weight gain at all, she put Robbie in the hospital for an evaluation. An array of blood tests were normal and a series of gastrointestinal x-rays—as it turned out, not the x-rays he needed—were performed and were also normal. The case manager on the pediatric floor recommended discharge after three days. The pediatric social worker, Naomi Siegal, disagreed, and Doctor Ricci requested authorization for extension of the admission.

Between his anxiety and the rising caffeine levels, Dan could barely rein in his agitation. He was out of his chair, pacing and re-reading without focus Siegal's concluding comments in the medical record. He sat in one of his conference table chairs, closed his eyes and intentionally slowed and deepened his breathing. He felt himself quiet. Opening his eyes, he tried again.

am particularly concerned about the quality of the interaction between this first-time mom and the infant, her apparent lack of technical feeding knowledge, and the minimal involvement and distance of the father. With no medical explanation for Robbie's failure-to-thrive, it is my recommendation that he remain in the hospital for a feeding trial, education particularly of the mother, further evaluation of family interaction, and possible skeletal x-ray survey if recommended by the attending physician. While I don't believe that referral to Child Protective Services is warranted at this time, I am concerned about the possibility of neglect, or even physical abuse. If he is discharged, at a minimum there should be frequent well baby visits and involvement of the public health nurses.

He returned to his desk and reached for the telephone as though it were a snake. He made his way through Information to the Oakland Children's Hospital operator, and then into the voicemail of his opposite number, their Medical Director.

"John, this is Dan Fazen at Memorial in Walnut Creek. I'm trying to follow up on Robert Wittman, the abused infant who died in your ICU yesterday. He was here for poor weight gain about a week and a half ago. I'm particularly interested in his x-ray findings. When you have a chance, please give me a call. Thanks."

He wasn't interested in the new injuries to the bones. He wanted to know if there were old ones.

It was 7:15 and he walked up two flights to UM, the Utilization Management office. He went to the "Case Management, Recent" file cabinet and began searching the W's. He knew there would be no surprises here but he wanted see the document. The one-page form was in its proper place. The patient and family, their address, phone number and other identifying data were recorded. The clinical entries were cryptic. Diagnosis: "FTT." Request: "extension of admission for further diagnostic evaluation." Case manager recommendation: "maximum inpatient benefit accomplished—remainder of eval can be done outpatient—recommend denial."

The last line of the form had two check boxes, "approved" and "denied," and a signature line. The "denied" box was checked. He stared at the signature. Black ink, strong hand. Easily legible. Back in Chicago at DeWitt Clinton Elementary his teachers had praised him for his penmanship. Patients and staff had told him for years that his handwriting was "good for a doctor." He had always liked the way his signature looked. This morning it sickened him.

⤙

The meetings began. Nervous aggregations of executives, middle managers, an occasional physician. Churning through the language of the regulators, the hospital policies, data reports, and committee minutes. Passing out and reviewing pound upon pound of stapled bond. Bundling specific clusters of patients' charts in anticipation of best guesses on areas of scrutiny. Listening to and editing canned presentations from overheads and carousels and laptops. Even staging aggressive mock cross-examinations to prepare the defenders of the citadel for worse case scenarios and malevolent site visitors.

Marion Lacey, the Director of Medical Records, sat at the end of the long table. Before her, five piles of charts rising nearly to her chin. Dan and a dozen others, the Medical Records Committee, were there to address how, and even if, physicians at Memorial documented in writing the verbal orders that they gave to the nursing staff. It seemed to him that the Joint Commission, the nation's guardian of hospital propriety, behaved as though it had pet peeves. He wondered how, among the thousands of things to scrutinize, this potent watchdog got a collective bug up its ass over a few particular things in each regulatory cycle. One of those things was doctors' verbal orders.

Marion reviewed the data. A layer of his awareness tracked the discussion. He heard the comments about developing a report card for the residents, threatening the surgeons' OR privileges, musing without effect about how to deal with the site visitors. It played like underscoring to his ruminations over the Wittman case. Even without the intensity of the distraction, he likely would have zoned out for signatures on verbal orders. It was one of those issues, and there were many, where if it weren't for regulatory risk, it wouldn't be an issue at all. No one's heart or abdominal organs are attached to countersigning, dating and timing verbal orders. The meeting lasted slightly over an hour. He didn't speak.

He was late for the Infection Control Committee. And while the subject matter was more compelling—at least it had something to do with the well-being of patients—the quality of his attention was no better. They were talking about patterns of postoperative infections: how they were related to specific surgical procedures, and particularly how they were associated with individual surgeons. He briefly engaged and then withdrew as the discussion turned to the effectiveness of the layouts of the presentation graphics. Under ordinary circumstances, he would have been grateful to be rescued from proceedings as dull as these. But when his pager began to vibrate, he felt nothing but anxiety. He had specifically told Clare to interrupt him if the call came from Oakland Children's.

"Hey John, thanks for returning my call so quickly." He was back at his desk. "As I told you in my message, the Wittman baby was admitted here for poor weight gain about two weeks ago. Workup for GI problems was negative." He'd already decided that he was not going to say more than necessary. "We're very interested in learning what happened to this baby."

"Dan, there's really nothing subtle about it. There was a complex, depressed skull fracture with subdural and intracerebral bleeding. Bruising on the face and the trunk. The child was essentially dead when he got here from Martinez. I mean he had a normal cardiac rhythm and oxygenated well enough with a ventilator, but there was essentially no cerebral perfusion. He was brain dead. We went about twelve hours and then pulled the plug. We did harvest for transplants, at least."

"Is it clear what happened?"

"Well, nobody's confessed if that's what you mean. But the injuries were obviously inflicted."

"That's just terrible. Anyway, thanks for the feedback." Then Dan posed it as though it were an afterthought. "John, do you know if there was any evidence of recurrent injuries? Fractures, anything like that."

"Absolutely. There were healed fractures at one of the wrists, radius and ulna, and there was something at the end of one of the femurs. No question that there was repeated injury."

One way or another, Dan wanted certainty. "Your radiologists, did they, uh, did they estimate the age of the fractures?"

"I saw the films myself. The skull was fresh. The stuff on the extremities was older. Lots of callus around the fractures. At least two, three weeks old. Maybe more."

It had an inevitability to it. He would have been surprised if they, he, had not been culpable.

"Dan, are you there?"

He lost the rhythm of the conversation. "Yeah. Excuse me. Uh, John, I appreciate the information. Really, thanks a lot. I, uh...let's stay in touch." He wasn't certain if he hung up before the man said goodbye.

He sat, still, for fifteen minutes. Eyes closed, the tips of his fingers resting above his eyebrows on each side, thumbs on his cheekbones, the weight of his chin and head taken on the heels of his hands and transmitted through his elbows to the surface of the desk. As soon as he had seen the item in the newspaper, the thought began to assemble. And as each bit of fragile uncertainty fell away, the thought pushed its way up through his failing bag of tricks. And his most important trick, the one he had to have, the one that let him think that he could keep his innocence in this place, could not camouflage or beautify or disappear the facts. The thought was out.

I killed that baby.

By the time he forced himself back into the schedule, it was early afternoon and he was twenty minutes late for the COBRA prep. Frost had decided that Jim Swain, the ER Director, would be the principal spokesperson with the Feds. This was to be a practice interrogation. Dan and three others playing the site visitors, with Swain in the hot seat. He had expected Frost to be at this one, and was grateful that he was not.

The session lasted nearly two hours. He asked the fewest questions, and compared to the others they were softballs. He was just hanging on. He wasn't so much specifically thinking about the Wittman case, as he was unable to think with clarity about anything. He spent the last thirty minutes of the meeting on his feet, leaning against the wall furthest from Swain, changing locations every few minutes, pacing. He drew a few quizzical looks, but no one commented.

By the end of the meeting, he felt like he was suffocating. Despite the fact that he was supposed to chair a Utilization

Management Committee meeting that was scheduled to have begun five minutes earlier, he had to get out of the building. He skipped the elevators taking the stairs two at a time up to the lobby level. Within twenty-five yards of the big glass double doors, he broke into a run and kept running until he got to his car. As he fumbled for his keys, he saw it. Another yellow envelope tucked under the wiper blade on the passenger side. Out of breath, out of focus, it took him a few moments to orient, to remember what this must be. He extracted it, got behind the wheel, locked the doors and started the engine. He had nothing linear that could get him to even an educated guess about what he was about to read. And he was so uncentered that something like intuition was out of the question. As he opened the envelope, he went to hope: that whatever this was, it would somehow make things easier.

Please.

From: frosttom@olympia.com

To: ██████████████████

Subject: DF

As discussed, have concluded that risk is unacceptable.
Strongly recommend severance before site visit.
Advise immediately.

He was walking counterclockwise. He had been on this path dozens of times, though never in leather-soled shoes. It was some kind of a tar and gravel composition, about eight feet across with a solid white stripe running down the center. To his right, on the upslope, were valley oaks and live oaks, and higher up, Monterey and Ponderosa pine. Their floor was the stuff of the golden hills, a sere yellow mix of grasses, wild oats, and thistle. The fire danger bulletins referred to it simply as "fuel." Poison oak, in spring-green camouflage, dotted the edge of the path on both sides. To his left the slope descended about fifty yards to 1.4 billion gallons of water, a not inconsiderable portion of the drinking supply for this part of the East Bay.

From the air, the Lafayette Reservoir looked like a Scottish terrier with its nose to the east, its ears to the north, and its rear end pointed in the general direction of the Golden Gate Bridge. On the ground, the path around the reservoir was a meandering oval, with grades hospitable to people and conveyances of all types and ages. While there was always a crowd on Saturdays and Sundays, on a weekday you could have the place mostly to yourself. On this afternoon, Dan would walk 10.8 miles, four times around.

He had made two calls between the hospital and the reservoir. "Clare, I'm coming down with some kind of flu or something. Call the UM folks and the Psych Department and tell them to go ahead without me. I'll, uh, I'll either be there in the morning or I'll call." With the second call he got to listen to his own voice. "Hi. We can't come to the…" He hung up. This was not answering machine material.

His first lap was the quickest. About forty-five minutes, his pace matching the sizzle of his autonomic nervous system. *Cracker motherfucker.* He was raging at Frost, careening from constructions of moral indignation to just vitriol. He imagined squeezing the man's skinny tab-collared neck with one hand, pinning his head against a wall, screaming into his ear from an inch away. Twice he broke into a short sprint—he'd had no intention of running—as though his agitated energy exceeded some kind of threshold that could contain walking. He discovered and rediscovered his aching hands, unclenching his fists each time. And he perseverated, relentless, on the question that he had come to this place to answer. . . . *What am I going to do? What the fuck am I going to do? Please, how am I going to do this?*

By the time he crossed the 2.5 mile marker, he had shifted. He wasn't certain when or exactly how, but his body was quieting and the pace was slowing. The gravel parking lot, the beginning and end of the loop, came into view. He tried to remember what Susan had said about her day. His mind, exploding fifteen minutes earlier, was now still, as though resting, exhausted. He stopped at the car, tried home and got the recording again. He would do this, to no avail, two more times.

The light was starting to change. He watched his shadow slowly lengthen and circle him as he walked. Over the next two hours he would figure it out. Not how to save his job, which was hopeless. Not even how to cut his losses, the financial ones anyway. The main idea came to him late in the second lap, the details in the third. The last time around was part victory lap, part list-making. From the lightness of his body, he knew he was right. Focused, he was oblivious to the falling temperature, the darkness, the lateness of the hour. He wasn't even distracted by the blisters forming from his utterly inappropriate footwear.

Back in the car, it took eight phone calls to reach his three critical people. He didn't start driving until this was done. They each agreed to help. He drove home via Fish Ranch Road, the back way to Berkeley from Contra Costa. It ess-curved steeply up to Grizzly Peak, and when he hit the crest, he could see that the sun had just finished, leaving a red-orange band across the western horizon. Behind him a nearly full moon was up about twenty degrees. He tried Susan again. This time she picked up.

"Where've you been?"

"Oh, hiking."

"What?"

"I'll explain in detail when I get there. This is, uh…this is a pretty big deal. I'm, uh, I'm not going to be working at Memorial. I can't. Look, I'll tell you everything when I get there."

"Jesus. Are you okay?"

"Yeah, I'm fine," he said. "Look, one thing. Don't answer the phone, all right?"

"Why not?"

"I'll explain that too. Just don't, okay?"

Winding the last few miles of Grizzly, he rehearsed his presentation to Susan—The Wittman case, the Frost email, everything that had gone before. And his plan. His last thought as he drove the fifty yards from the iron gate to his garage door was that his mother and father, each in their own way, would have loved what he was about to do.

The Summer of '55

FEARING THAT A NUN, A DARTH VADER FOR THE 1950'S, MIGHT reach through the vertical iron bars, abduct and do god knows what to him, little Danny never walked on the sidewalk next to St. Timothy's. The school and church, directly on his way between home and the nearest baseball diamond, was a Catholic enclave in a sea of middle-class Jews. Morrie, his father, always said *upper* middle class, but in truth those Jews were in the suburbs. This neighborhood was West Rogers Park. From the Fazen's house, it was four blocks to school and four to the Nortown Theatre, 2.7 miles to the lake, and 5.1 to Wrigley.

Whoever designed Chicago must have been thinking about garbage, and about coal. If you grew up there, you figured that everybody had alleys. The typical city block was a rectangle divided in half in the long direction by a paved alley. The garbage trucks picked up and the coal trucks delivered. And if your house or apartment building had a garage, it faced the alley, not the continuously landscaped street side. In New York City, the kids played stickball in the streets. But in Chicago, they were in the alleys with real bats, no gloves, and mushy gray softballs sixteen inches in circumference. Except for catch. That you did with gloves and real baseballs.

"Come on, dad."

The back of the house was still.

"Dad, ya comin'?"

"Hold your horses, son."

Danny stood in the center of the alley impatiently pounding his mitt. This was part of it. They always warmed up before going to a game.

Finally. "All right!"

"Okay kid, let's see whatcha got."

They were both wearing the royal blue cap with the embroidered red C. Starting out ten feet apart with soft toss, they inched backwards without breaking the rhythm of the exchanges, slowly widening the gap while increasing the velocity. They settled at about forty feet and the throws had enough on them to give a sweet audible pop when they went in just right. After a few minutes of smooth catch, Danny went into the next part of their routine.

"Okay, grounder!" "Pop-up!" "Liner!"

Though he was small, the shortest boy in his class, Danny was a decent athlete. He made it when sides were chosen, usually playing second base and batting late in the lineup. Behind the house with dad, he could make most of the plays. Of course the problem with catch in the alley was that there was no backstop. When he booted it, that hardball on pavement just kept on going. Danny would pivot, sprint it down, pivot again and let fly. It was these throws that challenged Morrie's athleticism. And the neighbors' property.

"Okay son. Let's go."

Morrie loved his new '55 Caddy, a white Coupe DeVille. A financially cautious man, he made an exception when it came to cars. He liked to point out that his older brother, his partner at the clothing store, only had a Buick. As usual, they parked near the Bryn Mawr station and took the el to Wrigley, the home of the Cubs. The Bears played there too, but they were more like guests.

In Chicago, baseball was a matter of geography—and race. If you lived on the North Side, you were a Cub fan. Period. The White Sox played on the South Side in Comiskey Park. If you made that trip, it was usually to see the Yankees and their great stars. Morrie didn't like to go there. "Too many *schvartzes*," he'd say. Rose, Danny's mother, would shoosh him. "Morrie, don't talk like that. I hate that. Daniel, don't listen to your father." In fact, Wrigley was Chicago's white ball park. Comiskey was at 35th and Shields, the poor, black, near-South Side. Danny felt foolish when his father would take his hand, walking as though they were late, from the parked car until they were through the Comiskey turnstiles. He'd otherwise stopped doing that since kindergarten.

Wrigley was safe. Jack Brickhouse, the first voice of the Cubs—Harry Caray was originally a St. Louis Cardinal—talked about the "friendly confines." This was a neighborhood ball park you could miss from a half a block away. No parking lot, no light towers, tucked tightly into one working class block of apartment buildings and storefronts. And unless it was a sunny Sunday doubleheader or they were playing a team like the Dodgers, no crowds. Sure, Ernie Banks was special. He was steady cheerful excellence, and an All-Star, but he never lit up the town the way Michael and Sammy would. He wasn't a phenom and neither, goodness, was the team.

The Cubs didn't just fail to contend. They displayed the kind of stable mediocrity, season after season, that emancipated the fans from hopefulness. And like a Zen paradox, Wrigley was a remarkably happy place. Nothing that happened on the field was particularly consequential. The Bleacher Bums made a fuss, but that was mostly the beer. Fans, with their backs to the players, chatted with friends. People strolled. They came late, they left early. Men in their business suits would show up for a few innings if the weather was good. Brickhouse's marketing pitch was "Come to Wrigley Field for an afternoon picnic."

But it thrilled Danny every time. The first sight of the green expanse, the men leaning out of the square openings in the big manual scoreboard in center field, people on lawn chairs on the roofs of the three-flats beyond the left field wall. And he, for one, paid attention to the game. His mitt was at the ready, although he never caught a ball. He used the little yellow pencil they gave you for free to record the details. The completed scorecard and the ticket stub would be added to the collection in his desk drawer.

He and his dad didn't talk much. Generally two trips to the concession stand were negotiated. For hot dogs and soda pop, and later for some kind of a snack. One of them would interrupt the silence three or four times an inning. "Wow, great play!" "How 'bout that!" "That stunk."

Though Danny understood the game well, better than his father, he would think of questions to ask. "Dad, why do the fly balls always curve toward the foul line?"

"I really don't know, son."

"You think the spin maybe?"

Eddie Matthews had hit a two run homer in the fourth, a low liner that just cleared the ivy and wrapped around the foul pole in right, and by the eighth it was four to one Milwaukee. Danny could sense his father's impatience.

"So whaddaya think? You wanna beat the crowd out?"

"Come on, dad. You always do that."

"Do what?"

"You always want to leave early."

"Well not if it's close."

"Come on, can't we stay?"

He had become accustomed to his father's restlessness. Morrie seemed to always want to get to the next thing. His mom could sit and savor, whatever it was. His dad conceded the rest of the eighth, and Danny the last Cub in the ninth, and they caught the first el north without much competition. Back in the car, Morrie asked his son if he wanted to make some extra money doing stock work at the store.

"Yeah, sure dad."

"Okay then."

"Dad, can we go to another game soon?"

Morrie was thinking about the store. "Sure. Sure."

Danny would return to Wrigley again and again. It was deliciously larcenous to cut afternoon classes in high school to catch a weekday game. And a few years after that, like the short stay businessmen, he and his fellow overloaded pre-med students would come down from Northwestern for a dose, a booster.

Danny was afraid of doctors. Actually of their needles. Turns out he was just a late bloomer, but there were years of anxiety and specialists and x-rays and blood tests before that was confirmed. He had been a good sized baby, and grew perfectly well for the first year. His doctor, in the fashion of the day, gave nutritional edicts down to the last detail, and claimed full credit for the robust growth and development of his patients. Little wonder that Doctor Irving Padnos became distraught when Danny's growth rate slowed dramatically after his first birthday. By the time he was five, he was the height of an average three year old.

Danny's mother Rose was in charge of his medical care. Morrie was fifty, sixty hours a week at the store, and anyway thought that all the concern about the boy's height was needless. His brother, Danny's uncle, had been tiny in grammar school and ended up a six-footer. "What's all the fuss, for chrissakes?"

Danny spent no small part of his childhood with his mother on buses and els, and in waiting rooms. They traveled to specialists at Northwestern and the University of Chicago and Michael Reese. When he was young, she would allay his fears along the way and distract him with stories and toys and coloring books. As he grew older, she began to talk to him about the world beyond Rogers Park and the clothing business.

"Daniel, this is a horrible thing." The temperature inside the CTA bus was surely over a hundred. Rose alternately read and fanned herself with the Sun-Times.

"What, mom?" It was the Friday before Labor Day. The summer of '55 had already had the highest recorded temperatures in

Chicago history. With the crush of people on the bus and the humidity, just talking was an effort.

"They killed this colored boy from Chicago," she said. "In Mississippi. Two white men beat, shot, and drowned him for talking to a white woman."

"Why would they do that, mom?"

"Cause they're filled with hate. And they're afraid."

The boy was fourteen-year-old Emmett Till. In the coming weeks she would tell Danny how the murderers were set free by the white jury. And she told him about school segregation, and that the Warren Supreme Court had outlawed it only a year earlier. And just a few months later she would read him the descriptions of the Montgomery Bus Boycott and Rosa Parks.

She wanted her son to understand social injustice. And she wanted him to know about her heroes. The largest picture in the house was a portrait of FDR over the living room sofa. She had her favorite quote from Saul Alinsky taped to the refrigerator door. "Change means movement, movement means friction, friction means heat, and heat means controversy. The only place where there is no friction is in outer space." She told him how Alinsky and John L. Lewis in the 40's organized the Chicago meat packers and improved the miserable working conditions in the Stockyards. When Albert Einstein died early in 1955, she made sure that Danny understood that he was opposed to the use of atomic energy for weapons. And that he was a pious Jew. And a few months later when Cordell Hull died, she told him about the United Nations, and why Hull had been awarded the Nobel Peace Prize.

—

"Danny, please be careful." His mother's cautionary send-offs were so ubiquitous and sweetly said, that at age eleven he didn't feel warned, only loved. Just a few years later, he would hate it. Objectively, it was a remarkably safe time and place. There were no weapons in schools. The experimental drugs were cigarettes and beer. Sexual adventure was leafing eight-pagers and first fantasies about the just sprouting girls. The boys talked about jack-offs, but not about jacking off. Rubbers were funny and bra straps were funny and falsies were hilarious. Within the neighborhood, you could walk anywhere, anytime. Including, in fact, St. Timothy's.

As for being the object of his parents' anxiety, Danny was triply cursed. First because he was Jewish. Sure, all mammalian parents demonstrated protective instincts for their offspring. But Jews had evolved, over millennia of persecution and murder and somehow survival, a seemingly genetic vigilance and caution which, for better *and* worse, transmitted to the children that the world was a dangerous place. And he was really small. Again and again, the doctors told them that there was nothing wrong with their son. That his short stature was "constitutional," whatever that meant. That he would be fine, and someday tall. Yet they kept asking him back so they could x-ray his bones and re-check his blood and his urine. "Rose, if he's so fine, why do they keep repeating all these tests?" "Look Morrie, they're the doctors and they say they're just being thorough." "Yeah, well they're sure being thorough with my money." And he was the long-awaited, prayed for, immeasurably precious, only child.

"Be careful, Danny."

"Bye, mom. I'll be playing ball."

He was out the kitchen door to the wooden porch and stairs, the shortest way to Greenbriar Park, the local ball field. And to Rose's horror, back the way he came in less than an hour, the front of his white tee-shirt wet with blood. He didn't want to cry, but the pain was too intense. Before the afternoon was out, Danny would get the novocaine, three stitches to his lower lip and an effortless extraction of his suddenly quite mobile left lower lateral incisor.

It had been embarrassing enough to whiff a ten mile an hour parabolic sucker pitch. The bat handle slid out of Danny's hands and came at the third baseman's legs like a slow motion helicopter blade. Larry Rosenman awkwardly jumped but the bat caught one of his shins, and he went down. Had there somehow been a choice, Rosenman was the last boy in the neighborhood that Danny would have wanted to piss off. True to form, the tall, mean-spirited kid treated it like an opportunity.

"You little asshole. Why'd you throw your bat at me? Huh?" Rosenman was walking straight at him, arms at his sides, glaring.

Danny stood in place, frightened. "Hey, it was an accident. I'm sorry."

Rosenman reached him, and with both hands to his chest shoved him backwards. "Fuck you, Fazen."

Danny barely kept his feet. "Hey, I said I was sorry. I didn't do it on purpose, for chrissake." The big kid shoved him again, this time knocking him down. He scrambled up, going backward, gaining maybe a yard of distance. He wasn't going to be able to talk his way out of this, and running was out of the question, humiliating, and anyway fruitless. The long-legged bully would be on him in seconds. As though hot-wired by fear and urgency, some reptilian place between his cortex and brain stem just took over.

He put his head down and exploded at Rosenman. Eyes closed, he felt the top of his head and shoulders crash into solid torso, their combined mass hitting the ground. He tried to rise, pushing off on his left hand, and swinging with his right, but didn't get the chance. Rosenman easily rolled him. Danny felt the weight on the front of both shoulders and two jolts to his face, no pain yet. He thought he saw a flash of light. He tried to get his hands in front of his head and suddenly the weight was gone. Two of the boys had pulled Rosenman off and were keeping him away. Danny sat up. This was his first and, as it turned out, his only fist fight. It had lasted twelve seconds. His mouth felt strange, numb and wet at the same time. He saw the blood on his shirt.

One of the boys leaned over him. "You okay?"

"Fuck yeah." For the moment, anyway, he felt pretty good. He had fought.

The four of them were sitting at the lime green formica table in the Rosenman kitchen. Morrie was still in his work clothes, a dark blue suit, white shirt, and floral silk tie. Danny was tucked in close on his left. His lower lip was three times the size of his upper with the ends of a thick black suture extruding from his mouth. Larry sat opposite, avoiding eye contact. Next to him, Sam Rosenman waited. At the door he had immediately apologized for his son's behavior. Morrie was not going to make it easy. "That's nice. Can we sit down?"

"Can I get you something to drink?"

"It's not a social visit."

The elder Rosenman was five inches shorter and maybe thirty pounds heavier than Morrie. He wore dark slacks, the kind with the expandable elastic belt, and a short-sleeve cotton shirt with 'Sam' stitched over the pocket. He more than filled his kitchen chair.

Morrie reached into his jacket and extracted a folded piece of white paper. Without speaking, he slid it across the table to Sam.

"What's this?"

"It's a receipt. From the dentist."

Sam read it, paused, reached into his pants pocket with his right hand and came out with a roll of bills. He peeled two twenties and set them on the table in front of Morrie. Danny watched his dad take the money without a nod of acknowledgement.

"Son." Larry was sitting, elbows propped, fists to his cheekbones, staring at the table. If he heard Morrie, there was no way to tell. This time louder, "Son." Nothing.

Danny was riveted. And then stunned. Sam suddenly pivoted in his chair, "Answer him!" Larry recoiled at his father's first movement, head to the table, face averted, forearms flung over his head.

"Don't! Please don't!" Larry was pleading.

Danny's heart was pounding. He watched his father lean back in his chair and silently stare across at the fat man. Sam tolerated about fifteen seconds of this. "What?" Morrie stayed fixed on him. "What?"

Morrie broke his gaze, looked to Danny, then Larry, and back to Sam. "I want to talk to the boys alone."

Larry was frightened. "What're you gonna do?"

"Don't worry, son. We're just gonna talk."

This time without eye contact, Morrie waited. Sam shrugged his shoulders and went into the living room.

Morrie spoke quietly. "I mean it, son. We're just gonna talk. There's nothing to be afraid of. Do you believe me?"

Larry looked directly at Morrie for the first time. "Yes, sir."

Danny watched his dad turn to him and then back to Larry.

"Larry, do you think that Danny threw that bat at you on purpose?" Larry hesitated. "Do you?"

"No, sir."

"Then why did you go after him?"

The boy's eyes filled with tears. "I don't know."

"You don't know?"

Larry shook his head.

Morrie thought about it. "You know, son. I believe you." He watched the boy for a few more seconds. "Larry, are you sorry you did it?"

"Yeah. Yeah, I am."

"Tell him. Tell him you're sorry."

Larry exhaled and looked up. "I'm sorry, Danny."

Danny smiled nervously.

Morrie turned to his son. "Come on, tell him you accept his apology."

"Yeah, okay. I accept your apology."

"Now both of you shake hands."

They awkwardly clasped hands and gave a single downward stroke.

"Now Larry, listen very carefully to me." He waited until he had the boy's eyes. "You will never harm Danny again. You will never threaten him. You will do nothing to scare or hurt him. Do you understand?"

"Yes, sir."

"Is that a promise?"

"I promise."

"Tell him."

"I promise, Danny."

Morrie extended his hand to Larry and the boy took it. Then he turned to his son. "Let's go."

On the way out, Danny watched his father approach Sam, who was reading a newspaper on the living room sofa. He leaned over and said something quietly in his ear. The man didn't answer.

⤙

Larry kept his word. After the episode, he and Danny mostly just avoided each other. On the way home from the Rosenmans that night, Danny asked his dad what he said to Larry's father. Morrie looked over from behind the steering wheel, "I told him that he was making his son mean."

Without a Net

HE HADN'T EXACTLY LIED TO THEM, HE JUST LEFT A FEW THINGS out. The hospital Audio-Visual Department was accustomed to short notice. They weren't going to question their senior medical executive about something so simple, the basics for a brief outdoor presentation to a small group of visitors. "You can set it up at the last minute," Dan told them, "a little bit before eleven. No need to clutter up the front lawn all morning." His nonchalance on the phone had been a piece of work.

"Test, test."

The tech turned up the PA volume.

"Test, test."

He was positioned so that his back was to the main entrance of the hospital. The videocameras, two to his left and one to his right, framed him and the lectern with its busy logo identifying Memorial and Olympia. There was a small microphone clipped to his tie, and three large ones, a 2, a 4, and a 7, clustered in front of him. He stood on the grass in full regalia—white coat, stethoscope, tongue blades, and reflex hammer. It had been almost twenty hours since he first read the Frost email. If you added up the stolen moments, he had slept perhaps two of them.

"Good morning everyone. My name is Doctor Daniel Fazen. I am the Vice-President for Medical Affairs at Walnut Creek Memorial Hospital."

Susan, Carly, Ben, and Mason Kanzler were sitting directly in front of him on metal folding chairs. Seated behind them were twelve other people, including Noah Sampson and James Colburn. Marty Sullivan, who had not set foot on the property since her forced resignation, was by herself in the back row.

"We've just distributed a copy of a letter that was faxed approximately thirty minutes ago to three regulatory agencies: the California State Department of Health Services in Sacramento, the Joint Commission on the Accreditation of Healthcare Organizations in Chicago, and the regional office of the federal Center for Medicare and Medicaid Services in San Francisco. The letter is an effort to accurately document the deterioration of medical care at Memorial since it was acquired by the Olympia Healthcare Corporation."

He was tired. And wired, loaded with coffee. Though his instinct had been to speak conversationally from notes, Kanzler insisted that he read verbatim from a statement. The way he was feeling, he was grateful for the text. Mason had come through for him immediately and generously. And so had his two other angels. Noah Sampson had not only delivered the Channel 2 news team but got full representation from his competitors at the NBC and ABC affiliates. And James Colburn, the young Contra Costa reporter, had been willing to get his opposite numbers from the Chronicle, the Tribune, and the Mercury News.

His reading copy was 14 font, bold, double-spaced with italics for emphasis. He had penciled in slashes to help him with the phrasing. Thinking about the final run-through and Kanzler's parting shot, at the last minute he hung a Post-It from the inside edge of the lectern. "SLOW DOWN!!"

"I have been affiliated one way or another with the Walnut Creek Memorial Hospital for over thirty years. Starting as a medical student and for the entirety of my private practice, Memorial has been my professional home. I admitted my patients here, I taught here, and I served on countless medical staff committees. The principal reason that I chose to practice in Alamo, and then in Walnut Creek, was not because I wanted to live out here. I chose to practice here because of my admiration and affection for this institution."

Mason had thought that he was starting with too much biographical material, that nothing should detract from the emphasis on the hospital. Dan insisted that he had to establish his credibility as a physician who had supported Memorial throughout this career. That as a loyalist, his criticism would be more resonant.

"Last year, prior to the acquisition by Olympia, Martha Sullivan, the long-standing CEO, asked me to leave private practice and take the full-time position of Vice-President for Medical Affairs. I accepted, with the explicit understanding that my principal responsibility was to defend the quality of medical care in the face of growing economic pressures on our hospital. I obviously do not know what the course of events would have been had Olympia not acquired Memorial. I do, however, know what has transpired since the acquisition."

He felt himself getting into a slow, comfortable rhythm. He was breathing more easily and his delivery, which started out monotonal and barely punctuated, was becoming expressive.

"The letter to the regulatory agencies that I have distributed describes, in some detail, episodes of preventable harm to patients. You will see that in all instances the identities of these patients have been protected. However, should the agencies choose to explore these cases, which I believe they will, they will have full access to the medical records. Though I will make reference to some of these specifics, my emphasis this morning will be on describing how the business policies and tactics of this hospital are putting our patients in harm's way."

He had no idea how he was doing. The journalists were unreadable, intermittently head down taking notes. He caught a reassuring smile from Susan, but that was hardly objective feedback. He paused, tamping and re-setting his text on the lectern.

"The largest operational cost at our hospital—any hospital—the biggest item in the budget, is the cost of nursing. The salaries and benefits of our employed nurses, along with the hourly costs of our extra-help nurses, is alone nearly 50% of the entire personnel budget. And it is in nursing that Memorial has been most seriously wounded. To reduce costs and increase profits, we have gone overboard in trading off RN's for LVN's and unlicensed medical assistants, we have understaffed patient care areas so that patient-to-nurse ratios are unacceptably high, and we have replaced talented veteran nurses with inexperienced new graduates at entry-level salaries. The overall negative effect on the quality of care has been profound."

Now he had his voice, and their full attention.

"Let me tell you what happens when you create insufficient nursing services in a hospital, when we overload veteran nurses, or ask less experienced staff to perform beyond their skills. They make mistakes—mental and physical errors. Errors of commission and omission. It is inevitable. They make medication errors, incorrect doses, or the wrong medication entirely. They fail to monitor patients adequately and changes in status are missed, which can be dangerous or even fatal. And ask yourself..."

He tried not to lose his concentration. He had looked up from his text momentarily and seen them. Frost and Reynolds were on the edge of the grass about twenty yards behind the reporters. They stood, each with their arms folded across their white shirts and ties.

"...ask yourself if you could be warm and attentive if you had twice the number of patients than you could reasonably care for.

The letter to the California Department of Health Services and the others outlines, in detail, specific instances of substandard patient care..."

Richard Reynolds was coming up to his left.

"...because of inadequate nurse staffing, and jeopardy to the nurses themselves."

Reynolds was standing next to him. He lost his focus, and his place in the text.

"Of the... uh... consequences of excessive cost reductions, uh... none has been as bad as, uh... excuse me."

Frost's lawyer had placed a note in front of him on the lectern. "Mr. Frost instructs you to discontinue this briefing immediately." Dan saw that Mason was on the move.

"Just a minute."

He unclipped his microphone, set it on the lectern, and headed to his left toward Kanzler. Reynolds followed. The two lawyers needed no introduction.

"Dan, what the fuck are you doing?"

"I'm, uh—"

Mason put his hand on Dan's shoulder and intervened. "I think it's pretty obvious, Richard. He's having a press conference."

They were speaking quietly, out of earshot.

"Are you his lawyer, Mason?"

"I am."

"Well, this is private property. And he is subject to the controlling authority here. And that's the Chief Executive Officer."

"Dan is also a senior executive at this hospital. Are you telling me he can't call a press conference?"

"He can't if his boss tells him he can't. And Mr. Frost is telling him he can't. So let's just send everyone home, right now."

Dan knew what Mason was going to say. They had talked through the possible scenarios hours earlier.

"I'm afraid not."

"Come on, Mason. This is private property. We can have Security shut this whole thing down. Don't be foolish."

"That's just fine," Mason said. "You do that. You have Security take Doctor Fazen out of here by force. Better yet, let's have the Walnut Creek Police Department come in and cuff him in front of the whole frigging Bay Area press corps. Maybe local coverage isn't enough for you. Let's escalate this up to CNN and Fox. Just how stupid are you people?"

Dan watched the two attorneys glare at each other.

Mason knew that Reynolds would back off. "Doctor Fazen is going to continue this press conference."

"Sorry for the interruption. The letter to the California Department of Health Services and the others spells out specific instances of substandard patient care because of inadequate nurse staffing, and jeopardy to the nurses themselves. Of the consequences of excessive cost reductions at Memorial, the reduction in nursing quality has, in my judgment, been the most damaging to patients."

He could tell that the attention of the reporters had been fragmented. The sidebar had piqued their curiosity and disrupted the flow of his presentation. There were whispered conversations, and a few were fully turned in their seats, following Reynolds as he rejoined Frost behind them. It occurred to Dan that the man's intention was simply disruption, that Reynolds hadn't been trumped at all.

He continued reading. The focus switched to sentinel events, and then to the suppression of information, which recaptured the journalists. Without specifically mentioning the Seldes incident, Dan told them how the administrative leadership exerted its power to protect physicians who were essential to the financial well-being of the hospital. And he slowed and over-enunciated *sanitize* in describing how the CEO wanted to approach a particularly damaging case.

Before revealing his personal plans, he read the final section.

"I want to take a few minutes to talk about the ways we refuse care to patients. We do not do this universally or randomly. We do it tactically, and these tactical choices are related to money.

If you are uninsured, you are unwelcome. If you have Medi-Cal, you are only slightly less unwelcome. If you have Medicare, you are welcome to come in, but you are unwelcome once you get in. If you have an HMO, well then it depends. And, yes, if you have good old-fashioned fee-for-service health insurance, uncommon these days, then come and stay as long as you'd like.

Despite the fact that a multimillion dollar foundation was created to support indigent care here—the law required it at the time of the Olympia acquisition—the hospital is intensely hostile to poor patients. Every effort is made to keep these people out. And if they do somehow get in, to get them out as soon as possible.

How does this harm people? How does this culture of refusal translate into damage, and sometimes death, of real patients? The letter to the regulatory agencies reviews several such cases. I will briefly describe two, both fatal."

Mason had advised him not to do it, not to talk about his own culpability in any detail. "Dan, I understand what you're trying to do. But it's unnecessary. And risky."

"Look Mason, this is not about me needing to confess out loud. This is about credibility. It's going to surface anyway that I formally denied the extension in the Wittman case. I believe the whole presentation is stronger if I, at least in this instance, hold myself accountable along with everyone else. Besides, it's the truth."

"The first involves an uninsured African-American gentleman who had fallen off a ladder and was experiencing chest pain. An evaluation in our Emergency Room demonstrated two rib fractures and no complications, and he was quickly sent via ambulance to the county hospital. He was essentially dead on arrival in Martinez twenty minutes later. The cause of death was a massively collapsed lung. In our hurry to get this uninsured patient out of our hospital, we did not take the time to have a fully qualified radiologist look at the chest x-ray, and we did not insist on a period of observation before putting him in the ambulance. Had we done either, he likely would be alive today."

He felt his anxiety. In his chest and in his armpits.

"The second case involves an infant, an HMO member for whom we were financially at risk. The baby was being evaluated for poor weight gain. There were factors suggesting that problems in the family might be responsible. Both the attending physician and the pediatric social worker recommended an extended admission—in this case beyond three days—so that they could get a better understanding of what was going on. The case manager, a person under relentless pressure from the hospital leadership to save money, recommended denial of the additional care."

He paused and looked at Susan.

"I personally authorized the denial and the infant was sent home."

Now he shifted to Mason. If there was any frustration or disapproval, he couldn't see it.

"Approximately one week later the baby was pronounced dead at Oakland Children's Hospital. The cause of death was non-accidental trauma to the head—fatal child abuse. And the studies at Children's indicated that, had we x-rayed the child's bones while he was at Memorial, we would have discovered that he was a battered child. Those x-rays were part of the recommendation of the attending pediatrician. Had we, had I, approved the extension of that admission..."

He looked back to Susan, her lips pressed tightly together, nodding encouragement.

"...I believe that infant would be alive today."

He followed the instruction he had made in the margin to pause at this point. He didn't take long. Enough for a deep breath and some housekeeping at the surface of the lectern.

"Perhaps later than I should have, I have concluded that I am unable to embrace the values of the new leadership at Memorial, and that I cannot, will not, meet their expectations of me. I have also concluded that there is no likelihood that their values or behavior will change. Therefore, I will not continue in the employ of the Olympia Healthcare Corporation. Effective immediately, I resign as Vice-President for Medical Affairs. This will be in writing to the CEO before the end of the day."

Mason had suggested that he also not do what he was about to do. They had a prolonged debate about it. Dan argued that it was a press conference, and that at a press conference you were supposed to take questions. Mason thought that it was both unnecessary and risky. They wound up compromising.

"I would be glad to take a few questions. However, I will not answer any questions about specific patients or cases."

"Doctor Fazen, I believe you said that you could no longer embrace the values of the hospital administrators. What values are you talking about?"

"Well, first let me say that I hope that I never embraced them. I think that what I said was, or what I meant to say was, that it took longer than I would have liked to get clarity about our differences. I believe that Olympia is first and foremost committed to making money for its shareholders, and that the quality of medical care is a distant second. I don't think that there's anything wrong with a business making

money for its investors, or in fact a healthcare business making money for its investors. But their promise to the community must be that they will not sacrifice quality of care in service of profit. I have seen enough of this organization to conclude that, regardless of what they say in their ads and their marketing materials, they do not value quality health care and patient safety in a way that is meaningful."

"Doctor, have any of the regulatory agencies begun investigating either of the cases you just described?"

"As I stated, I'm not going to answer any questions about specific cases."

"Sir, I don't think that anyone would disagree with the characterization of your actions today as extraordinary. I cannot recall in three decades of covering the health care beat a physician executive turning in his own hospital. Sir, please forgive the question, but are you personally retaliating against Olympia for something they've done to you?"

Dan thought about the Frost email. He responded as dismissively as he could.

"That's a simple no."

"Doctor, in retrospect do you regret having left practice to go to work for Memorial?"

"Well, insofar as going to work for Marty Sullivan and an independent non-profit Memorial, I have no regrets at all. Now, should I have stayed on with Olympia?..."

It was too complex to formulate on the fly, so he just said the first thing he thought of. Later, he decided it was perfect.

"...that will be between me and my conscience."

Mason was pointing to his wrist watch.

"Okay, this'll be the last question."

He pointed to James Colburn.

"Doctor, what are you going to do? What are your plans?"

That was a lot easier.

"Mr. Colburn, I think I'd better look for a job."

Epilogue
Relax and Breathe

Oakland, California, ten months later

FIRST HE TAP-TAPPED IT WITH HIS INDEX FINGER AS HE LISTENED. Then, with a few moments of brisk friction against the palm of his hand, he took the cold surprise out of the metal and plastic disc.

"Relax and breathe."

Dan had done this thousands of times. Blocking out the ambient noise, holding the edges of the stethoscope just so against the chest, resting his left hand on the elderly gentleman's shoulder, hearing the sounds as regular rhythmic turbulence. He needed but one inspiration and one expiration for each of eight areas front and back.

"Mr. Williams, you're not smoking, are you?"

"No no, doc. Haven't had a cigarette in two months, not since you told me."

"Because you still sound a little congested."

"I swear, doc."

The examination rooms at the county clinic were utilitarian, worn but spotless. Dan had this and one other, with a small office between for deskwork and conversation.

He slid the green speculum into the man's ear canal and looked at the ear drum.

"Are you taking your pills?"

"Yes, sir. I'm taking the blood pressure pill and the cholesterol pill and the little yellow aspirin."

"And the vitamins?"

His deal with his new boss, the Chief of Internal Medicine at Oakland County General, was simple. Nobody wanted these Saturday mornings. He'd do them in exchange for Thursday afternoons off and—this was non-negotiable—no administrative assignments.

"How about exercise? Are you doing your walking?"

He was palpating the right upper quadrant of James Williams' abdomen, listening to the man's description of his morning stroll at Lake Merritt, looking at the clock on the wall—it was nearly noon—and thinking about the party.

—

ATM, flowers, wine, cleaners, ice, candles, the cake. He scratched them off the list, one by one, as he made his crooked way home. Susan had balked, but this was not just any birthday. Dan knew that if he persisted, she would eventually give in to a big bash for her fiftieth. Now she was excited, everybody was coming. Carly, with her unusual boyfriend, and both of her rarely seen siblings. Susan's inner circle, the Berkeley psychotherapy crowd, her music people, her family from Sonoma. Ben, of course, and Marty. Mason Kanzler and his wife. Even ex-Olympia board member C.J. Corbett, Dan's clandestine correspondent, his guardian angel.

The bakery on Piedmont Avenue was his last stop. With care, he set the pink cardboard box on the right front seat, and drove home as though the big birthday cake were truly a fragile thing.

Home was North Oakland. They'd been there for five months, a perfectly serviceable three bedroom on an oak-lined street in the flats near the Berkeley border. No view at all in the Grizzly sense, but a nice back yard, some beautiful woodwork in the living room and dining room, and a renovated kitchen. As it came into view, he said to himself what he'd repeatedly said aloud about this latest house. There was nothing unpleasant about it.

Susan was cutting flowers by the front door as Dan pulled into the driveway. In denim overalls and a white tee-shirt, she walked toward the car, wiping her hands with a rag and smiling.

"Happy birthday, Tone."

She leaned through the open window and kissed him on the mouth.

"You got everything?" she asked, looking around the packed interior of the car.

He slid his hand into the pocket of his windbreaker, touched the ribboned box, and thought about the improbability of it. Three letters to Paris, then three to Athens—no recriminations, just a family history and a plea. He'd abandoned all expectation when it arrived at his office, tarnished and crystal-cracked in flimsy, failed bubble-wrap. The craftsman in Sausalito charged him through the nose, but Daniel had it now, pristine, his heartfelt long shot. Susan's family wristwatch, her *Nightingale*.

"Yep," he said. "I've got everything."

Acknowledgements

I am grateful, above all, to my wonderful wife Gayle for her loving encouragement, editorial input, and remarkable patience. Without her support, this audacious foray into fiction would not have been possible. My other indispensable ally has been James McManus, a great writer, the real deal, who inspired, edited, cajoled, blurbed, and pitched—a relentlessly generous mentor. And many thanks to my other craftmasters, Ed Stackler and Rebecca Lowen, who provided invaluable writerly guidance; to my little writers' group—Danielle Wood and Edo Mor—for their countless hours of smart and caring feedback; to the early believers—Nancy Baumgartner, Byrd Leavell, and Rick Broadhead; to my pals and co-conspirators from the Squaw Valley Community of Writers; to Ingo Brauer for his legal input (even though the courtroom scenes didn't survive the revisions), and finally to Connie Shaw and Timm Bryson at Sentient for their belief in *Standard of Care*, their friendship, and their collaborative creativity in bringing the novel to fruition.

About the Author

Photo: Lily West

DAVID KERNS' career as a pediatrician has been largely devoted to the care of abused and neglected children. He is currently Adjunct Professor of Pediatrics at the Stanford University School of Medicine. He is also the Medical Director for the Center for Child Protection, Department of Pediatrics, at the Santa Clara Valley Medical Center in San Jose, California, where he has served over the years as Chairman of the Department of Pediatrics and Chief Medical Officer. In addition, he has been a Resident Scholar at the Rockefeller Foundation Bellagio Study Center. He was educated at University of Illinois at Champaign-Urbana and Northwestern University School of Medicine.

Dr. Kerns has published 35 academic journal articles as well as essays and book chapters in the field of pediatrics, and has co-authored a pediatric CD-ROM on child sexual abuse. Aside from writing and doctoring, he has occupied himself as a semi-pro musician, with incarnations as both a rock drummer and a blue-grass banjo player.

David Kerns lives in Oakland, California.

For more information, see his website, www.davidkerns.com.

Sentient Publications, LLC publishes books on cultural creativity, experimental education, transformative spirituality, holistic health, new science, ecology, and other topics, approached from an integral viewpoint. Our authors are intensely interested in exploring the nature of life from fresh perspectives, addressing life's great questions, and fostering the full expression of the human potential. Sentient Publications' books arise from the spirit of inquiry and the richness of the inherent dialogue between writer and reader.

We are very interested in hearing from our readers. To direct suggestions or comments to us, or to be added to our mailing list, please contact:

SENTIENT PUBLICATIONS, LLC
1113 Spruce Street
Boulder, CO 80302
303-443-2188
contact@sentientpublications.com
www.sentientpublications.com